LIBRARY OF CONGRESS CATALOGING-IN-PUBLICATION DATA

Chapman, Gary D., 1938–
   It happens every spring : four seasons / by Gary Chapman & Catherine Palmer.
      p. cm. — (Thorndike Press large print christian fiction)
      ISBN-13: 978-0-7862-9623-1 (lg. print : alk. paper)
      ISBN-10: 0-7862-9623-2 (lg. print : alk. paper)
      ISBN-13: 978-1-59415-194-1 (lg. print : pbk. : alk. paper)
      ISBN-10: 1-59415-194-6 (lg. print : pbk. : alk. paper)
   1. Marriage — Fiction. 2. Ozarks, Lake of the (Mo.) — Fiction. 3. Large type books. I. Palmer, Catherine, 1956– II. Title.
PS3603.H367I86 2007
813'.6—dc22
                        2007012897

Published in 2007 by arrangement with Tyndale House Publishers, Inc.

Printed in the United States of America on permanent paper
10 9 8 7 6 5 4 3 2 1

FOUR SEASONS

IT HAPPENS EVERY SPRING

GARY CHAPMAN & CATHERINE PALMER

THORNDIKE PRESS

An imprint of Thomson Gale, a part of The Thomson Corporation

Detroit • New York • San Francisco • New Haven, Conn. • Waterville, Maine • London

This Large Print Book carries the
Seal of Approval of N.A.V.H.

IT HAPPENS EVERY SPRING

FOR MY HUSBAND, TIM,
with whom I have shared all the
seasons . . .
and how grateful I am for our summer
love!

ALSO FOR CC McCLURE,
beautiful woman, friend, and bookseller.
Thank you for urging me to write about
the lake.

C.P.

Years later, when they were grown up, they were so used to quarrelling and making it up again that they got married so as to go on doing it more conveniently.

C. S. LEWIS
The Horse and His Boy

NOTE TO READERS

There's nothing like a good story! I'm excited to be working with Catherine Palmer on a fiction series based on the concepts in my book *The Four Seasons of Marriage.* You hold in your hands the first book in this series.

My experience, both in my own marriage and in counseling couples for more than thirty years, suggests that marriages are always moving from one season to another. Sometimes we find ourselves in winter — discouraged, detached, and dissatisfied. Other times we experience springtime, with its openness, hope, and anticipation. On still other occasions we bask in the warmth of summer — comfortable, relaxed, enjoying life. And then comes fall with its uncertainty, negligence, and apprehension. The cycle repeats itself many times throughout the life of a marriage, just as the seasons repeat themselves in nature. These concepts are described in *The Four Seasons of Marriage,* along with seven proven strategies to help couples move away from the unsettledness of fall or the alienation and coldness of winter toward the hopefulness of spring or the warmth and closeness of summer.

Combining what I've learned in my counseling practice with Catherine's excellent writing skills has led to this series of four novels. In the lives of the characters you'll meet in these pages, you will see the choices I have observed people making over and over again through the years, the value of caring friends and neighbors, and the hope of marriages moving to a new and more pleasant season.

In *It Happens Every Spring* and the stories that will follow it, you will meet newlyweds, blended families, couples who are deep in the throes of empty-nest adjustment, and senior couples. Our hope is that you will see yourself or someone you know in these characters. If you are hurting, this book can give you hope — and some ideas for making things better. Be sure to check out the discussion questions at the end of the book for further ideas.

And whatever season you're in, I know you'll enjoy the people and the stories in

Deepwater Cove.

Gary D. Chapman, PhD

ACKNOWLEDGMENTS

One evening after a book-signing event, I was sitting at a restaurant with CC McClure, manager of Downtown Book and Toy in Jefferson City, Missouri. After I had related several stories about my life in a small community on the Lake of the Ozarks, she suddenly stopped me and asked, "Why aren't you writing about the lake?" Well, because I hadn't thought of it . . . and I probably never would have if CC hadn't suggested the idea. In fact, I might have forgotten all about it, but a few weeks later, a note came from CC again urging me to write about the lake. So, dear friend, here's your book. And thank you so very much!

Through the process of writing *It Happens Every Spring,* many people encouraged and supported me. On a summer afternoon in Denver, the Lord led Dr. Gary Chapman — a complete stranger to me at the time — right into my path on a crowded conference-room floor and cleared the way for us to discuss the idea of partnering on a writing project. Thank you, Gary, for embracing the vision that your God-given concept of *The Four Seasons of Marriage* and the seven strategies for healing broken marriages could come alive through fiction. What a joy it is to partner with you in this project!

Ron Beers and Karen Watson of Tyndale House Publishers first had the foresight to pair a nonfiction author with a novelist. I am so grateful for your hard work in taking this fiction series from concept to reality. Kathy Olson, my amazing editor, is a gift from God. I can write with confidence, knowing she will help shape my words into a story worth reading. My deep thanks to everyone at Tyndale: marketing, sales team, public relations, warehouse, and all who partner with me in this ministry.

My family provides the cocoon in which I feel safe to dream, plot, and write. Thank you, Tim, for nearly thirty years of marriage. How grateful I am that your careful pen edits each word of my manuscript before it goes into the mail. Bless you for taking on so many responsibilities at home so that I can be free to work. Geoffrey and Andrei, I am so proud of my two sons — heavenly miracles, both of you. I love you all so much.

Catherine Palmer

CHAPTER ONE

The night lightning struck a power pole on the west side of Lake of the Ozarks, Patsy Pringle knew right away there would be trouble in Deepwater Cove. The sizzling bolt of brilliant radiance brought a deafening clap of thunder and knocked out the electricity in all of the neighborhood's twenty-three houses. Lightbulbs blinked off, computers fried, televisions died, and dogs scooted on their bellies to hide under beds.

Up the road from the cove, at the Just As I Am beauty salon in the little town of Tranquility, Missouri, the blow-dryer in Patsy's hand whined down to nothing, bringing Esther Moore's weekly set-and-style appointment to a sudden end.

"Well, I'll be," Patsy said. "Good thing you were my last appointment of the day. I'm going to have to shut her down."

"Nuts," Esther muttered as she patted her damp hair. "I'd better head home and

17

rescue Charlie. My husband couldn't find a candle with a search warrant."

Patsy fished a flashlight from the drawer at her styling station and snapped it on. As she helped the older woman locate her purse and keys, she worried about the widows in the neighborhood. Deepwater Cove was home to seven of them, ranging in age from sixty-three to ninety-four. This early in March, many would have had their electric heaters on during the storm. She hoped they could find enough blankets to stay warm.

"I'll bet Boofer is beside himself," Esther said. "That mutt is too fat to get behind the sofa these days. He'll be howling and Charlie will be bumping his bony old knees on the coffee table trying to find the dog. The power company probably won't get the lights back on for hours. They never do. Well, bye, Patsy. Charlie will be itching to get out in his golf cart and check on the neighbors."

"Tell him to be careful," Patsy warned. "The rain is starting to freeze up."

She frowned as she pictured the elderly man maneuvering icy, narrow roads in the lake community's preferred mode of transportation. Deepwater Cove boasted fifteen golf carts, though the nearest eighteen-hole course was all the way over in Osage Beach. A reliable golf cart could carry a fishing pole, a tackle box, a minnow bucket, a stringer of crappie, and a dog. It could get a person to the lakeshore, the mailbox, a neighbor's house, or clear around the cove and back again. The logic was simple, Patsy acknowledged. If a golf cart could take you somewhere, why walk?

As she raised an umbrella and led Esther Moore through the driving downpour toward her car, it occurred to Patsy that right away both women had worried about the neighbors. Plenty of other things could have come to mind — drainage ditches overflowing, roofs leaking, tree limbs snapping off in the wind. But, no, the people were first. Of course neighbors would check on each other. That's just how it was in Deepwater Cove.

"A little storm won't stop Charlie once he gets out in his cart," Esther shouted over the howling wind. " 'Neither snow, nor rain, nor heat, nor gloom of night stays these couriers from the swift completion of their appointed rounds' — if I heard that once, I heard it a million times. Charlie wasn't a mailman all those years for nothing."

Brenda Hansen was in the basement painting a dining-room chair when lightning struck the electric pole right outside her house on Sunnyslope Lane in Deepwater Cove. Startled by the peal of thunder and the sparks shooting through the darkness, she dropped her paintbrush on the floor. The cat, who had been curled up with his tail over his nose in the cold room, yowled, leaped straight up, and landed with all four feet in the tray of pink paint. The instant his paws hit the chilly liquid, he squalled again, bounded out of the tray, and darted for cover.

"Oh, Ozzie, now what?" Still jumpy from the earsplitting thunder, Brenda looked toward the electric pole.

A man stood just outside the basement's sliding glass door. Tall, thin, dark. Another burst of zigzag light brightened the sky, and she saw his beard and long hair and dripping pants. He was staring at her.

"Steve!" she cried out. Realizing instantly that of course her husband wasn't home, she ran for the stairs and grabbed the rail. Falling, stumbling, scraping her shins, Brenda catapulted herself up to the main floor of the house. "Lord, help me. Lord, Lord, please help me," she prayed out loud as she felt her way through the living room in the dark.

Had she locked the basement door earlier today? No, she had pushed back the glass and pulled the screen across to let in fresh air and ventilate the paint fumes. What if the man was inside already? What if he came after her? Was that him following her up the stairs?

Brenda couldn't see a thing as she lurched across the tiled foyer. Just as she reached for the dead bolt, someone pounded on the large, double-paned window set into the insulated-steel front door.

It was him.

She could just make out his shape — towering and unkempt — on the porch. She slammed the bolt and fell back against the wall, sure she was going to be sick.

Where was the cell phone? How soon could the sheriff get to Deepwater Cove? Eight minutes, someone had told her once. Just long enough for a person to die.

"Knock, knock, who's there?" The voice outside the front door was deep, male, and eerily loud. Though the thermal window in the door kept out the weather, it certainly didn't buffer the sound of the man's words as he called to her, "It's me, Cody!"

Brenda shut her eyes and swallowed. She didn't know anyone named Cody. Especially not a tall, bearded, serial strangler who roamed quiet lakeside neighborhoods on rainy nights. She should run down to the basement again, pull the sliding glass door shut, and try to lock it.

"I can see you right there," the man called over another roll of thunder. "Hi, I'm Cody!"

Brenda pressed her back against the foyer wall and began to slide away from the door. Where was Steve when she needed him? Off showing a house to someone in the middle of a spring thunderstorm. He would come home with a big sale under his belt and find his wife lying in the foyer, murdered.

"Do you have any chocolate cake?" the man outside asked, tapping more softly on the window. "I'm hungry, and I like chocolate cake. A lot. Triangles are okay, but I like squares better. Because you get more icing thataway."

Brenda thought her cell phone was probably in her purse. She couldn't remember the last time she had called anyone. Or gone shopping, for that matter. Life had been so empty lately. She hadn't had a reason to pick up her purse in days, but she always kept it on a low table in the foyer. She took a sideways step along the wall.

"Can you hear me, because I'm asking about chocolate cake." The man tapped on the window again. "Because I'm wet and hungry. My daddy told me that anyone might give you food, but only a Christian would give you chocolate cake, too."

Her heart thumping half out of her chest, Brenda glanced at the window in the front door. The man had cupped both hands against the glass and was peering at her through them.

"No!" She shook her head furtively, unwilling to look at him but unable to stop herself. "Go away!"

"Are you a Christian?" he asked. The question held a plaintive note. Another flash of lightning made his long, tangled hair glow. He had blue eyes and filthy teeth. "I'm hungry."

She shook her head again. "Go! Shoo! Get away from my door!"

"Okay." He drawled out the word in a Missouri backwoods accent. *Oh-kye.*

As the man's shoulders sagged and he turned away, Brenda lunged for the corner of the foyer. In the darkness, she knocked over the hall table, discovered her purse wasn't there, and curled up in a ball on the frigid tile floor.

This was just like Steve, she fumed. Leaving her alone so he could show off one of his listings. They rarely ate dinner together anymore. He never seemed to have time for her. And when he was home, all Steve could talk about was closing costs and termite inspections and septic tanks.

Brenda hugged her bent legs and rested her forehead on her knees. For what seemed like the hundredth time, she wondered what had gone wrong. She had eagerly awaited her "empty nest" life and had looked forward to all kinds of activities — redecorating the house, volunteering at church, joining the local garden club, and sewing to her heart's content. Maybe she could fulfill her dream of one day starting a little interior-design business.

Even better, she and Steve would have unlimited time together once the kids were on their own. They could travel, dine out together, go to movies, entertain guests, and take regular sunset boat rides.

But it hadn't turned out like that at all. Steve was never at home, and without someone to share her plans with, they began to seem pointless, far-fetched, even boring.

Christmas had come and the kids arrived home from school, but they left again quickly — bright eyed and eager to get back to their friends and classes. Nowadays, Brenda had trouble getting out of bed and finding things to do. It was so quiet and lonely in the house. If the kids had still been around, she never would have fallen apart over a simple Missouri thunderstorm or a stranger at the door. You couldn't collapse if someone needed you.

Now she was all alone in the big, empty house with some crazy man on the front porch. He would probably cut her into pieces and throw her in the lake, and who would even care?

"Because I saw Jesus downstairs in your basement." He was back at the door, knocking on the window again. "I did. I saw Him. He was looking at me."

"Jesus doesn't live in this house!" she shouted. "Go away! Just leave me alone!"

"Because I saw Him. That's why I asked about the chocolate cake."

"You can't have my chocolate cake, okay? I made it for . . . for . . ." Who *had* she made the cake for that afternoon? She was on a perpetual diet. Steve usually took clients or colleagues out to dinner at the country club.

"Are you a Christian?" the man asked. "Because my daddy said —"

"Listen, what is your problem, mister?" Suddenly angry, she leaped to her feet. "You can't just go knocking on people's doors in the middle of a rainstorm when the electricity's off! You can't just ask for chocolate cake! And for your information, Jesus does *not* live here!"

He brushed his finger under his nose. "Okay."

"So go away before I call the police!"

"Okay." He scratched his head. "I'm hungry. Do you have any kind of food? Because if Jesus doesn't live here, I could eat potatoes. Or bread."

"Are you even listening to me?" she asked him through the window.

His face lit up in the darkness. "Oh! I forgot the magic word: *please.* That's what I did wrong. I knew I must have forgot something. Hi, I'm Cody. *Please* can I have some chocolate cake? *Please?*"

Curious in spite of herself, Brenda stopped shivering and studied the creepy figure on her porch. Freaky long hair. Big, bushy beard. Weird blue eyes. Why did he speak like that — like a little boy? Adults didn't talk about "the magic word." They didn't come begging for chocolate cake in the middle of the night. They certainly didn't claim to have seen Jesus in the basement. He must be schizophrenic or psychotic or something like that.

"Hi, I'm Cody," he said again. "What's your name?"

"Brenda." She had no idea why she told him.

"How old are you?"

"You can't ask that. It's not polite."

"Okay." He turned away.

Brenda stepped toward the door. "Wait. Just hold on a second, all right?"

He turned around and pressed up against the window again. Making a tunnel with his hands, he looked at her.

Sure she was completely nuts, Brenda fumbled toward the kitchen. She found a box of matches, lit one of the many scented candles she kept around the house, and then cut a perfectly squared piece of cake. *"Triangles are okay, but I like squares better,"* the man had told her. Who talked like that?

She should be hunting for her cell phone and calling 911 instead of cutting cake for the murderer on the front porch, but so what? Sliding the portion onto a small plate, she added a fork and a napkin. Then she carried the candle in one hand and the cake in the other to the front door.

"I thought you went away," he said. "I thought you pro'ly left me."

"I brought you some chocolate cake. Now, go sit on the porch swing over there."

He smiled. "Chocolate cake! I love chocolate cake!"

27

"Sit on the porch swing. I mean it. Sit down and don't move."

"Okay." His shoulders slumped and his muddy shoes crossed the wooden deck to the swing.

Brenda could hear the rain pouring outside as she unlocked the door, quickly set the plate and candle on the welcome mat, and then shut the door again. When she turned the lock, the electricity in the house suddenly came back on.

"Hey!" Cody said, gazing up at the porch fan with its central light fixture. He focused on Brenda. "Hey! Look!"

She nodded. "You can get the cake now. It's by the door."

"I'm not allowed to touch candles," he told her. "Because fire is hot. Because it can hurt you."

"Then don't touch the candle. Just get your cake."

He stood, looking tall, bushy, and frightening again. Wearing only a yellow T-shirt, a faded blue zippered jacket, a pair of ragged jeans, and grubby sneakers with holes in the toes, he looked as wet, bedraggled, and forlorn as a stray dog. *He must be about to freeze,* Brenda thought.

Bending over, he lifted the cake from the plate. In two bites, it was gone. "Chocolate cake!" he said, beaming at her. Dark crumbs coated his crooked teeth. "I knew you were a Christian."

"You're right," Brenda said through the locked door. "I am a Christian."

"Because I saw Jesus in your basement."

"No, you didn't. He's not here, Cody."

She studied the man as he licked his fingers. He must be some homeless person. She had read in the newspaper that many of them were mentally ill. Maybe he was harmless after all. Feeling less fearful with the brightly lit foyer and porch, she let out a breath. "Are you still hungry?" she asked.

He looked up in surprise. "Yes, I am! I could eat another piece of chocolate cake."

"I'll fix you some dinner. Wait there on the porch swing. Don't move."

At least she would have something to tell Steve when he came home tonight, Brenda thought as she returned to the kitchen. Her husband had zero interest in the chairs she was painting downstairs. Or anything else she did, for that matter.

Working day and night during the fall, she had sewn brand-new slipcovers for the sofa and two armchairs. He hadn't noticed. She waited three days before calling her handiwork to his attention. Then he had said, "Brenda, if you wanted new furniture, why didn't you just tell me? I'm making enough money now to buy you a whole new living-room set."

As if that's what she had wanted. Brenda took two pieces of baked chicken, some leftover green-bean casserole, and a dollop of mashed potatoes from the refrigerator. Setting the plate in the microwave, she felt her anger and hurt grow as she set the timer and punched the Start button.

When the kids were growing up, Steve had worked in sales at an auto-parts store, and he had eaten up all the details of what the family had done each day while he was away. He wanted to see every drawing and read the kids' book reports. He rough-housed with Justin and piggybacked Jennifer and Jessica all through the house and yard. He laughed at the stories of their shenanigans, and in the evenings, he even listened to Brenda's plans for the weekend or a coming school holiday.

But Steve didn't care about the pink-and-yellow-plaid chairs she had been painting for the dining room. Plaid was very tricky — various-sized bands of glazed color going this way and that. He would have no idea how hard it was to paint. Who thought about the intricacies of plaid?

Steve wouldn't notice how the dining

chairs matched the napkins and placemats she had sewn. Or how all of it coordinated with the new slipcovers in the living room.

"Pink?" he had said when he finally focused on the sofa with its beautiful print of roses, ivy, trellises, and butterflies. "Well . . . I guess I can learn to live with it."

Learn to live with it? What kind of a comment was that?

"It wasn't Jesus after all."

The voice in the kitchen knocked the breath right out of Brenda's chest. She turned to find the long-haired stranger standing less than five feet away. Streaks of mud trailed from his shoes back across the living room toward the stairs that led to the basement.

The sliding glass door. The unlocked screen.

Brenda grabbed the knife she had used to cut the cake. "I told you to wait on the porch swing!"

He took a step backward and held up his hands. "Whoops. Are you mad at me?"

"Go outside. Get out right now. I mean it!"

"Because I went around the house to check on Jesus, and He wasn't there. It wasn't Him after all, and you know how I figured it out?"

31

"Cody, you may not stay in this kitchen. Go out the front door over there. Do it now."

"It wasn't Jesus. It was me." He smiled, chocolate-cake crumbs still filling the crevices of his teeth. "The door was like a mirror. When I looked in the basement, I thought it was Jesus, but it was me. Just me in the glass, like a mirror. Can you see how I got confused — with my beard and hair all long? It was me, not Jesus. That's funny."

"It's not funny that you came into my house without asking. Now go outside this minute."

"Okay." He looked at the floor as he turned away. "I thought you might give me some more chocolate cake even though Jesus doesn't live downstairs."

"I'll give you some dinner . . . and cake . . . if you'll go outside."

"It's warmer in here."

"But you can't stay. You're not invited."

"Okay." Cody shrugged, then dragged his muddy shoes back across the kitchen and through the foyer. "You are the nicest Christian I ever met. And you are the only lady I ever knew with a pink cat."

"A pink cat?" Behind him, Brenda carried the plate of steaming food, unlocked the door, and gave him a gentle push back onto the porch. It *was* cold outside.

"For your information, my cat is gray. Here, take this," she ordered, handing him the plate.

Then she picked up the candle from the welcome mat, retreated, and locked the door again. As Cody sat on the porch swing to eat his dinner, Brenda raced down the stairs and locked the sliding glass door.

When she turned around, she noticed what she had missed on her way down. Muddy footprints mingled with a pattern of pink paw marks that covered the basement floor. And on the coffee table, where her three children had propped their feet while watching television, sat one miserable — and very pink — cat.

Charlie Moore's teeth were chattering as he drove his golf cart past the Hansen house. With the electricity back on in Deepwater Cove and all the neighbors safe and sound, he was eager to get home to Esther. Before he set out on his appointed rounds tonight, she had packed him a thermos of water — cold, of course, since the power was off and she couldn't make coffee. And she had put some of her famous chocolate-chip cookies in a Baggie for him. Those were long gone now.

A mug of hot chocolate sure would taste good, Charlie thought. He knew Esther would have the stove on and the water heating when he walked in the front door. He would ask for two marshmallows even though it was against the rules for his diabetes. Esther would give them to him too, because she'd realize he was about frozen to death. Besides, if a man couldn't have marshmallows in his hot chocolate, what was the point?

"Now, what in the dickens . . . ?" Charlie muttered as his golf cart crept to the top of Sunnyslope Lane. He pushed the brake pedal, put the cart in reverse, and looked over his shoulder as he backed down the hill. There was a *man* sitting on Steve Hansen's front porch. He was eating off a plate and rocking so hard in the wicker swing that it looked like the whole porch might come down.

Glad he had decided to leave his dog, Boofer, at home, Charlie parked beside a large lilac bush that was just beginning to leaf out and set the brake. He could see immediately that the swinger was *not* Steve Hansen. Steve kept his dark hair cropped short and his face neatly shaved. These days, he usually wore a suit and tie, because he was always driving around the lake to show houses listed with his real-estate agency. He had gotten a little thicker around the middle, but who didn't as the years went by?

The fellow on the porch was as skinny as some old alley cat. He wore a yellow T-shirt with the word *Cheerios* printed on the front in bold black letters. His brown beard and curly hair hung long and tangled. Charlie would have considered going home for his gun if the man hadn't looked so goofy sitting there swinging his legs back and forth like a little kid.

Flipping open the glove compartment in his golf cart, Charlie took out a can of Mace. A mail carrier knew to be careful at all times, no matter what. He slipped the can into his pocket and gingerly stepped down onto the wet road.

As Charlie walked toward the Hansen house, the swinging stranger looked up.

"Hi, I'm Cody!" the man called out. "Guess what. She's got chocolate cake inside! Squares, not triangles."

Wary, shoulders tensed the way they did when he was facing a growling dog, Charlie stepped onto the porch. "Cold night to be without a coat," he remarked, keeping his voice casual. When the stranger didn't respond, Charlie asked, "So, is Steve

Hansen home?"

"I'm Cody!" The bearded man stopped swinging and held out his empty plate. "Look. It was chicken and potatoes and green beans. And more chocolate cake. I ate two pieces, so you know what *that* means."

Charlie gripped the Mace can in his pocket. "No. What does that mean?"

"It means she's a Christian. Because my daddy told me that anyone might give you food, but only a Christian would give you chocolate cake, too."

"I see." This guy clearly wasn't all there. Anyone could tell that from the get-go. But was he dangerous? "So, who gave you the cake?"

"Her." He pointed toward the Hansens' front door. "*She's* a Christian even though Jesus isn't in the basement."

"How 'bout that. Well, I believe I'll just check on her, then. Make sure she's okay after the big storm."

Charlie carefully crossed the porch. The man might look like a half-drowned alley cat, but he could turn out to be as mean as a junkyard dog. You never could tell. Charlie pressed the doorbell.

For a moment, the horrible thought crossed his mind that something might have happened to Brenda Hansen. She was without a doubt the prettiest female in Deepwater Cove — except for Esther, who would always be the most beautiful girl in the world to Charlie. But Brenda was young — probably still in her forties — and she had spunky, short blonde hair and sparkly green eyes. She was always out working in the garden or washing windows or mowing. The Hansen home never collected the large, dangling black spiders that inhabited the eaves and screened porches on most of the lake houses. Brenda took her broom to them every night, and she made sure her driveway was swept and her porch was neat as a pin. Steve never helped her with that kind of thing anymore, not since his work kept him so busy. Charlie sure would hate to think Brenda was in trouble without her husband around to protect her.

Just as he was working up a full head of worry, Brenda emerged through the foyer with a mop in one hand and a wet pink cat under her arm. She peered through the window that was set into her front door.

Spotting Charlie, she put the cat down and gave him a bright smile. "Hey, there, Charlie!" Brenda said as she opened the door. She glanced over his shoulder at the porch swing. "I guess you've met Cody."

Charlie nodded and quirked an eyebrow

at her. "You okay?"

"I am now that the lights are back on."

"Want me to call the sheriff?"

She leaned one shoulder against the doorframe and spoke in a low voice. "I don't think so. Have you ever seen him before?"

"No, but folks do come out of the woods sometimes, you know. They can live in the hills and hollers for years without attracting a bit of attention, and then something brings them back into the public. The sheriff would take him off your hands. I really think you should notify the authorities, Brenda."

"Oh, here comes Steve," she said. As a sleek silver hybrid car pulled into the Hansens' driveway, the garage door rose. "He missed all the excitement."

"Steve won't want someone like that hanging around Deepwater," Charlie predicted. "Might drive down real-estate values, you know. That husband of yours is sure stirring up things with his business. Heard he hired a secretary and took on a couple of agents. You folks have got such a pretty house here that —"

"Thank you, Charlie." Brenda cut him off as her husband walked up from behind her.

Steve Hansen had come into the house through the garage, and Charlie felt surprised to see him suddenly there. Steve peered around his neighbor to have a look at the stranger.

"Hey, Charlie," he said, putting his arm across his wife's shoulders. "Quite a storm, huh? Who's that on the porch?"

"It's Cody." Brenda spoke as if a skinny man wearing a Cheerios T-shirt and sitting on her porch swing were the commonest thing in the world. She shrugged out from under Steve's arm. "I fed him dinner. He likes my chocolate cake."

"What?" Steve stared at her in disbelief. "Who is he?"

"Cody," Brenda repeated. She smiled at Charlie again. "Thanks for checking on me. It's nice to know someone cares."

Charlie glanced at the man on the porch. Cody was licking his plate. "I guess I'll get on home to Esther, then," he said. "Give me a call if you need anything."

"We're fine." Brenda tilted her head a little, the way she used to when she was talking to one of her kids. "Everything's fine, Charlie. It really is. Just fine."

Gripping his can of Mace, Charlie stepped past Cody and started back to his golf cart. He might ask Esther for three marshmallows tonight.

Chapter Two

The next morning, Patsy Pringle almost lost her temper. She was repairing a set of acrylic fingernails for a regular client at the time. It seemed that no one who came into the Just As I Am beauty shop could talk about anything but the stranger who had appeared on the Hansens' front porch during the storm. By ten o'clock, Patsy had just about had it up to here. It was all she could do to focus on her work.

Some people said the man's name was Cody. Others called him Colby. One woman kept calling him Cory. He had been described as everything from a Mexican to a hippie to a hillbilly to a drunk. He had bushy black hair, long brown hair, filthy blond hair. He was fat, skinny, tall, short, young, old. He was creepy, menacing, sweet, innocent, and dumb. If Esther Moore hadn't come in for a redo on her set-and-style this morning, Patsy would have concluded the man was a figment of everyone's imagination.

Now Esther sat over in the tearoom and repeated the story to anyone who would listen. A sunny, glass-windowed area on the far side of the salon provided three tables, plenty of chairs, a wide choice of teas, and countless goodies for Patsy's clientele. She had planned it as a place of relaxation, quiet reflection, and spiritual refreshment. Esther and the women gathered around her had other ideas.

Several people claimed to have seen the fellow during the storm. Some said he had been spotted in the lake area even before that. Evidently he had knocked on quite a few doors during the rain, but only Charlie had actually talked to the man. This made Esther queen of the henhouse, forcing the others to gather around her for grains of information they could take home to their own little nests and savor in private.

"Property values will go right down the drain," she was telling two of the Deepwater Cove widows who had joined her for a cup of Earl Grey. "You can't have someone like that wandering around your neighborhood. It's just not right."

Patsy fought the urge to march right over to the radio and turn up the volume. She didn't play Christian music at the shop for nothing. In the local newspaper, Patsy pointedly advertised the Just As I Am salon as "a faith-based beauty experience." On the sound system, she alternated a Christian station with CDs of Christian recording artists, including her favorite local trio, Color of Mercy. A stack of free pamphlets explaining the path to salvation waited by the cash register for anyone who wanted one. Uplifting, decent women's magazines filled the shelves in the waiting area. She had painted the tearoom a soothing pale lavender and had hung lace curtains at the windows. A hand-lettered copy of Jesus' words in Matthew 11:28 — "Come unto me, all ye that labor and are heavy laden, and I will give you rest" — hung right over the hot-water urn.

Anyone would have thought that so much Christianity floating around would keep the gossip to a minimum. But no. Every day, in walked the women buzzing about this, that, and the other. Young Ashley Hanes would arrive for her manicure and start jabbering about her husband's buddies and all the trouble they were causing their wives. Kim Finley brought her twins in for haircuts and the next thing you knew, she was discussing the women in her office, sharing details from their lives. And then there was Esther Moore. It didn't matter how old or how young they were, Patsy mused; these women took one step inside Just As I Am and started jabbering and squawking and fussing like a bunch of blue jays around a birdbath.

Patsy had opened for business when she was twenty-five, and not too long after that, she had been just about ready to take down her sign and close the shop. Then one of her regulars mentioned how safe and comfortable she always felt at the salon. It was a place to unwind. A place to get things off your chest. A place where you could talk, and people would listen. More than that, at Just As I Am, you always knew someone would care. That had been ten years ago, and Patsy had come to tolerate — if not enjoy — the chatter.

Today she gritted her teeth and concentrated on the French manicure she was applying while the women discussed this latest development in the neighborhood. They not only talked about the stranger and how his presence affected the area, but every woman wanted to offer an opinion as to what *she* would have done if he had stood on *her* front porch. There would have been calls to the sheriff, shotguns taken down from racks, and hostile dogs let out to run the fellow off. No one could imagine actually opening the door the way Brenda Hansen had. Or *talking* to him. Or, heaven forbid, *feeding* him.

Only when the entire salon suddenly fell silent did Patsy look up to find that Brenda herself had walked in the front door. You would have thought it was the Easter bunny. Blow-dryers went dead, chatter ceased, and everyone turned to gawk.

"Well, hey there, Brenda," Patsy greeted her. She flipped on the dryer over her client's wet nails. "I haven't seen you in ages. Where've you been keeping yourself?"

"I've been . . . busy."

Brenda was a quiet woman these days — not like when her kids had been at home. Cute, bouncy, spunky, she had always been the sort of woman people admired and sought out as a friend. She could do any kind of artsy-crafty thing, she loved children, and she kept her flower gardens so pretty that folks were always stopping by to compliment her. And sweet . . . she was so sweet that if you kissed her cheek, you'd taste sugar.

But this past fall, Patsy had noticed that Brenda seemed to be dragging around as though something had let the wind out of her sails. Unlike in past years, she didn't bother to rake up the leaves from her big maples and oaks. No one ever saw her sweeping the front porch anymore, and she hadn't decorated her house with the usual Christmas zeal — no candy canes lining the driveway or strings of white lights in the bare tree branches.

What troubled Patsy the most was that recently Brenda had kind of let herself go. Today she was wearing a pair of old faded jeans and a raggedy sweater. She hadn't bothered with makeup, and her hair was downright shaggy.

"You want a trim?" Patsy asked hopefully.

"Could you work me in?"

"Let me take a look at the book." Patsy crossed to the desk where her stylists listed their appointments. She scanned her schedule for the day. "If you'll give me ten minutes to finish these nails and tidy up my station, Brenda, I can do you myself. You want the usual?"

"Yes, please."

As Brenda settled in the waiting area, Esther approached, carrying a teacup. Esther was a dear woman, Patsy knew, but she sure could pry.

Wearing a motherly expression, Esther sat down beside Brenda. "Charlie said you had

45

quite an adventure last night."

"I lost my electricity," Brenda told her. "But I guess everyone did."

"It took Charlie forever to find his flashlight. I thought he never would get out to the golf cart to go check on the neighbors. He told me he was pretty worried about you."

"When the lightning hit, Ozzie jumped up and landed in a paint tray. I'm doing my dining-room chairs in a pink-and-yellow plaid."

Esther never missed a beat. "Yes, but what about that *man?* Charlie said the fellow like to scared him to death."

"That was Cody." Brenda turned a page of the magazine in her lap. "He was wet and hungry."

"And you fed him?"

"I heated some leftovers and gave him a piece of chocolate cake."

"Well, who on earth was he?"

"Cody. That's about all I know."

"What did Steve do after Charlie left your house?"

Brenda's face grew somber for a moment. Then she shrugged. "He went to bed. He works so hard, you know."

"Yes, but . . . but . . ." For once in her life Esther had run out of words.

"You ready, Brenda?" Patsy asked. She had swept her station and put away the dryer and curling iron from her last customer. "Come on over."

Brenda stood, laid down her magazine, and then faced Esther. "Cody slept on our porch swing last night. And if he's there again tonight, you can tell Charlie not to bother him. We don't mind a bit."

With that, she lifted her chin and carried her purse over to Patsy's station.

Steve Hansen pulled his Honda Civic hybrid to a stop at the gas pump in front of Pete Roberts's Rods-n-Ends. A month ago, the store next door to the beauty salon had reopened under new ownership, and everyone in Deepwater Cove had breathed a sigh of relief. Not only were the two gas pumps back in service, but Pete had stocked the shelves with lures, tackle, snacks, wakeboards, skis, sunscreen, coolers, minnow buckets, and even a few swimming suits and towels. If it could be used at the lake, Rods-n-Ends had it.

A single wall separated Patsy Pringle's small, glass-windowed tea area from Pete's store. But that was as far as the similarities went. Lately Pete had been talking about selling pre-owned Jet Skis, johnboats, and even a few four-wheelers and motorcycles. He was already repairing small engines in his extra room, and he felt that fixing up and selling secondhand vehicles would keep him in business during the slow months. Steve agreed.

At Lake of the Ozarks, multimillion-dollar homes, marinas, golf courses, and country clubs tended to overshadow the harsh reality faced by many of the area's year-round residents. Mobile homes and sagging houses with leaky roofs hid in the woods along roads that led to high-end condominiums and gated communities. Parent-teacher night filled the local school's parking lot with an odd mix of rusty old junkers and luxury sedans. Steve knew there wasn't much of a middle class at the lake, and it was tough on those who tried to make a decent living.

Bagnell Dam, built in the 1930s, had plugged up five rivers and created a body of water that now boasted 1,200 miles of shoreline. Restaurants, arcades, antiques shops, grocery stores, bars, and tattoo parlors proliferated, but these businesses failed at an alarming rate. Turnover in the strip mall at Tranquility was too high for comfort, Steve believed. He had been considering a move into commercial real estate

— and keeping that little mall alive was one of his major goals.

Congratulating himself once again for his wisdom in buying a hybrid, Steve ran his credit card through the slot on the gas pump. As he began to fill the tank, he saw Pete Roberts saunter out from the store.

"Hey, Steve. How's it going?" Pete wandered over and started washing the Honda's windshield. "Sell any houses today?"

"I'm closing on one next week, and I've got another that's just about ready to go to contract. It's a great market for both buyers and sellers right now." He made his voice sound as cheerful as possible. "What's new with you?"

Pete Roberts, a newcomer to Deepwater Cove, might be a good-looking man, but it was hard to tell under his beard. If he really wanted his business to succeed, Steve thought, he needed to lose some of that beer belly, shave his beard, and put on a pair of khakis. Old, worn-out jeans didn't look professional. And he ought to wear a long-sleeved shirt to cover up those tattoos.

"Folks have been in and out of the store all day," Pete commented. He began wiping the streaks from the windshield. "Sold a lot of minnows and a fair number of worms. They say fishing's been pretty good. You

49

been out much?"

"No time for fishing these days. The business keeps me going nonstop."

"Everybody's talking about some fellow who showed up on your front porch last night in the storm," Pete said. "You get a good look at him?"

Steve grimaced. News traveled way too fast in Deepwater Cove. He recalled the heated discussion he and Brenda had gotten into the evening before. It seemed lately that was the only kind of talking they did.

Brenda had once been bright, energetic, and fun. But she was growing more and more unpleasant, and the whole situation confused him.

Just when she should have been her happiest, she had begun to turn sour and snappy. On top of that, she had lost so much weight that she looked downright haggard. Steve had always admired the soft curves and rounded femininity that Brenda bemoaned while gazing at herself in the mirror. "Look at these hips," she would lament, but he loved them. A woman ought to be shapely, he thought, with gentle mounds and silky hollows in all the right places.

It bothered Steve that his wife wasn't eating right, taking care of herself, or looking at the sunny side of life. These days, entering their house felt like stepping into a chill wind off the lake. When Brenda emerged from the kitchen or the basement — her eyes distant and her hair straggly — he felt like he had come home to the Ice Queen.

Last night Steve had been frustrated and worried. Why on earth had she thought it was safe to open the front door and hand a plate of food to a complete stranger?

She had told him there was paint and mud all over the basement floor. Then she started crying.

By that time, Steve was so upset with her that all he could do was go to bed and hope it blew over by the next day. He had left the house this morning before Brenda was up.

"I saw the fellow on the porch," Steve told Pete. "Pretty hard to miss. I figure he was just some homeless guy, cold and hungry. Brenda gave him a bite to eat, and he was gone this morning."

"You got yourself a fine wife there," Pete observed. "Not too many women would be brave enough to do a kind deed like that."

Steve studied the bearded man for a moment. "You married, Pete?"

"Twice. I'm single now. Quit drinking three years ago after one too many DUIs and a little jail time. I took a business class at the tech school in Springfield. Got things turned around pretty good now, but I'm not looking for another wife. I'm sure you're grateful for yours, though. Brenda stopped in for gas today and bought a cooler, and I thought to myself, now that's a good-hearted woman. And pretty, too."

"Yes, she sure is," Steve agreed, picturing his wife's tear-streaked cheeks and swollen nose from the night before. He handed Pete two dollar bills for the windshield. "Well, you have a good evening now."

Pete smiled and shook his head. "Glad to be of service," he said. "You keep your money and come see me the next time you manage to empty that hybrid's gas tank."

"It'll be a while," Steve said with a laugh.

Pete was a decent sort of fellow, Steve thought as he pulled away from Rods-n-Ends. Passing the beauty shop next door, he saw that the lights were still on and Patsy Pringle was doing someone's hair. It gave him a good feeling to envision people working in their stores and salons, building up the local economy, making life better for themselves and everyone around.

As he drove away from the town of Tranquility toward Deepwater Cove, Steve reflected on the long journey of his own life. Growing up poor, marrying young, and having three kids — one right after the other —

had forced him to abandon all thoughts of college. He had worked long and hard selling auto parts, coaching Little League teams, helping with the youth group at church. He had enjoyed his kids, and Brenda had done a great job with them. Steve wouldn't be a bit surprised if Jennifer got married and went off to be a full-time missionary. Justin and Jessica were making progress in college, and Steve couldn't be prouder.

Best of all, Steve had come up with the idea to sell real estate on the side to defray the college expenses. He truly believed that God had given him that desire.

As it turned out, his experience peddling auto parts had helped him become an outstanding salesman. He took a course on how to sell property and went to work for an agency in Tranquility. Before he knew it, he was making sufficient money to quit his regular job. Soon he was earning enough to pay for all three kids' college and a couple of new cars. The next step had been to start an office of his own. And now he had a secretary and two sales associates.

So why did he have to walk through the door and run smack-dab into Brenda's cold shoulder? Why couldn't she be satisfied with her husband and glad to see him at the end of the day? As Steve pulled his car into the garage, he almost wished he could turn tail and run.

Brenda used to greet her husband with "hello" and a kiss. Today she ignored him and kept stirring something on the stove. Steve hung his coat in the hall closet, kicked off his shoes, and went looking for the local newspaper. He liked to check the real-estate section and find out what his competition was up to. Settling into a recliner, he flicked on the TV and scanned the paper. He could hear Brenda in the kitchen banging pots and pans around. Well, if she didn't want to talk, that was fine with him. A cop show was coming on in a few minutes, and he would watch that and then head for bed.

Of course, Steve would have preferred if Brenda had come into the living room, sat down in his lap, and let him put his arms around her and tell her all about his day. About the couple who had discussed listing their big lakefront house near Tranquility with his agency. And the folks who had come by the office to see pictures of his highest-priced homes. And the lady whose dog had upchucked something green and nasty on the carpet in one of the condos he was showing her. It might have been nice if his wife had offered him a piece of her chocolate cake — which she knew he loved — and asked him how the new computerized record-keeping program was working out. But no, she was giving him the silent treatment.

His cop show came on, and Steve got sleepy. He was just about to doze off when he heard Brenda open the front door. Glancing in that direction, he saw her heft a big white cooler with a blue lid out onto the porch. She pulled the door shut behind her and didn't come back in.

Steve frowned. It was one thing for Brenda to ignore him, but now she was acting strange. He eased out of the recliner and padded over to the door. Through the front window, he could see Brenda sitting on the porch swing. And she was talking to *him.*

The stranger!

His heart suddenly racing, Steve threw open the door and stepped outside. Bad enough to have a vagrant in the neighborhood, but this was too much.

"Brenda?" he said.

"Oh, Steve, it's you." Her voice was crisp, like a chill wind that cut right through to his bones. "Would you like to meet my new friend?"

For a minute, Steve couldn't make anything come out of his mouth. He stared at the skinny man, a young fellow with a tangled beard and long hair. The man stood with one of the Hansens' stoneware bowls in his grimy hand.

"Hi, I'm Cody!" he said, breaking into a grin. "I got some soup tonight. Lots of it. I've been hungry, but now look!"

He bent and flipped open the cooler's blue lid. Inside sat two stacks of full, lidded soup bowls; several Baggies of sandwiches; and a few boxes of fruit juice. "And chocolate cake!" Cody continued. "Because my daddy told me that anyone might give you food, but only a Christian would give you chocolate cake, too. That means she's a Christian. What's your name?"

Steve managed to put on his best Realtor smile and held out his hand. "I'm Steve Hansen."

"How old are you?" Cody stuck out his left hand and awkwardly shook Steve's right. "I'm getting older now, and my daddy told me it's time to make my way. 'Make your way, Cody.' That's what he told me. How old are you?"

"I'm forty-five," Steve said, glancing at Brenda.

"Hey!" Cody plopped down on the swing. "Same as her! Forty-five years. What's your name, lady? I forgot already."

"Brenda Hansen. I'm married to Steve."

"Okay." Cody sipped a spoonful of soup. "Forty-five years. That's pretty old. I'm not that old."

"How old are you?" Brenda asked in a soft voice.

Cody studied her. "I'm not forty-five years."

"No, you're younger."

"Okay. This sure is good soup. Look!" He flipped open the lid of the cooler again for Steve. "It's full to the brim! You could eat it for forty-five years. She gave it to me, because I was hungry. And chocolate cake, too. Three pieces!"

The tension began to slide out of Steve's shoulders. He could tell right away that this fellow was neither drunk nor criminal. He was just simple, that's all. Childlike. Still, you couldn't be sure he was harmless. Pete Roberts at Rods-n-Ends had been right to call Brenda good-hearted. She was kind to help out a hungry person. But she never should have opened the door without Steve around, and what was she thinking — buying a cooler and filling it with soup and sandwiches?

"Brenda," he said, "could I talk to you inside for a minute?"

She lifted her chin, stared straight at him,

and said, "I'm visiting with Cody. Sorry."

A flood of icy rage spread through Steve's chest. "I see."

"We're chatting. You can go on back in and watch your TV show."

Steve sucked down a deep breath. "Brenda, I want to talk to you inside the house. Now."

She shrugged. "Did you try a sandwich, Cody? They're turkey and cheese. I think you ought to have one tonight. And keep the lid on your cooler. You don't want to let all the cold air out."

Steve stared at his wife. He felt like she'd stabbed him through the gut with an icicle. Did he deserve this kind of disrespect? this contempt? What had he done but work hard and give her everything she could want? Now she was sitting on the porch swing feeding a bushy-haired stranger and treating her own husband like a pesky gnat buzzing around her head.

"Where do you live, Cody?" Steve barked out. "Do you have a house around here?"

Cody spoke through a bite of turkey sandwich. "My daddy told me it's time to make my way. 'Make your way, Cody.' That's what he told me."

"Where's your daddy now?"

The young man hung his head. "Well . . .

it's time to make my way."

"Cody's not sure where his father is," Brenda explained, her voice gentler toward Steve for the first time in days. "I think he's been wandering around for a while. He told me his daddy used to make him shave, but they haven't been together lately. Judging by his beard, I'd say it's been a long time since Cody last saw his father."

The whole time she talked, Brenda looked at Cody instead of at her husband. Steve felt invisible. "I've put a few blankets and a pillow in a backpack for Cody," she continued. "I told him he's welcome to sleep here on the porch swing if he wants, or he can go camp somewhere. At least he'll be warm."

With that, she stood and patted the young man on the shoulder. "Good night, Cody. I hope you sleep well."

"Thank you." Cody stood up. "What's your name? I forgot again."

"Brenda."

"Thank you, Brenda. You're forty-five years old."

"That's exactly right." She smiled. "And how old are you?"

"Twenty-one," he blurted out, as if surprised to hear it himself. "My daddy said, 'You're twenty-one, Cody. Time to make your way.' "

"Well, what do you know?" Brenda said. She glanced at Steve as she passed him. "Cody is twenty-one years old."

The front door shut behind her, and Steve stifled an impulse to throw the bum off his porch. A decent family couldn't have a vagrant lolling around all night. Maybe Cody was slow, but he was an adult, and he needed to go to a homeless shelter or something. Steve didn't have to put up with this. He ought to just run the guy off and get back to his evening routine.

"Wow," Cody said from the porch swing. "This is the best soup I ever ate in all my life. And look! Chocolate cake too. Brenda is a Christian, because she gave it to me. I love chocolate cake."

Disgusted with himself, Brenda, and even Cody, Steve turned on his heel and stomped back into the house. He shut and locked the door. This was great. Steve could just hear Charlie Moore chatting with the neighbors as he made the rounds on his golf cart: *"There's a bum sleeping on the Hansens' front porch. He's there every night. Brenda feeds him, and Steve puts up with it. Can you believe that?"*

Nobody in Deepwater Cove would want a simpleminded bum loitering around. People

60

felt safe in their little neighborhood. They enjoyed being able to leave their doors unlocked by day and their windows open at night. The low crime rate at Lake of the Ozarks was part of what drew so many people to buy second homes there. Million-dollar homes. You just couldn't have a hairy, unwashed nut job wandering around the place.

"Brenda?" Steve walked into the bedroom. She was in the adjoining bathroom. He knocked on the door. "Brenda? I want to talk to you right this minute."

She threw open the door, stepped out, and stalked to the bed. "I'm tired," she announced over her shoulder. "Good night."

"Tired? Tired from what?" In disbelief, Steve watched her pull back the comforter and slide into bed. "What have you done today besides make soup and sandwiches for a bum?"

Brenda's eyes narrowed. "The only bum I know is standing in my bedroom."

"What? Now you're calling me a bum? How many bums do you know who can buy a house like this . . . put kids through college . . . and leave you at home to do as you please?"

Brenda switched off the light beside her bed. Turning away from him, she drew the comforter up to her neck. "Good night, bum."

"Brenda, listen . . . I don't know what's going on with you, but things had better start changing around here." He crossed to her side of the bed and switched her light back on. "You can't just shut me out like this. There's a stranger on our front porch, and if you think you can —"

"The only stranger around here is you, Steve Hansen," she said, sitting up in bed. Her eyes glittered with an ice-cold green light. "I never see you. I don't even know who you are anymore. And if you want something to change, well, your wish is about to come true. You know what's changing? Me. I called a carpenter, and he's coming over next week to give me a bid on remodeling the basement. I'm feeding a poor, cold, hungry man who doesn't know where he is, and I plan to keep on feeding him until someone shows up to claim him or he figures out what to do with himself. I got my hair cut today, and I washed the cat, and I finished painting the dining-room chairs. And guess what else is different? I don't need you. I don't need anyone or anything. I'm fine by myself, so just leave me alone, and don't you dare touch me. This discussion is over."

With that, she snapped off the light again. Steve stood in the darkness and stared down at the lumpy shape that used to be his wife.

CHAPTER THREE

At the salon a few days later, Patsy Pringle was putting the finishing touches on a beautiful manicure. Young Ashley Hanes had the prettiest hands in Deepwater Cove, and she enjoyed drawing attention to her new wedding ring. Patsy couldn't imagine how Brad Hanes had paid for that glittering one-carat rock on his wife's finger, but maybe the construction business was more profitable than a person might think. Summer was on its way, and new houses would be going up left and right. With Ashley working as a waitress at one of the country clubs and Brad on the building crew for a big home just the other side of Tranquility, they might be pulling in a fair amount of cash.

"What did you call this color?" Ashley asked, gazing at her hands. "Rose something-or-other?"

"Tea rose." Patsy leaned back and admired

her work. "It's a pretty shade on you. Flattering."

"Brad loves my long nails," Ashley said. She gave a shy giggle. "He thinks they're hot."

"I wouldn't know about that. But if Brad likes something, then you better take good care of it."

"Were you ever married, Patsy?" Ashley asked suddenly.

For a split second, Patsy considered retorting that such a thing was no one's business but her own. Then she thought about the ladies chatting over in the tea area, the stylists primping and cooing along with their clients, and the Christian music playing softly in the salon. At Just As I Am, no one could claim privacy. If a subject came up that was a matter of interest to others in the cozy little salon, you simply had to talk.

"Never have found a husband," Patsy replied with a sigh. "I guess I still could — I'm still this side of forty — but Mr. Right hasn't come through the door yet. When I was closer to the marrying age, I was busy taking care of my mother and her Alzheimer's disease. I was going to cosmetology college and working long hours over in Osage Beach. Even if a man had been interested in me, I didn't have time to date, much less get serious with anyone."

"I wish you could have found a guy like Brad," Ashley said. Her brown eyes reminded Patsy of pots of melted chocolate. "He is awesome. It's like being married to my best friend. Every morning I wake up next to him, and I'm just so shocked, you know? Brad Hanes is really my husband! I actually married him! And when his truck pulls up to the house at night, I practically shiver. I never thought marriage would be this wonderful. Brad is the greatest thing that ever happened to me."

Patsy smiled. "I'm glad you're so happy, sweetheart. I remember you coming into the salon with your mother when you were a little girl, and I thought to myself, that child deserves a good life."

Beaming, Ashley held her nails under the dryer. "Brad and I are talking about having a baby," she said in a low voice. "Don't tell."

"My lips are sealed," Patsy assured her. She studied Ashley for a moment, feeling a warm glow radiating from the young beauty with her auburn hair and lovely smile and graceful hands. It was like watching a rose bloom. Or an exquisite fern leaf uncurl.

Brad Hanes had come into the salon a few days earlier for his once-a-month haircut, and Patsy sensed she was in the presence of a young buck in the springtime. Brad was just full of himself — face tanned from working outdoors, shoulders broad and strong, blue eyes glowing. He acted as though marrying Ashley had crowned him king of the world. Every time her name came up in conversation, he smiled slyly, as if he were the only man in the universe to discover the joys of marital bliss.

The young couple was talking about remodeling their little house on the second tier at Deepwater Cove, Brad had confided to Patsy. He said Ashley wanted to take some college classes and become a kindergarten teacher. Brad had bought himself a new truck. And now they were hoping for children.

"You just enjoy that husband of yours," Patsy said, giving Ashley's shoulder a pat. "Brad is a good man, and he's going to make you a very happy woman."

"I know," Ashley sighed. "Look at my ring. Can you believe he bought this for me? And we have our own home and the truck. We're way ahead of most of my friends. But I'll tell you something. . . ." She leaned across the manicure table. "Brad's not thrilled with the situation over at the Hansens' house.

That creepy guy, you know? With the beard?"

"I know," Patsy said. Did she ever.

"They say he's been sleeping on the Hansens' porch. I heard that Steve wanted to call the sheriff, but Brenda wouldn't let him. Brad told me he was walking down to the lake a couple of evenings ago, and he saw Steve and Brenda in their backyard so upset they were practically yelling at each other. Can you imagine that? I always thought they were the perfect couple. Their house is so pretty . . . all that work they've done on it. And the flowers, too. Did you know Brenda's been feeding that homeless guy?"

"I suspect he's hungry."

"Brad doesn't like having a stranger in the neighborhood. He won't let me take my ring off when I'm doing dishes, and he locks the truck up tight every night, including the toolbox. We bolt all the doors, too."

Patsy sensed the conversation had crossed the line from concerned discussion to outright gossip. "Charlie Moore told Esther the fellow was just simple in the head," she assured Ashley. "I don't think you and Brad have a thing to worry about."

"Maybe not." The young woman studied her nails again. "Tea rose. It's a pretty color.

I hope I can keep from banging them up. Being a waitress is not easy on a manicure; that's for sure."

Patsy began to clean up the nail station. She had a client coming in for a perm in a few minutes, and it was always hard to find time to keep the floor swept, the counters cleaned, and the windows washed. All that hair spray!

Working more than fifty hours a week left Patsy on the verge of exhaustion, but what choice did she have? To her, Just As I Am was more than a beauty salon. It was a ministry. She had labored long and hard to buy a place of her own and build a loyal clientele — and God had blessed her beyond measure.

As Patsy grabbed a broom and went to work on the floor, Ashley laid her manicure money on the front desk and sauntered over to the tea area. The young woman did most of her waitressing at night. That gave her time to relax and visit while she was at Just As I Am. A wave of gratitude welled up inside Patsy as she covertly studied the women sipping cups of Earl Grey tea and nibbling shortbread cookies. Never in her wildest dreams had Patsy imagined having a tearoom, but it had become one of the most profitable parts of her business.

The whole thing had started off with only a hot pot and a few tea bags. She didn't charge, even though it meant doing a whole dishwasher load of mugs every night. Pretty soon, Patsy had noticed women carrying chairs into the glass-windowed alcove so they could hear each other over the hair dryers. She'd bought a little table and some pretty chairs for the sunroom. Then another table, and another. She hunted in antiques shops for china teacups and saucers. And then she got the idea to paint the walls between the windows a soft shade of lavender.

Before she knew it, women were arriving before their hair appointments and staying afterward to chat over cups of tea. Finally, Patsy had purchased a large stainless-steel urn that kept the water just at the edge of boiling. She started asking twenty-five cents for tea bags. Then she began baking goodies at home and selling them from an antique glass counter case she bought at an auction. Now she oversaw a regular cottage industry of local women who baked for the tearoom. They brought in banana bread, blueberry muffins, cinnamon rolls, you name it. Patsy charged a small commission and gave the women the rest of the money.

These days, the little Just As I Am tearoom

was famous all over the lake area, and Patsy sold china cups, teapots, tablecloths, stationery, candles, and tea-themed gifts. She had raised her prices enough that she had been sure people would gripe, but they didn't. If she ever lost her salon, Patsy thought she might be able to keep the tearoom open as a stand-alone business. But the two went together so perfectly, and the ladies loved it. Even some of her male customers had been known to drop an English Breakfast tea bag into a cup of hot water and sit around chewing the fat for a while after they'd gotten their haircuts.

As Patsy put away the broom, it occurred to her that over the years, the salon had become her own little garden — and the women were the flowers and trees and growing things she nurtured there. Ashley Hanes was a rose in bloom, a ripe strawberry, a bluebird's song. Everything about that girl said springtime — excitement, joy, hope, trust, anticipation, and most of all, love. Ashley fairly glowed with awakening.

Esther Moore, seated across from Ashley and talking the poor girl's ear off, radiated contentment. She was a golden sunflower, a soft sweet peach, a chirping robin redbreast. When she walked into a room, it felt like summer had arrived. Patsy knew it was because Esther and Charlie were so comfortable together, so relaxed. While Ashley and Brad were so crazy in love they were just about to burst, Esther and Charlie had settled into a calm, unflappable unity.

Patsy loved her garden of women. Over in the far corner sat Kim Finley with her twins, Lydia and Luke. A dental hygienist, Kim sometimes got off work early enough to meet the school bus when it stopped at the strip mall in Tranquility. She and the kids would walk over to the salon for teatime before she drove them to their tidy gray house in Deepwater Cove to start on homework.

At a young age, Kim had weathered a rough divorce from the twins' father, Joe Lockwood, and she had spent several years as a single mom. When Derek, a State Water Patrolman, entered her life three years ago, Kim had fallen deeply in love and married quickly. Patsy knew from cutting Kim's hair so often through the years that Kim and Derek had experienced a few rocky patches too.

Kim wore a soft resignation on her face. She made Patsy think of autumn — beautiful, but a little tired. Kim was a windblown shock of wheat, a ripe apple hanging heavy on the tree, a mourning dove that gathered her little ones close about her and cooed in the wind.

The young women, the children, the widows, the jovial men . . . Patsy treasured them all. As she crossed to the desk to check that her stylists were caught up on all their appointments, the front door opened.

It was Brenda Hansen. Winter had arrived.

When Brenda walked into Just As I Am, she felt every eye in the salon fasten on her. And when Cody shuffled through the door behind her, she heard an audible gasp.

Well, so what? She didn't care if people were scared of Cody or disliked having him in Deepwater Cove. The stranger who had showed up at her door during the power outage was the best thing that had happened to Brenda in a long time. Cody was a child — a sweet, slightly confused little boy who needed looking after. And Brenda had decided that God had given him to her as a mission.

"Hey, Patsy," she said.

The salon's owner hurried to the front desk as the pair approached. Look up the word *nice* in the dictionary, folks said, and you'd see Patsy Pringle's picture. With her exaggerated hourglass shape, pretty face, and hair whose color changed on a whim,

Patsy was a fixture at the lake, and everyone counted on her. If her shampoo, set, and style couldn't lift a woman's heart, her warm tearoom certainly would. More than once, Brenda had gone to the salon just to sit in a corner, sip tea, and read magazines. It sure beat pacing the floor waiting for Steve to come home.

"I didn't expect you back here so soon," Patsy told Brenda. "Your cut still looks great to me. In fact, I think that's one of the best cuts I've ever given you. Let me look at the left side there. Oh yes, that's perfect." She focused on Brenda's companion. "And who's this?"

"Hi, I'm Cody!" The young man held out a dirty hand.

Patsy shook it firmly. "Welcome to Just As I Am. You must be the fellow who's been sleeping on the Hansens' porch."

"Okay." Cody nodded. "Because Brenda is my friend. She makes me chocolate soup cake."

"Soup and chocolate cake," Brenda said in a low voice. "Cody's words sometimes get tangled up."

"Oh, mine do too." Patsy smiled. "Just last Sunday the deacons were trying to put my name on the kitchen committee, and I said, 'Sorry, boys, but I don't want to be on the commitchen kitty.' Can you beat that? I thought those fellows would never stop laughing."

Brenda chuckled, appreciating Patsy's kind attitude even though Cody's presence had obviously upset the regular flow and rhythm in the salon.

"I love my cut," Brenda told her. "I was wondering if you could trim Cody up a little. Maybe give him a shave. He says he used to shave when he lived with his father. I think this beard is just too thick for him to manage right now."

"I look like Jesus," Cody announced. "I thought Jesus was in Brenda's basement, but it was me."

"He saw his reflection in the sliding glass door," Brenda explained.

Patsy tilted her head. "Come to think of it, Cody, you do look like Jesus."

"Because I'm a Christian."

"Is that why you look like Him?"

Cody nodded. "Okay."

Patsy laughed. "I'd love to shave off those whiskers, Cody, but I'm afraid I've got a perm coming in right now. Of course, if you and Brenda could wait a little while . . . I . . . uh . . ."

Patsy glanced at the sunroom, apparently realizing that having Cody sit down among the tea-sipping ladies was probably not the best plan. "We've got all kinds of magazines in the waiting area," she said, gesturing toward a row of five chairs that lined one wall. "I keep men's magazines in stock too. Fishing, hunting, boating. All that."

Brenda squared her shoulders. "Cody and I will have a cup of tea and wait for you to do the perm," she said. "Then you can work on his hair and beard while she sits under the dryer."

"Well —" Patsy swallowed — "all right. We've got chocolate cake in the counter. Help yourself."

"Chocolate cake!" Cody's blue eyes brightened. "My daddy told me that only a Christian would give you chocolate cake. Are you a Christian?"

"I certainly am," Patsy said. "That's why I named this salon Just As I Am. My favorite song in the whole world says that Jesus loves us just as . . ." She stopped speaking and gazed at Cody. Her eyes misted. "He loves us just as we are. No matter where we come from or how we've acted or what we look like. God loves us all."

"Okay," Cody said.

"You and Brenda step over there for a cup of tea and some chocolate cake. I see my perm just driving into the parking lot."

"Thanks," Brenda said. For a moment, she covered Patsy's hand with her own. Then she nudged Cody toward the tea area.

Young Ashley Hanes was sitting with Esther Moore at one table. Kim Finley and her twins, Luke and Lydia were at another. No doubt they had come into the salon this afternoon for haircuts, Brenda mused. Their mother always kept the ten-year-olds scrubbed, pressed, and looking adorable in color-coordinated outfits.

Brenda steered Cody to the empty table and pointed him to a seat. She sensed everyone staring as she arranged her coat and purse on the opposite chair. The moment Cody sat down, Kim began gathering up her children, wiping their mouths, and urging them to put on their jackets. Red-haired Ashley went as pale as a ghost. Esther looked annoyed.

"Hey there, Esther." Walking past the table toward the hot-water urn, Brenda greeted the older woman. "And how have you been, Ashley?"

"Fine," they said in unison.

"That's Cody at the table. You've probably seen him around."

As she bent to fill two teacups with hot water, Brenda heard someone come up beside her. She didn't have to look to know it was Esther. With her glossy white hair and sweet smile, Esther Moore had a kind heart and was loved by the neighbors in Deepwater Cove. But Brenda knew the woman had strong opinions about everything. Her husband, Charlie, had been a mailman before retirement. Now instead of letters, he carried gossip from house to house. If he wasn't driving around in his golf cart gathering up hearsay, he was down at the dock fishing for rumors. And, of course, every tidbit had to be filtered, sorted, organized, and officially stamped at the grand post office — Esther.

"How are you getting along these days, Brenda?" Esther dropped some change in the basket and took another tea bag. "I hardly ever see you out and about. Seems like the last time we talked was the day you came in to get your hair cut."

"That's right," Brenda said. "When the weather warms up a little more, I'll probably be in the yard. Have you seen my pansies? They made it right through the winter this year. I don't think I lost a single one."

"I noticed that." Esther used a pair of tiny silver tongs to drop a sugar cube into her cup. "You always have such a pretty yard. Charlie thinks it's the nicest in the whole neighborhood. We love those baskets of petunias you hang by the door, and last year you had so many roses!"

"It was a bumper year, all right." Brenda was about to head for the sweets when Esther put out her hand.

"Brenda, I ought to tell you that Charlie's been a little concerned about your friend."

"Which friend?"

Esther looked flustered. "Uh . . . *him.*" She glanced over at Cody. "As a matter of fact, several of us in Deepwater Cove aren't quite sure what to make of the situation. You know . . . him sleeping on your porch swing."

Brenda clamped her mouth shut to keep from saying something she might regret. All these months of emptiness — sitting alone in her house missing the children, cooking meals that nobody would eat, painting and sewing on furniture that didn't matter to anyone — and the first time anyone in Deepwater Cove acted like they *cared,* it was to complain! No one had stopped at the house to visit her. No one had asked why she'd let the fallen leaves molder on the lawn or the spiders move back onto the porch at the end of the summer. No one wondered how she was getting along without her children there.

"You can tell Charlie that Cody is very comfortable on the swing," Brenda said. "I appreciate his concern. It's sweet of him to care about my friend."

Esther stood gaping as Brenda walked to the glass counter and took out two pieces of chocolate cake. Carrying the cake to the table and then returning for the tea, Brenda kept her focus on Cody. He was scratching his head with the pointed tines of a fork while studying himself in the stainless-steel napkin holder.

"I sure do look like Jesus," he said when Brenda sat down. "Like in the Bible when He was sitting on that rock with all the kids on His lap and around His feet. 'Suffer the little children to come unto me, and forbid them not: for of such is the kingdom of God.' Mark 10:14. I look like Jesus on that rock."

"Not for long. I'm eager to see what Patsy can do with your hair." Brenda pushed Cody's tea and cake in front of him. As he warmed up to her, he had become more verbal, and much of his conversation showed a fairly high intelligence. He could cite many Bible verses.

"That beard has to go," she told him. "No one can see what you look like."

"I'm twenty-one," Cody said. "Time to

80

make my way."

"You're an adult, all right. I wish we knew where your father went off to."

Picking up a clean fork, Cody leaned forward in the chair and lifted a bite of chocolate cake to his mouth. "Make my way," he said glumly. "Time to make my way."

"Why did your daddy want you to leave?"

"I'm twenty-one. Time to make my way."

Brenda sighed. They had been through this conversation many times, and it never got them anywhere. She had no idea how long Cody had lived with his father, or where. Nor did she know what had possessed the man to send this man-child into the world alone. Surely Cody's dad must have known the young man would have a difficult time surviving on his own.

"I'm a sweeper," the young man said suddenly. "I kept the trailer span. That was my job. I kept everything span."

"You lived in a trailer?"

"Until we moved out and lived in our car. In the trailer, I swept the floor with a broom. Like her." Cody pointed a finger at one of the stylists who was brushing shorn hair from her last cut into a dustpan. "I can mop, too. With a mop and a bucket and water. My daddy says I keep everything span."

"Now, Cody, where was this trailer? Was it near — ?"

A deafening, floor-shuddering buzz suddenly blasted through the salon, cutting off Brenda's words. Walls shook. Ceiling fixtures swayed. A row of teacups leaped off a shelf in unison like a team of synchronized swimmers diving into a pool.

As the cups shattered on the floor, a look of horror darkened Cody's face, and he clamped his hands over his ears. The buzz grew to a roar that sounded like the end of the world. Both of Kim's twins began to scream as Patsy Pringle came running into the tearoom.

"What on earth?" she cried. "What on earth?"

Cody let out the wail of a wounded animal. He bolted from the table, knocking over his chair, and ran through the salon as though a bear were after him. As Brenda tried to steady the plates and teacups rattling on their table, she watched him fling open the door and vanish.

"Oh, my stars, not again!" Patsy hollered over the roar. She flung a handful of pink plastic curlers to the floor. "That does it. I will not stand for this!"

She turned and dashed out the salon door

behind Cody. Still holding on to the table, Brenda saw the buxom salon owner march past the window toward Pete's Rods-n-Ends, the tackle shop that had recently opened next door. Then, like every other customer in the salon, Brenda raced after Patsy.

The only difference was, Brenda was looking for Cody. And he was nowhere to be seen.

Empty cars sat parked in front of the various businesses that made up the strip mall, while other vehicles streamed up and down Highway 5 through Tranquility, which was nothing more than the row of stores, a bank, a grocery, a bar, and two restaurants. A line of trees, just beginning to leaf out, rimmed the parking lot.

Brenda sensed Cody would have headed for protective cover.

"Now you just come with me!" Patsy Pringle was saying as she hauled a burly, bearded man out of the tackle shop by one of his beefy arms. "Take a look at what you did to my tearoom, mister. And while you're at it, you can explain yourself to my customers!"

"I started up a chain saw — that's all," the man said. "Just to see if it worked."

"You might as well have cut right through my wall with that crazy thing," Patsy snapped. She waved a hand toward the group of women who stood on the sidewalk in plastic capes, curlers, and layers of tinfoil. "Come on back inside everyone. This Einstein is Pete Roberts, our new neighbor."

The man reminded Brenda of a Saint Bernard being dragged down a sidewalk on a leash. He gave the ladies a sheepish smile as Patsy pulled him into the salon.

Brenda hurried over to the line of trees. "Cody?" she called. "Cody, it's all right. You can come out now. That loud sound was just a chain saw in the store next door."

Nothing in the woods stirred except a gray squirrel. It leaped from a stump to a low branch and then scurried up the trunk.

"Cody?" Brenda yelled again. "It's me, Brenda. You can come back now. Everything is safe!"

She stood for a moment, feeling almost as awful as she had the fall day when Justin and Jessica drove off to college. Emptiness sucked through her like a vacuum. She tried to breathe, but couldn't.

"Cody!" she called, more softly now. She knew it was useless. "Come back, Cody. Please come back."

CHAPTER FOUR

Steve Hansen had a plan. A foolproof plan. He had closed on a lucrative sale that morning and finished his office work early. This meant he would get home in time for supper — an event he was determined to avoid. So he would greet Brenda with a shouted hello. Hoping she wouldn't come looking for him, he would quickly change into jeans and a T-shirt, grab his fishing pole, and head down to the dock.

After work, he had stopped by Rods-n-Ends and asked for a dozen minnows. Like most bait-shop owners at the lake, Pete always scooped out about twice that many — plenty enough to keep Steve busy until well after dark. He also bought a rotisserie hot dog and a can of soda. He would eat while he fished.

If things went well, he would be able to head for bed without ever setting eyes on his wife. That would be good. Her project to save a local drifter from homelessness had come to an abrupt end the other day. Every time he asked what was wrong, Brenda stared at him from beneath hooded eyelids as if he was supposed to read her mind. These days she barely spoke to him, and she shrank from his touch. Forget about the two of them doing anything in bed but sleeping. Brenda had made it perfectly clear she was not interested.

As he switched off the car engine and listened to the garage door go down, Steve closed his eyes, leaned his forehead on the steering wheel, and tried to pray. He had loved Brenda from the minute he first laid eyes on her. They had been high school sweethearts, and up until the last few months, she had been trim, pretty, smart, fun loving, and as sweet as a slice of warm pecan pie.

What was wrong with Brenda lately? Why wouldn't she ever talk to him or touch him?

Frustrated, realizing that his prayer had come to nothing, Steve opened the car door. The handyman Brenda had hired was supposed to start on the basement remodeling today, and Steve fervently hoped that project would improve his wife's mood.

As Steve opened the door from the garage to the kitchen, he heard a sound that hadn't been in the house in months. Brenda was laughing.

"All right, all right," she said with a chuckle. "If you say so. I think it's kind of extravagant, but why not?"

"You deserve it, so you ought to have it," a deep voice answered her.

Steve rounded the corner to find his wife standing in the foyer with a tall, lanky fellow in a sweat-stained ball cap, a paint-spattered shirt, and an even dirtier pair of jeans. The man's focus shifted to Steve, and his expression sobered a little. "Howdy. I'm Nick LeClair, A-1 Remodeling." He held out his hand. "You must be the famous Steve Hansen."

Steve shook his hand. "Did you and Brenda work out a plan for the basement?"

"A crafts room!" Brenda exclaimed, her green eyes sparkling. "It was Nick's idea. I explained how the basement had been the playroom when the kids were little, and then it became the teen hangout, and that I just didn't know what to do with it now. All their trophies are down there, and school pictures, and the wide-screen TV. The puzzles and LEGOs . . . you know? Nick and I were looking at the paw prints where Ozzie had jumped into the paint, and he asked me why they were pink. So I showed him my chairs!"

"Which chairs?" Steve asked. He had no idea what Brenda was talking about — paw prints, chairs, pink paint. What on earth was a crafts room, and why did the Hansens need one?

"The dining-room chairs." The emerald sparkle in Brenda's eyes faded to a dull, wary olive. "The ones I painted."

"Oh." Steve glanced across the foyer into the dining area. Sure enough. Pink plaid chairs. Where had those come from?

"Nick thinks they're wonderful," Brenda said. "I showed him the slipcovers I'd sewn for the couches. He knows a lady who hired someone to make a set of slipcovers, and he says hers aren't nearly as professional looking. Our house has been mostly contemporary, you know, but I've been wanting a change. I told Nick my thoughts, and he says with a little paint and a few alterations, we can easily go cottage."

Steve stared dumbly at his wife. He had no idea what she was talking about, but at least some life had come back into her eyes.

"Cottage," he repeated, nodding sagely. It was a trick he'd learned years ago. If he couldn't remember, didn't understand, or couldn't make himself care what his wife was talking about, he simply repeated her last word. Worked like a charm. She never knew he was paying no attention.

This time, Brenda rolled her eyes. "Nick knows several store owners who are interested in painted furniture too. He thinks I should continue perfecting my art."

"Perfecting your art?" Steve mouthed. When had painting chairs and draping sheets across furniture become an art?

"We can cover the floor in a neutral vinyl," Nick was saying now. "Then we can divide the room into work zones for Brenda. We'll use different shades of paint and a few built-in dividers to separate each area. It won't take much — time or money. We can give her a sewing spot with a big table where she can spread out her fabric. Then we can create a painting space where she'll be able to drip without causing any problems. I've got an idea for a large, shallow metal tray that will allow her to put the furniture safely on the floor. She told me about her gardening, so I thought we could set a potting area next to the sliding glass door. And that ought to just about take care of her."

Steve blinked, trying to work his head around potting, sewing, and painting zones. All day he had been thinking about closing costs and mortgage rates. Phrases like *your dream vacation home* and *fishing, floating, and fun* and *lakefront beauty* had been zipping around in his brain. He had photographed three houses, one of which was about to collapse on its foundation, and had spent hours trying to get good shots from flattering angles.

What on earth was a potting area?

Steve rubbed his temples. For the first time since he'd walked into the house, he noticed that Brenda was wearing a pretty purple shirt and a pair of black slacks. It looked like she might have done something with her hair, too. The edges were different.

Deciding the best thing to do at this point was follow his original plan of action, Steve mustered a smile for his wife. "Well, that sounds interesting," he said. "Looks like you've got your work cut out for you, Nick. Write us up an estimate, we'll take a look at it, and then we can talk some more." Turning to his wife, he continued speaking. "I guess I'll head down to the lake and wet a line, Brenda. I haven't been home early in a while, and Charlie Moore tells me the crappie are really biting these days."

"Nice to meet you, Steve," Nick said. "You've built yourself a great reputation here at the lake. I wouldn't be surprised if you got the Realtor of the Year award at the banquet this Christmas. Congratulations."

Steve nodded to acknowledge the compliment; then he hurried toward the bedroom. He could hear the excitement return to Brenda's voice when she began conversing with the handyman again. Well, if it made her happy to pot, sew, and paint, then that was all right. Maybe she would get back to normal eventually.

In fact, now that Steve recalled the situation, Brenda had looked like her old self today. Maybe even better. He decided to revise his plan and only fish for a little while. If Brenda was happy about the basement remodeling, maybe she wouldn't push him away in bed again tonight. In fact, the more he thought about it, the more Steve felt sure good things were right around the bend.

Brenda sat cross-legged on the floor of the basement and looked around her as the cat curled up in her lap. It might be okay. Fixing up this room — banishing memories and starting afresh — could be the start of those dreams she had envisioned would fill her empty nest. Discouragement and confusion had waylaid her in the fall, but it was almost spring now, and maybe this remodeling project was the answer to her prayers. For weeks, maybe even months, she had been asking God to give her some kind of direction in life.

Brenda missed the kids so much. She had taken great satisfaction in guiding them from infancy to adulthood. Ballet, cheerleading, soccer, football, school plays, the church youth group — Brenda had participated in everything that had interested her children. She had worked on homecoming floats, sewed costumes, dried tears, bandaged cuts, baked well over fifty birthday cakes, and endured endless sleepovers. If not driving the kids from one event to another, she had stayed busy behind the scenes or cheering from the sidelines. After they left last fall — the last of them off to college at last — she had hardly been able to go down into the quiet, echoing basement.

But as desperately as she missed the kids, as much as she grieved over her quiet, empty house, she knew she could have borne it if only Steve were here to go through the transition with her. Surely he must miss their children too. And yet just when Brenda needed him the most, just when she thought they could rediscover who they were as husband and wife, Steve had deserted her too.

Ever since he bought the new office building and hired a staff, her husband had turned into a walking zombie. Wearing a blank expression, he left the house every morning just after seven. Pale, frowning, tense all the time, he usually appeared at some late hour of the evening. He rarely called home and then it was to ask if Brenda had heard from the kids or to tell her he would be late again. If she didn't know how focused he was on his work, she might have thought her husband was having an affair.

Then Cody had magically appeared at the house, and somehow he began to fill the hole in her heart. Since he had fled, she worried about him constantly, but no one in Deepwater Cove had seen him again. With her children and Cody gone, what did Brenda have left? Who was she?

And then today, Nick LeClair had showed up. With his cheerful smile and warm blue eyes, Brenda liked the man immediately. It was one thing to build houses based on an architect's plan. Or to sell houses that someone else had built, as Steve did. But Nick had vision. He could see past the sagging sectional sofa, the popcorn-embedded area rug, the TV set, the shelves lined with sports trophies, the bulletin boards covered with blue ribbons and prom photographs. And what he saw was Brenda.

Why couldn't Steve be that way? They'd been married forever, yet he treated her as though she didn't exist. Even tonight, when he'd come home early for once, all he could think about was racing to the lake to fish. Brenda had considered strolling down to the dock and sitting with him, but she decided against it. Why should she give up time to be with him when he couldn't bother to spend even five minutes with her? He treated her like an old dishcloth, used up and dirty and fit for nothing. He never asked about her day or bothered to find out how she was feeling. Her hopes of the two of them going out to dinner, seeing movies, and boating together had come to naught. In fact, she couldn't remember the last time the two of them had spent any special time together.

"Brenda?"

His voice carried down the stairs into the basement. She glanced at the sliding glass door, remembering the night Cody had stood out there and thinking of the way he had run screaming into the woods. The sound of Steve's shoes on the steps made her want to do the same thing. Run. Just run.

He held a stringer of crappie in one hand as he stepped into the basement. Holding it up, he gave her a warm smile. "Six! Big ones too. Charlie was right — fishing's great."

"I don't know when you think we'll ever eat those," she said, instantly regretting the harsh tone in her voice. But she couldn't keep back the words. "I guess you'll expect me to fry them up some weekend when Justin and Jessica come home."

His smile faded. "We could eat them. You and I."

"When? You're never home." She stood and brushed the dust off her black slacks. "Maybe you should give them to Charlie Moore. He and Esther eat a lot of fish. I'm sure they'd appreciate it."

Steve looked at his stringer. Brenda knew he had come home feeling like the hunter in from the range, the warrior back from the battlefield. Usually he cleaned the fish before he returned to the house, but tonight he had brought his catch to show off. His trophy. She was supposed to *ooh* and *ahh* over the stringer of dead fish as though he'd just rescued his family from the brink of starvation.

"I'll come home early tomorrow."

"No, you won't. You already have a dinner scheduled, remember? Ashley Hanes told me you keep a table reserved at the country club six nights a week, and you only cancel it once or twice a month."

"Ashley? The redhead?"

"Brad Hanes's wife, yes. Jessica's friend. They live directly across the cove from us on Shadyside Lane, in case you've forgotten. You sold them their first house."

"I know who they are. I've seen Ashley at the country club. She's a waitress in the evenings. Red hair."

"Yes, red hair! It's obvious you've spent more time looking at her lately than you've spent with me." For some reason it infuriated Brenda that her husband had noticed a waitress's hair.

Steve took a step toward her. "Why would you say such a thing, Brenda? You know I love you."

"How am I supposed to know that? Because you bring in all this money? Because you go to church with me on Sundays?"

"Church hardly makes a difference in our marriage these days. You sit through Sunday school with your mouth practically sewn shut. Don't you have any ideas or opinions?"

"Of course I do. You know my faith is important to me. I've always been loyal to God, and I've tried to follow the Bible's teachings. But what's the point in commenting on something I've heard a thousand times? All they do in church is play the same tape over and over. I could recite that stuff by heart."

"If you *had* a heart," he snapped back. "You're as cold as ice toward me, Brenda. Why are you treating me this way? How can you think I don't love you? I'm your husband. We had three children together."

"The kids! Having babies together is supposed to show that you love me? I had your babies a long time ago, Steve. If you think I'm supposed to count on that . . . when they're not even around . . . and don't call . . ." She suddenly fought tears.

Steve reached out to her. "Honey, is that what's wrong? You're missing the kids?"

"Don't touch me!" she shouted, backing away. "You have no idea who I am or what I need. You know nothing about me, so don't claim you love me!"

"But I do love you, sweetheart." He crossed his arms over his chest and stared at her. "Maybe you stopped loving me. Ever consider that? You wouldn't touch me with a ten-foot pole. You never let me kiss you anymore. And forget about bed!"

"Bed! I've served your needs long enough, Steve. I'm not here just to indulge your every whim." She took a step toward the staircase. "You're selfish — that's what you are. The whole world revolves around you, and you wouldn't need me at all if it wasn't for that bedroom up there."

"But I do need you!" he cried out, moving toward her again. "I feel like if I could just hold you and touch you, we could overcome all this frustration inside you."

"Inside *me?* I don't care if you never touch me again. That won't resolve the problem."

"Well, what is the problem, for pete's sake?"

"It's you! You and your self-centered focus on selling houses. You just want to make more money, hire more secretaries and agents, build a bigger office building, and become the greatest and most amazingly wonderful real-estate agent at Lake of the Ozarks. What are you trying to prove?"

She set one foot on the bottom step, and Steve caught her arm. "The problem is *you!*" he barked back at her. "You drag around this house in your bathrobe. You give me the cold shoulder. You do everything in your power to make me miserable. And I haven't done a thing but take care of you and the kids better than just about any husband I know. A lot of good it's done me!"

"Let go of my arm," she snarled.

"You'd better snap out of it, Brenda!" he shouted.

"Snap out of what? You haven't even taken the time to find out what's going on with me. You want to do your precious real-estate thing, come back to the house after dark and sleep with me, and then go out the door at sunrise and chase after more money. And if you think I'm going to respond to someone who yells at me —"

"Okay, honey, I'm sorry," he said, trying to pull her off the step toward him. "That was totally wrong of me. I shouldn't have shouted. It's just that I hate the way things have been going between us. I'm sorry I've been so focused on my job. I guess I figured you'd be proud of me."

"I am." She kept one hand on the banister as he moved closer to her. "I'm thrilled that you're doing well. But what about me? What about us?"

"Well, I'm home tonight. Let's turn the lights out, get into bed, and see what happens."

"Let me go. I have to spend some time looking over the paint samples Nick brought with him today."

"Paint? No you don't." He jerked her toward him. "We're married, remember? The least we can do is sleep together."

"Here, sleep with these!" she cried, grabbing the stringer of crappie and giving a mighty swing. The fish hit Steve's arm with a resounding smack. He let go of Brenda and stumbled backward.

Bursting into tears, she dropped the fish on the floor and ran up the stairs.

"Men!" Patsy Pringle said as she clamped a hot curling iron around a strand of Esther Moore's fine white hair.

"Can't live with 'em, can't live without 'em," Esther finished. "I remember a few times when I thought I'd be happy if I never saw Charlie again. Now I can't imagine what I'd do without him. It's not that he changed his ways or that I gave up my dreams. We just got comfortable with each other. Satisfied, you know?"

"I know I'd be satisfied if Pete Roberts sold every last minnow and fishing rod out of that store next door and moved away from Tranquility forever," Patsy said. "He started up a weed whacker the other day, and I nearly gave Steve Hansen a Mohawk."

Esther chuckled. "I think he messes around with those loud engines just to get your goat."

"What do you mean by that?"

"Charlie was in Rods-n-Ends the other day to buy some minnows, and he brought up the chain-saw incident to Pete. Charlie mentioned how your antique teacups fell off the shelf, and Kim's twins started screaming, and Brenda Hansen's hobo ran out of the salon hollering like he'd seen a ghost. Pete just laughed. Said he gets a kick out of watching you storm into his store and give him what for."

Patsy slid the curling iron into its slot and glared at the wall dividing Just As I Am from Rods-n-Ends. "Pete thinks it's funny to scare my customers?"

"According to Charlie, it's all about *you.* Pete likes irritating you, because then you rush over there and stir things up. He says he never knows whether you'll be a redhead or a blonde when you come in. Pete thinks you're as cute as a bug's ear when you get all riled up."

"Cute?" Patsy snatched the curling iron again and began clipping stray tendrils of Esther's hair onto the heated barrel. As steam rose from the gelled and sprayed white curls, she fumed. "I am not cute when I get mad. My cheeks get pink and my nose starts to drip and my eyebrows take on a life of their own. I don't see why that man would want to upset me when all I've done is be nice to him from the moment he moved in next door. I sent him over a mug of coffee and two doughnuts the day he opened for business the first time. I even wrote out a little card that said, 'Welcome to the Tranquility Strip Mall. May you be blessed with lots of gas and many bait buyers. Love in Christ, Patsy Pringle.' Now how much friendlier can you get?"

"Ouch!" Esther gasped as the curling iron singed her scalp.

"Oh, I'm sorry, honey." Patsy released the clump of hair and began fanning Esther's head. "It makes me furious to think that Pete would set up his machine-repair area right next to my tearoom. After he started up the weed whacker and scared the living daylights out of me, I had to work nearly half an hour to fix what I'd done to Steve Hansen's hair. I thought I'd never get both sides even. I cannot have that kind of racket going on while my ladies are trying to drink their tea. I was here first, and if that man runs me out of business, I don't know what I'll do."

"Relax, Patsy. No one's going anywhere. Your clientele is so loyal we'd all move to Timbuktu with you if you decided to pull up stakes. Pete Roberts isn't about to scare us off." She patted her hair as she eyed Patsy in the mirror. "If you want to know what I think . . . well . . ."

"Well what?" Patsy demanded.

"I think he's got a little thing for you. He's teasing you the way boys do, Patsy. Trying to get your attention and make you notice him."

"Pete Roberts is no boy! He's at least forty, and I hear he's been married twice and was an alcoholic so many years his liver's pickled. Oh, what am I doing? I don't mean to gossip about anyone, but I am not a teenager playing silly flirting games. I am a businesswoman, and I've worked too hard to . . . to . . ."

Esther reached up and laid her hand on Patsy's arm. "Your nose does drip when you get mad, doesn't it?"

Patsy sniffled as she began rummaging through a drawer. "Where is my pick? People are always taking things out of my station. I've lost a pick and two combs and no telling how many bobby pins. I had a wedding last Saturday morning, and I couldn't find a bobby pin to save my life. Have you ever tried to style an updo without bobby pins? That bride was determined her hair would be at least a foot high, and I must have spent an hour hunting for some way to hold it in place. Curls and braids and daisies. Oh, let me tell you, I just about had a fit. I finally had to go into the back room and hunt through all the boxes until I found some new packs of hairpins. It was a nightmare."

"Maybe you like him just a little bit too," Esther said. "He's very nice. He keeps his stock organized and his shelves dusted. Charlie said Pete has the cleanest minnow tank at the lake, and you know Charlie has seen them all. If you want to catch crappie, there's something to be said for healthy, lively minnows."

Patsy clamped her mouth shut and began finger-combing Esther's hair into place. As she worked with the curls, she did her best not to think about Pete Roberts next door. Though she had tried to be kind to him, she could find no excuse for his behavior.

Esther Moore was dead wrong about him. Maybe Pete was nice to his customers and kept a tidy store. Maybe he had used his blasted weed whacker on the flourishing dandelion patch in front of her beauty salon the other day. And maybe Patsy had seen him eyeing her from his pew at LAMB Chapel the past three Sundays in a row. But that did not mean he had a "little thing" for her. And she certainly didn't like him. Not even a little bit.

"Oh, that looks so pretty," Esther spoke up as Patsy began spraying the style into place. "You always do such a good job. It's no wonder everyone in Deepwater Cove and most of the west side of the lake comes to

Just As I Am. You have the power to transform us all! In fact, I think Brenda Hansen is looking better than she has in months. When that homeless man she was taking care of ran away, I predicted she would go right down the drain. But she sure has perked up. Maybe it's that new haircut you gave her."

Patsy shrugged. She had enough to worry about with Pete Roberts threatening to start up one loud engine or another next door. Which made her think about poor, simple-minded Cody and how scared he had been when he ran out of the salon that day. Which led her to wonder what had really brightened up Brenda Hansen so much. Her husband hadn't seemed too thrilled when he came in for his monthly haircut — he said their basement was all torn apart and some handyman had practically taken up residence in the Hansens' house. Which brought Steve's glum face to Patsy's mind and led her to recall how hard she'd had to work to repair his haircut. Which took her right back to Pete Roberts and his infernal weed whacker. That man was just about all she could think of these days.

CHAPTER FIVE

Brenda tore off a strip of blue, low-tack painter's tape and began to edge the molding around the staircase in the basement. It had taken the best part of two days to tape the windows, doors, floors, and ceilings, but she didn't mind. Nick LeClair kept his radio tuned to a country station, and Brenda had discovered to her surprise that she liked the twangy Southern music — especially the ballads. She had grown up in St. Louis listening to rock and pop, but some of the country songs almost made her cry. She told herself it was hormones.

Lately, everything had seemed a little out of whack. At forty-five she was probably too young for menopause, but maybe not. Her emotions had leaped onto a roller-coaster ride that never stopped. Feeling almost as crazy as she had in her teenage years, Brenda swooped up into giddy happiness one minute and then plunged into tears the next.

It was Steve's fault.

After their fiasco the night he brought home the stringer of fish, they hadn't touched each other and had barely spoken.

"You just saved my bacon!" Nick exclaimed as he stepped through the basement's sliding door this morning. "I've got the paint, and you've done the taping!"

"I was wondering where you were," Brenda said. She rose from the floor and faced him.

Nick wore his usual chambray work shirt, jeans, boots, and baseball cap. He wasn't handsome like Steve, he drawled like a hillbilly, and sometimes he messed up his grammar, but Brenda had come to enjoy the man's jovial company. In fact, she went to bed each night replaying their conversations in her mind, and when she woke up the next morning, she waited to hear his pickup crunching the rocks on the driveway.

"I asked the hardware store to shake up the paint," he was saying as he crossed the basement floor, "and then I realized we couldn't start on the Serene Green sewing zone until we'd taped it off. But there you go, girl, always one step ahead of me."

Brenda laughed. She liked the way Nick

called her "girl," as though she were just a kid. They had discovered they were only a year apart in age, but that was about the only similarity between them. Brenda had grown up in the same house and neighborhood with the same set of parents and siblings all her life. Nick seemed to have been riveted together from various bits and pieces, like one of those whirligigs Missouri gardeners built to the keep the crows away.

He had been raised with parents, stepparents, brothers, sisters, half brothers, half sisters, stepbrothers, stepsisters, cousins, family friends, and the occasional stranger all living under one roof. But that roof had altered through the years as changes in the family structure moved him from rental houses to trailer parks to apartments. Once he had even lived in his car for nearly a year.

Along the way, Nick seemed to have lost parts of his tacked-together self. While splitting kindling, he had cut off half of an index finger. A little sister had drowned, and then his parents got divorced. During Nick's rodeoing days, his first wife had left him. "My heart wasn't the only thing that got broke," he had told Brenda, his blue eyes misting with tears as he spoke. During that brief period, he had snapped his leg three times and shattered an elbow. Later, his second wife had miscarried his first son. And part of his left ear was gone, lasered off during a brush with skin cancer.

Still in his second marriage, Nick LeClair now lived in a mobile home near Camdenton, had grown children, and loved his two grandbabies. Though he didn't go to church, he said he believed in God. Family and faith weren't the only things that enriched his life. Though he had barely graduated from high school, Nick informed Brenda proudly that he never once considered going to college.

"Didn't need it," he assured her, "because I have the gift of vision."

Nick insisted he could look at a bare slab foundation and see an entire house right down to the plumbing and wiring. He could remodel a room in his mind without even needing a blueprint. And, he told Brenda, he could see right through people.

"You're a bona fide artist," he drawled as he carried cans of paint through the basement door and set them on the concrete floor. "I'm not kidding. When the paint guy at the hardware store saw the colors you had picked out for the basement, he liked to have had a cow. He told me every one of those greens was used on a video the paint company sends out to help train the salespeople. Neither of us could tell the difference between one shade and another when we looked at the samples, but once we had them all mixed up and we opened the lids, we could see it was a perfect range. I told him, I said, 'That lady I'm working for is an artist, pure and simple.' And he said, 'Let me tell you what, Nick; I do believe you're right.' Not only did you get the colors right, Miz Brenda, but you're a whole step ahead of me with the taping."

He straightened and grinned at her, his cloudless blue eyes shining in the sunlight that streamed through the basement windows. Nick might have broken a few bones and plastered his arms with tattoos, but there wasn't a thing to mar the man's perfect white teeth. Unlike most of the construction workers Brenda had met through the years, he didn't smoke. His mother had died of emphysema, Nick explained, and that made up his mind for him at an early age. Still smiling, he stripped off his jacket and hooked his hands in the pockets of his jeans.

"Well, I'm ready to change your life, girl." He reached down and picked up a paint roller. "You ready?"

Swallowing, Brenda stepped toward him and took the handle. "Let's do it."

Steve flipped shut the door to his gas tank and hurried into Rods-n-Ends. There was serious business afoot, and he wanted to discuss the situation in the privacy of the tackle shop. For days now, gossip had been swirling around the lake like a nasty green oil spill. He had heard rumors in Deepwater Cove, Tranquility, and even as far away as Camdenton and Osage Beach. Steve figured if anyone knew the true story it would be Pete Roberts.

As the front doorbell tinkled, the burly man glanced up from a table full of engine parts in his repair area. "Well, if it isn't Steve Hansen, the king of real estate," he boomed. "How's it goin', my friend? Did you finally run low on gas? I swear if you start a trend with that hybrid of yours, you'll run me out of business in no time flat."

Steve worked up a smile. "No chance of that. Besides, you've got boats, four-wheelers, and Jet Skis to fill."

"Hey, did you hear the news?" Pete hopped up and made his way toward the cash register.

"I might have," Steve said. "Are you talking about the . . . uh . . ."

"I'm talking about the NASCAR hauler that stopped by here the other day. I tell you what — you should have been here, Steve. It was no ordinary trailer. It was a monster."

"Is that right?" Steve tried to muster interest. NASCAR was a popular sport at the lake, and now that he recognized Pete's enthusiasm, he noted the display of calendars and photographs of brightly colored, decal-covered stock cars on the tackle-shop walls. Pete even had framed autographed pictures of various drivers lined up in a row near his workbench.

"It was an official NASCAR Craftsman Truck Series transporter," Pete went on, beaming as if Dale Earnhardt himself had just stepped down from heaven for a visit to Rods-n-Ends. "The driver let me have a look inside, and it was something else. In the front, the crew has a private office with a TV and a sofa. Behind that, in the upper level, I could see the two trucks sitting there like royalty. Beautiful! Below them was storage for parts and tools, and the crew even had a set of lockers. I don't think the president of the United States gets as good care as a stock car. I would have given my right arm for a look under the hood of one of those babies. You ever seen a NASCAR engine? The trucks have cast-iron, 5.7-liter V8 engines with aluminum cylinder heads. Each one has a maximum displacement of 358 cubic inches. Can you believe that?"

"Pretty amazing," Steve said. He had begun to think stopping at Rods-n-Ends had been a bad idea. Trying to repair the ever-widening gulf with Brenda, he had volunteered to come home in time for supper. She wanted to discuss activities and plans for the upcoming spring-break vacation. Their two younger kids, Jessica and Justin, would be home from college, and Brenda wanted to make a special occasion of it.

Warming toward her husband for the first time in weeks, Brenda had told Steve she would bake lasagna for their dinner tonight. She knew he loved her lasagna, and Steve hoped this signaled an end to the hostile attitude she had been clinging to all this time. Brenda said she planned to serve dinner in the dining room instead of the kitchen — another sure sign of a thaw in her antagonism. Before leaving the office this evening, Steve had put a sticky note on his dashboard, reminding himself to take a look at the progress on the basement, make a few nice comments about the plaid chairs she had painted, and remark on the matching place mats she had sewn.

"The torque is 535 feet per pound at 6,000 RPM for those trucks, you know," Pete was saying as he rang up Steve's gas sale. "That means the engine can produce horsepower in the range of 750 at 8,000 RPM. Now that's something to see."

"I guess so," Steve said.

"You and Brenda ever been to a stock-car race?"

"Never have."

"It's the number-one spectator sport in the country. Bet you didn't know that."

"Well, that does surprise me." Steve gave a nod as he pushed his credit card back into his wallet. "Maybe I can talk Brenda into it one of these days."

"I doubt you'll have much convincing to do. She's a live wire, that woman. In and out of here at least once a day having me sharpen her scissors, fill up her gas tank, or load her down with hot dogs and sodas. She nearly bought out all my coolers to store the kids' trophies, medals, and ribbons. Said they'd be better protected in coolers than in plain old plastic boxes from the discount store. In fact, Brenda was here when the transporter drove through. Said she'd love to go to a race."

"*My* Brenda?"

"Yep. I don't know the last time I saw a woman with so much energy. That must be quite a basement you've got over there in Deepwater Cove."

Steve stared blankly at Pete. Never in a million years would he have described his cold, silent wife as a "live wire" full of energy. Lately when she spoke to her husband at all, it was to say something bitter and resentful. Most of the time, though, Brenda stayed withdrawn into the chilly little igloo she had built around herself.

Not knowing how to respond, Steve pushed his hands down into the pockets of his khaki slacks and turned to gaze out the front windows of the shop. He couldn't imagine that Brenda presented herself to the world as a warm, happy, interested participant in lake life — willing to go to a stock-car race, for heaven's sake! — when she never gave her husband anything but a cold shoulder.

Brenda reserved her bouncy zest for a tackle-shop manager and a stock-car trailer!

Icy anger flooded through Steve's chest as he thought about all he had done and given and meant to her. What was he getting in return? Zero.

Clearly there was a problem, but it wasn't him. It was Brenda. If this dinner tonight didn't produce some changes in her behavior, Steve had decided to tell his wife she needed to make an appointment to talk to their minister. Pastor Andrew might recommend a doctor or a counselor who would be able to help her. For all Steve knew, this difficulty grew out of her starting menopause. Or having a midlife crisis. Whatever the cause, Brenda's attitude was the effect. And Steve was sick to death of it.

"Here's your receipt," Pete said, handing him a scrap of curled paper. "You know, if you and the wife want to make an outing of it sometime, just let me know. I've been thinking about asking Patsy Pringle to the races. We could all go together."

It took a moment before Pete's words sank in. "I don't think Patsy is the NASCAR type," Steve said, glancing at the wall that divided the bait shop from the beauty salon next door. "Besides, Pete, I'm a little surprised you think Patsy would go out with you. Last time I was over there for a haircut, you started up a weed whacker, and she nearly scalped me. She didn't have a lot of kind words for you. I get a feeling she thinks you irritate her on purpose."

Chuckling wryly, Pete shook his head. "Women! Can't live with 'em, can't live without 'em."

"That fits my Brenda to a tee." Steve started for the door, then hesitated as he recalled the original reason for his visit to the store. He had been hoping to clear up some information and make sure that Pete and Patsy were both in agreement with him on the situation.

"Say, Pete," Steve said, turning back, "there's a rumor that's been floating around the lake these past couple of weeks."

"A rumor?" Pete's ruddy complexion suddenly paled. "About . . . about Brenda?"

"No, about the strip mall. I hear someone has rented the empty space next door to the beauty parlor."

"Oh, that!" Pete blew out a breath. "Yeah, I heard a fellow was putting in a movie-rental place."

"*Adult* movies. Triple-X videos, pornographic magazines, and other kinds of trash."

"Triple-X?" Pete's eyes widened. "Are you sure?"

"That's what I've been hearing. How do you feel about a business like that moving into Tranquility?"

"I can tell you right off the bat — I don't like the idea. We have enough trouble with the bar up the road. Fellows start drinking around three o'clock every afternoon.

Sometimes they come over here for gas, and it's all I can do to let them drive home. Don't get me wrong. I know how it is — been there myself, and I'll be the last one to sit in judgment. But that bar is not good for the area. If we start having the kind of creeps a porn shop would bring in . . . well, it would just set a tone. You know what I mean?"

"I agree completely, and I'm sure Patsy would go along with you on that."

"At least there's *one* thing we could see eye to eye on!"

"I know Dr. Hedges wants nothing to do with an adult-movie business anywhere near his chiropractic clinic. I'm not even sure the tattoo people would want pornography around."

"You can't count on that, Steve." Pete stroked his thick beard. "Tell you what . . . I'll talk to Patsy and see what she thinks. But you know the laws around here better than any of us. Would we have any say in who moves into the strip mall?"

"It's private property," Steve told him. "The owners can rent to anyone they choose."

"Even if the rest of us don't want them?"

"If you got together as a group, you'd have some influence, I'm sure." He paused for a moment. "You know, I've heard the strip mall could be for sale to the right buyer. If an upstanding person bought it, then he could keep the undesirable businesses out."

"That won't be me," Pete said. "I'm trying to be upstanding and all, but I barely make my rent. I know Patsy Pringle doesn't like me doing small-engine repair next door to her tearoom, but sometimes that's all that carries me over from week to week. I'm hoping business picks up during the summer, or I won't last through the year."

"You'll do great with your bait and tackle once the weather warms up. People will be flocking here for gas, too. No question about that."

"Maybe *you* can find a buyer for the mall," Pete suggested. "That would be a great idea — make you a bundle on the commission, too. You have anyone in mind?"

Steve shrugged as he lifted a hand in farewell. "I'm not sure. I guess we'll just have to see, won't we?"

As he headed toward his car, Steve glanced back over his shoulder at the row of storefront windows glittering in the setting sun. If things went well tonight . . . if life took a turn for the better . . . well, he just might have someone in mind after all.

■ ■ ■ ■

Brenda slid the lasagna out of the oven just as Steve's car pulled into the garage. *Good.* For once, he had followed through on his plan to come home.

All day she had been expecting her husband to call with one excuse or another. A potential client wanted to show him a million-dollar home that he might want to list with Steve. Or he had forgotten a last-minute meeting with a termite inspector. Something like that. At six, the phone had rung, and her heart sank. But Steve was only calling to say he had stopped at Pete's for some gas and would be there shortly.

The thought of having Justin and Jessica home for a whole week thrilled Brenda, and she was eager to talk to Steve about it. Working on the basement had helped her begin to feel almost like she used to — eager to make plans for the family, excited about projects they could do together, hopeful that the kids would have a wonderful time and would want to come back more often.

Jessica used to come home on weekends. But because of a new boyfriend, she had come home only once since Christmas break. Justin rarely called or visited. He had made new friends, a new life, and — as he enjoyed telling his parents — a new home there in Springfield. And as for Jennifer, she was a short-term missionary in Africa. Other than the occasional e-mail, she might as well be a stranger to her parents.

"Smells great!" Steve said as he stepped into the kitchen from the garage. "I've been thinking about that lasagna all day."

Despite her best intentions, a retort flew into Brenda's mind. *I'm surprised you didn't prefer to have dinner with one of your clients at the country club.*

But she managed to bite her tongue. Thank God!

All day Brenda had been praying that she and Steve could have a civil, even amiable, evening together. As she and Nick LeClair painted the basement walls, she had tried to keep her thoughts on her husband and her children. She was a good wife, Brenda reminded herself. A loving mother. A faithful Christian. A kind neighbor. She and Steve had been married so many years that surely they could weather this unpleasant chilly spell between them.

"Just the way you like it," she said, forcing a cheerful tone to her voice as she hung the hot pads on their hook. "Extra ricotta cheese and loads of meat sauce."

"Thanks, honey." He paused and looked at her. His eyes went soft as he reached out and ran one hand down her arm. "You look beautiful."

She tried not to shrink from his touch. "I've lost nearly ten pounds."

"How'd you manage that?"

"I'm not hungry these days. So busy, you know."

"Pete Roberts told me you're always in and out of his place buying hot dogs and sodas."

Bristling, she turned away. "That's not all I buy from him. I got storage containers from Rods-n-Ends for the kids' trophies and art projects. The hot dogs are for Nick."

"The basement guy?"

She took a large bowl of tossed salad from the refrigerator. "Nick loves the rotisserie hot dogs from Pete's place. I usually buy him a couple on my way back from the hardware store. Seems like I have to run to town for supplies nearly every day. Nick has gotten so used to me bringing him hot dogs, he doesn't even carry his lunch from home anymore. He likes my chocolate cake, too."

"He does? Huh." Sounding slightly befuddled, Steve wandered over to the hall closet, where he hung up his jacket and set down his briefcase.

Brenda carried the salad bowl into the dining room. The garlic bread would be just about warm by now, and she hoped Steve would wash up without her having to tell him. Sometimes the man stood around like a little kid, expecting her to do everything for him and give him basic instructions for managing the world. Well, she wasn't his servant. Or his mother. She had her own life.

"Have you seen anything of that other fellow who liked your cake?" Steve asked, following her into the dining room like a puppy at her heels. "The guy who slept on our porch for a few nights last month?"

"Cody. Patsy Pringle told me that people have said they saw him down in the woods or across the lake. But he hasn't been back to Deepwater Cove. I've worried a lot about him. I even asked at church if Cody had dropped by the Good Samaritan closet to get a coat or some food. But Pastor Andrew said he hadn't seen anyone of that description."

"I'm sorry, Brenda," Steve said, closing in behind her. "I know you really cared about him."

She stiffened as he took her shoulders. "You're glad he's gone. Don't deny it, Steve."

His hands froze. "I didn't want anything bad to happen to him."

"No, of course not." She stepped away from him and headed back to the kitchen. "Nick tells me that people like Cody can survive in the woods even through a cold winter. They have instincts, he says. They find warm places, and they know how to get food. Nick lived in his car once, so he ought to know. He insists it's not as bad as people might think. Of course, Nick is very different from Cody. Nick is brilliant, and Cody wasn't even sure of his own last name."

"Nick is brilliant?" Steve asked, padding after her into the kitchen. "You talked to him about Cody?"

"Of course I did. What do you think I do around here all day? Talk to myself?"

That had come out much harsher than she intended. Brenda shook her head, swallowed down the regret, and lifted the lasagna from the stove top. "Go wash up, honey," she said gently. "The bread is hot. We'll talk while we eat."

As Steve vanished into the powder room, Brenda mentally formed another prayer. She could *not* go into this evening with a bad attitude toward her husband. The atmosphere just had to get better between them. For one thing, the kids were coming home, and Brenda didn't want them to suspect that anything was troubling their parents' marriage.

For another, she really wanted to find a way to get along with Steve. True, he had allowed a deep passion for his work to take Brenda's place in his life, and sometimes the thought of ever genuinely *liking* her husband or enjoying spending time with him again seemed almost impossible. But they had been through a lot together in the past, and they couldn't risk losing what they had worked so hard to build.

Steve stepped back into the dining room and sat down at the table across from Brenda. As always, he took her hands and bent his head to bless their meal. It should have felt normal and comforting, but Brenda couldn't help wanting to pull away and shove her hands into her lap. From the time his work began to consume him, Steve had done everything in his power to alienate her, and now he wanted to pretend things were exactly the same as ever. But they weren't.

This man had abandoned his wife. He had left her in the dust as he raced off after fame and money. The thought of it stuck in her throat, and she almost didn't notice when he said, "Amen."

"So," Steve began as she cut a rectangle of lasagna. "It's amazing how well you matched these chairs to the place mats, honey. Plaid."

She glanced across the table at him. "Do you like the colors?"

"Sure. Yellow is nice. And pink, too. Yeah, I think they're fine."

"Fine?"

"Good is what I mean. Or *pretty* would be a better word. The whole house looks very pretty, Brenda."

"Do you like the slipcovers, too?"

He studied the living-room sofa for a moment, and Brenda couldn't help but feel that he had never even noticed the hard work she had put into those slipcovers.

"Wow," he said. "I didn't know you could sew like that. I mean, I *knew* you could sew. I always knew you were very good at sewing. You made those Easter dresses for the girls every year. But slipcovers."

"Are you sure you wouldn't rather have new furniture?" she asked, throwing his words back at him. "You told me I could have bought new furniture."

"Well, you could. If you wanted to."

"Then you don't really like the slipcovers."

"No, that's not what I mean. I love the slipcovers. But if you want new furniture, we can afford to buy it. I'm bringing in a lot of money, Brenda, and business is picking up as the weather warms. You know that big house over on the other side of the Tranquility strip mall? They listed it with me. I've already gotten a few nibbles from buyers too. You wouldn't believe how many people are out looking for property. Condos are still moving well, of course, but your really high-income people are looking for large second homes. These people want lakefront lots with a great view, and they'll pay top dollar. The west side of the lake is going to grow; you can bet on that. This is where we'll start seeing a big jump in the real-estate market. Local businesses should profit too. If we could move in a few more chain restaurants and some nice gift boutiques —"

He caught himself and grinned. "Listen to me running on and on. It seems like months since we've sat down together and talked."

"I know," Brenda said, fighting the next retort that sprang to her lips. She forced a smile. "Listen, I wanted us to discuss spring break, remember? The kids will both be home a week from Saturday. Can we get the boat out, Steve? spend a day on the water like we used to?"

He took a bite of lasagna and chewed in silence for a moment. "I don't know if I can take off a whole day," he said finally. "A morning, maybe. People prefer to look at houses in the afternoons and evenings."

"Morning? Justin won't even wake up till noon, and Jessica's not much better. I was hoping we could drag them both out of bed and leave the house about ten. I'll pack a picnic lunch, and we can fish, read, play games, work puzzles — whatever — all afternoon. If it's warm enough, you and Justin will want to get out the wakeboard, and Jessica will be sunbathing. We could all do some tubing. Then we could take the boat over to one of the lakeside restaurants for dinner. That would be fun."

"It sounds good, but I don't know, Brenda. We'd have to work out which day. I've already got a pretty full calendar."

"What? Steve, you *knew* which days to keep open for spring break! I told you weeks ago."

"I can't stop working just because the kids are home. Realtors have to stay on top of the market. If you drop the ball, people will take their business elsewhere. I'm juggling a lot of projects right now, and it's only going to get more intense this summer."

"So what are you telling me? You don't want to spend time with your children? You'd rather sell houses than be with your family?"

"Brenda, that's not fair. Of course I want to spend time with you. I just have to balance everything."

"Is this what you call balance — eating supper at home one time in the last two months?"

"Brenda, please."

"Never mind." She held up her hand. "Excuse me; I forgot to get the bread out of the oven."

As she hurried into the kitchen, Brenda's eyes filled with tears. How much more plain could he make it? Steve absolutely loved his work, and he wanted to devote all his time to it. As for her and the children, well, he had relegated them to the back burner of his life. Only . . . since the children were already gone, that meant the last person sitting on the back burner was Brenda.

The faithful, subservient wife.

She yanked the bread from the oven and dumped it into a cloth-lined basket she had prepared. "Justin is able to drive the boat," she said as she strode back into the dining room. "He can take his sister and me out onto the lake. I'll run the boat if the kids want to wakeboard or tube. Then the three of us will head for dinner at one of the restaurants."

"And I could meet you there!" Steve concluded. "You can call me on the cell phone when you get ready to head for the restaurant, and I'll drive over."

"You would really do that?"

"Sure!"

"Miss a day on the water with your children?"

"Wait, I thought . . . I thought that's what you were suggesting — that I could meet you at the restaurant."

"Oh, you are the most thickheaded man in history!" She tore off a slice of garlic bread and set it on her plate. She hadn't been able to eat a bite of the lasagna she'd worked most of the morning to prepare. "I told Nick you'd be too busy to go out on the water with us. Sunday will be the same way, won't it? We'll all sit in church together like happy little Hansens, and then you'll drive off to show your precious properties."

"Weekends are the best times to hold open houses."

"Weekends are for family!"

"Our children are grown, Brenda. It's not like we have to plan anything for them to do this spring break. They can drive, operate the boat, ski, wakeboard, or whatever they want all by themselves. Tell them to bring their friends to the lake for a few days, and that will keep the whole crew busy."

"You'd like that, wouldn't you? Everyone out of your way so you can work?"

"Brenda, for pete's sake —"

"Nick told me you were driven. He said he saw it in your eyes the minute he met you. He's right. You have one thing on your mind, Steve, and that's making money. Rising to the top of the heap. Winning the Realtor of the Year award. I told Nick about our dinner tonight, and he said you would probably be too busy to spend time with us over spring break. Nick thinks —"

"What does this Nick guy know anyhow?" Steve said, throwing his fork down on the plate. "He's a handyman!"

"Nick LeClair is my friend! He's here every day. He listens to me. He thinks I'm creative and intelligent and interesting. Nick says I'm an artist, and guess what — I am!"

"Brenda —"

"But you wouldn't know anything about that, would you? You don't care about my life anymore. You care about selling houses and making money and eating dinner at the country club. Forget your kids. Forget your home. And forget your wife!"

"Brenda, I told you I liked the slipcovers." He pushed back his chair to reach for her as she grabbed her plate and headed for the basement. "I know you're an artist. I said I thought the dining-room chairs were nice. Where are you going?"

"Where does it look like?" she shouted back up the stairs. "I wanted us to talk about spring break, and we did. You made your priorities clear. Since we're finished with our discussion, I'm eating the rest of my meal down here."

In the basement, Brenda set her plate on the plank between the two sawhorses Nick had placed in the center of the room. She could hear the kitchen door slam upstairs as Steve left the house. In a moment, the garage door rose and his car pulled away.

Brenda wiped her cheeks as she stared through her tears at the uneaten lasagna, cold garlic bread, and limp salad. As a shiver of pain ran through her, she sank to her knees on the chilly concrete floor and sobbed.

CHAPTER SIX

"I am ready for this week to be over!" Patsy worked her blow-dryer through Kim Finley's short brown hair. "This has been the longest week I can remember. The tea shop never was empty for a minute, and the goodies disappeared so fast I could hardly keep up. People streamed in and out of here — appointments, drop-ins, and a lot of folks just stopping by to chat. I don't mean to complain, but these days by Saturday night, I'm just about to keel over."

"I know what you mean," Kim said. "The dentist's office is nuts right now. I appreciate you working me in at the last minute today."

"Oh, I'm not referring to you, honey! You and the twins can come in anytime. Your hair doesn't take but a few minutes, and the kids tickle me to death. It's all these other people. Sometimes I think I ought to change my sign to Grand Central Station."

Kim laughed. "It's just because it's spring, I imagine. Derek says a lot of people are already coming down to open their lake homes for the season because it's been so warm. He expects the Water Patrol to have their hands full. I'm sure all the locals want to get their hair taken care of before the holiday. Lydia can hardly wait to wear the Easter dress we bought this afternoon in Camdenton. She really does look like a princess in it."

"I have no doubt about that. The child is gorgeous. She could win a beauty contest."

"Oh, I'd never do that to her. She's so shy. Now Luke! That boy wouldn't have any trouble on a stage, but I doubt he would win a pageant. I never know what will come out of his mouth. Little boys . . . they are something else."

"How is Derek getting along with him lately?" Patsy asked, aware that Kim and her husband had been married only three years. The twins' father was in and out of the picture, usually stirring up some kind of hullabaloo, and poor Derek seemed to be struggling to handle his role as husband and father.

"Every time he comes in here, he brags on the kids," Patsy continued. "He says Luke reminds him of when he was a boy."

Kim turned her head to admire her new cut as Patsy fingered the last tendrils into place. A beautiful woman, Kim had her hands full as a dental hygienist, mother, and wife. In fact, the more Patsy thought about it, the more she marveled at how her clientele managed so many roles in life. Not only did most of them work full-time jobs, but they had husbands and children, and they took on all kinds of volunteer work at the schools, helped out at their churches or clubs, and kept tabs on their friends. And Patsy thought *she* was tired on a Saturday night!

"Derek enjoys the twins," Kim was saying as Patsy removed the plastic cape from her shoulders and gave it a shake. "He'd like for us to have a baby, too, but I just can't picture it. Everything has to go like clockwork or our system starts to break down. Lately Luke has been sick a lot, and he's had to miss several days of school. It's a nightmare for me to have to call in to work and ask for the day off right as the office is opening up. With lake traffic building up already, Derek can't take time away from his job with the Water Patrol, and then Lydia has to be picked up from school and driven to dance lessons on Tuesdays and to piano on Wednesdays. My ex is no help at all."

"Are they ever?" Patsy sighed. "The trouble with divorce is that you never really do end the relationship. It may change a little, but you're still stuck with each other in one way or another. At least, that's the conclusion I've come to after listening to my clients all these years."

"You're right," Kim said as she picked up her purse. "But I am *so* glad not to be married to my first husband. That was a total nightmare. With Derek, things are still hard, but at least the kids and I are safe."

"Was your ex that bad?"

"You can't imagine."

Patsy shook her head. "Why can't people be nice to each other? You would think folks would want to try to get along, wouldn't you? And not do things to hurt or irritate each other? Is that so hard? Folks can be downright awful."

As she punched the buttons on her cash register, a familiar form crossed in front of the salon window. "Oh, speak of the devil," Patsy said in a low voice. "Here comes Pete Roberts from next door. That man is liable to drive me to drink. What can he mean by coming over here when he knows good and well I'm shutting down for the day?"

"Esther Moore told me Pete likes you," Kim spoke up. "Charlie says Pete thinks you're cute."

"Well, I don't care who said what. You would think Deepwater Cove was the gossip headquarters of the world. Kim, your hair looks beautiful, and I'll be praying that Luke gets to feeling better. You give him and Lydia suckers from me, okay? Now, hurry up and escape while you can. I'll get rid of this intruder lickety-split."

Patsy handed a couple of bright red lollipops across the counter to Kim just as Pete Roberts pushed open the door to Just As I Am.

Reaching out, Kim covered Patsy's hand for a moment. "Thanks, Patsy," she said softly. "Thanks for cutting my hair . . . and for listening."

"Praying, too. Don't forget that. I pray for all my clients."

Kim smiled. "I count on it."

"Evening, Mrs. Finley," Pete said, tipping the brim of his cap at Kim as she hurried by. "Tell Derek that Charlie Moore caught a whopper yesterday out in the cove. He used a four-pound test line to cast a 1/64-ounce jig under a lightweight float. The water's so muddy these days that I'm recommending the chartreuse jig-n-float."

"How big was Charlie's fish?"

"Nearly three pounds. Largemouth bass." Pete kept walking toward the salon desk. "I saw the thing myself. Charlie came over to the shop to show it off. Lunker."

"I'll tell Derek."

Kim waved as Pete turned to face Patsy. "How much you want to bet I'll have a run on those chartreuse jig-n-floats tomorrow afternoon?"

"Sunday's the Lord's Day," Patsy reminded him. She turned her shoulder and went to fetch her broom. "You shouldn't even open Rods-n-Ends."

"A tackle shop can't be closed on a Sunday! I'd get run out of business for sure."

"At least you'd have a clear conscience."

"And an empty wallet. Don't you remember what the pastor said in his sermon a couple weeks ago? Jesus told the disciples that the Sabbath was made for man, not man for the Sabbath. Besides that, Sunday's supposed to be a day of rest. If folks want to go fishing on a Sunday afternoon, they need bait. And why not a good ol' boy like me to sell it to 'em?"

"It's your decision," Patsy said. She tried to keep her focus on tidying up the shop for the two-day break. Her stylists were long gone, and everyone in the lake area knew

Just As I Am would be shut tighter than a drum on Sunday and Monday every week. But Tuesday mornings, Patsy opened early and made sure the place looked clean, fresh, and neat as a pin.

The few times she had come face-to-face with Pete Roberts since Rods-n-Ends opened, he had been standing behind the workbench in his shop. Furious as she was about the noise, she had hardly paid attention to how the man looked. But now, with both Kim Finley and Esther Moore whispering that the man was sweet on her, Patsy found it difficult to keep from giving him the once-over.

Truth to tell, Pete was not a bad-looking fellow. What had at first appeared to be an oversized middle now turned out to be something more like an extra-large, out-of-shape T-shirt hanging from a pair of massive shoulders. Maybe that beer belly wasn't quite as pronounced as she had imagined.

Pete still carried the hulking demeanor of a grizzly bear. His dark brown hair needed a good cut and even some thinning. If he had a jawline or cheekbones at all, the beard ought to go. And that cap could use a run through a washing machine.

But he did have startlingly blue eyes, a genuine smile, and a deep voice that settled into Patsy's bones like warm honey. Hitching up his baggy jeans, he plopped into one of the stylists' large black chairs and leaned back comfortably, as though expecting to begin a nice little conversation.

"I'm shutting down for the week," Patsy told him. "I hope you didn't come over for a cut."

"Nah. You go ahead and finish your sweeping." He tapped his fingers on the vinyl arms of the chair. "I already locked up next door."

"How's business these days?" she asked.

"Picking up. You?"

"Busy all the time. Of course, I've been here in this same spot for years. People know me."

"I don't know you much at all. You still mad at me about the weed whacker?"

"Can't say I'm happy. My tea area brings in a lot of customers, and they want to relax. The last thing any of us needs is one of your machines starting up."

"I heard you lost a bunch of teacups."

"Antiques. They fell off a shelf thanks to your chain saw."

"Sorry about that. You want me to pay for 'em?"

"I can't replace antiques at the dollar discount store, Pete. It took me several years to collect all those. One of them belonged to my grandmother."

She glanced over and saw that he had hung his head and was staring glumly at his fingernails. Carrying the dustpan to a wastebasket, Patsy noticed the words she had painted behind the desk.

Just As I Am . . .

"Don't worry about those cups," she said, swallowing her frustration. "They were just for show anyhow. People use the ones on the table across the way for their tea. You want to try a cup? Earl Grey is relaxing at the end of a long day."

He looked up, surprise lighting his eyes. "Me?"

"Men drink tea here all the time."

Though Patsy's voice had been light and welcoming, she couldn't deny that she really didn't want to serve this grizzly bear who had ruined her peaceful sanctuary. But . . . Just as I Am. That was how God accepted people. Jesus had died for folks just as they were. The Holy Spirit filled hearts that way too. If God did it, Patsy ought to at least try.

"Come on over to the tearoom," she said. "I'll fix us each a cup."

Pete pushed himself out of the chair and edged across the salon toward the lavender alcove as though entering forbidden territory. He perched on the first chair he came to and put his hands in his lap as though he was afraid to touch the lace tablecloth.

Patsy set two Earl Grey bags into cups and filled them with steaming water. "Milk and sugar?" she asked.

"Well . . ."

"It's best that way. Might as well give it a try."

She went ahead and fixed his cup. Then she set a shortbread cookie on his saucer and carried it over to him. As she settled down in the chair across from Pete, she decided this might be just the thing to ease the tension between them. He would see how special teatime could be, and then maybe he would quit revving up engines next door.

"I always say a teatime prayer," Patsy told him. Without waiting for a response, she bowed her head. "Dear Lord, thank You for this Saturday evening when we can look forward to a day of worship and rest. And thank You for Pete Roberts, my next-door neighbor. In Jesus' name we pray . . . amen."

"Amen," he intoned in his deep baritone. Stirring his tea, he cleared his throat. "Us being Christians and all . . . well, that leads me to the reason for my visit. The other day,

Steve Hansen stopped by for gas. He mentioned a problem. A rumor."

Patsy gave an involuntary gasp. "About Brenda?"

"That's what I thought at first too. But that's not it."

"Wait a minute . . . what did you think at first?"

"That he wanted to talk about Brenda."

"Oh." Patsy clamped her mouth shut. She didn't know what Pete had heard about the Hansens, but some unpleasant tidbits had drifted her way over the past few weeks. The last thing Patsy wanted to do was spread rumors, so she decided to take a sip of tea.

"Steve told me the store next door has been rented," Pete said. He paused a moment before adding, "To an adult-movie place."

Patsy's mouthful of tea went down the wrong pipe, and she began to cough. "You're kidding! Here? Why would anyone want to put a place like that way out here in Tranquility?"

"Exactly because it's *way out here.* People don't want to be seen walking into an adult-movie store on the main street of Osage Beach or Camdenton. No, this is exactly the kind of spot that attracts that kind of business. It's off the beaten path, and folks can keep their comings and goings private. Steve Hansen is opposed to the rental place moving in, and so am I. Dr. Hedges doesn't want it anywhere near his chiropractic clinic. I don't know about the tattoo folks. Where do you stand, Patsy?"

"Opposed, of course!" She took a big sip and managed to get it down right. "What's next? We've had the bar for years. Someone put in a strip club down the road a while back. I think it got torched, but they rebuilt it anyhow. If we have to put up with an adult-movie place in our mall, it'll start to give the whole place a reputation."

"A *tone.* That's what I told Steve Hansen. It would set a tone that we just don't want. But since we're renters, we don't have any voice in the matter."

"We most certainly do!" Patsy exclaimed. "If the owner wants his building rented out, he'll have to listen to us. And I'll do whatever it takes to keep that adult-movie place away from here."

The corner of Pete's mouth tilted up. "Now that's exactly what I thought you'd say. You're a fighter, Miss Patsy Pringle, and I like that."

Suddenly uncomfortable, Patsy focused on the lace curtains and realized that she and Pete Roberts were all alone at the mall.

Their cars were parked side by side, and no doubt people could see their silhouettes in the tearoom. She pursed her lips for a moment. "Listen, I need to get home. My sitcom is on in less than an hour, and I haven't even finished cleaning up in here."

"What about dinner?"

"I eat popcorn and carrots for supper. Healthy, you know."

"No, I mean what about having dinner with me? Tonight?"

"I can't," she said before she even had time to think about it. "I'm busy."

"Watching TV and eating carrots and popcorn?"

Patsy felt her cheeks grow warm. "Pete, you're a nice man and a good neighbor . . . well, for the most part I've felt okay about you being next door. But I'm not interested in having dinner with you."

"Tonight? Or ever?"

She hesitated only a moment. "Tonight. And you never told me what you're going to do about the movie store."

"Fight it, of course. I'm rounding up support from the other stores and the community." He fished a sheet of folded paper from the back pocket of his jeans. "This is a petition I wrote up. I made copies. It kind of surprised me, but the guy who runs the tattoo parlor wants nothing to do with a place like that. And Dr. Hedges is about to have a fit over it moving in right next to his chiropractor joint." He paused for a moment. "That's a little joke. Chiropractor *joint* . . . get it?"

Patsy rolled her eyes. "Let me take a look at that petition," she said, taking the grease-stained document from his hand. After skimming it, she nodded. "I'd be happy to ask my clients to sign this. I'll put it on the desk next to the cash register — right beside my *Plan of Salvation* pamphlets."

Chuckling, Pete rose and returned his chair under the table. "That hit the spot. What do I owe you?"

"Not a thing. I'm glad you dropped by, Pete." She began walking him toward the salon's front door. "See how restful and rejuvenating a cup of tea can be?"

"I don't know about that, but it tasted delicious." He smiled at her. "Mind if I ask you a personal question, Patsy?"

She stiffened. "I guess not."

"What color is your real hair?"

"Well, for heaven's sake, what kind of a question is that?" She fingered the gelled auburn spikes she had worked into place that morning. "I don't remember. Mousy brown or something. Who cares?"

"I do."

"If appearance really mattered to you, Pete Roberts, you'd realize that you need to shave off that awful beard and get a decent haircut."

"My beard is awful?"

"A bird could build a nest in there."

He fell silent for a moment. "You're a fighter, Patsy . . . and you're honest, too. I like that a lot." Shaking his head, he eyed her with a worried expression. "So, do you think something might be going on between Steve and Brenda Hansen? And maybe the handyman, too? Like folks are saying?"

"I don't gossip," Patsy said firmly.

"But you *do* pray."

She nodded and spoke in a low voice. "I do. I've been praying for them."

"Me too," he said. "Well, good night, Patsy. I hope I see you in church tomorrow."

She watched him walk out the door and went back to her cleaning. As Patsy sprayed the desktop with lemon wax and gave it a wipe, she saw Pete cross the sidewalk in front of the salon window. Now that she had gotten a closer perspective on the man, he didn't look nearly as much like a grizzly bear as she had thought.

She glanced into a mirror and studied her

auburn spikes. Maybe next week she would try a softer brown.

Brenda took a step backward, set her hands on her hips, and surveyed the basement. Her hope of spending hours sewing, painting, and decorating was about to come true. The dream that one day she might pursue work as an interior decorator seemed almost within reach.

She could hardly believe it was the same place. Everything that once said teenage rec room was gone. In place of the sectional sofa and big-screen television set stood a long worktable with Brenda's sewing machine at one end and the cat curled up comfortably at the other. Over the table hung a Peg-Board with spools of thread, scissors, rotary cutters, seam rippers, and all her favorite tools. She had plenty of room to lay out a length of fabric, pin on a pattern, and cut the pieces. A set of open shelves beneath the table held multicolored fabrics and patterns she had gathered through the years. An overhead light fixture bathed the area in a bright glow that ensured her eyes would never get tired.

With the sewing zone completely outfitted, she could put together slipcovers, pillows, curtains, tablecloths, and place mats.

If she chose, she could stitch dresses, mend torn jeans, or replace buttons. While her own children had outgrown the need for those things, there were plenty of kids in the cove whose busy moms might welcome such a service.

This afternoon, Nick was finishing up the crafts center. She watched him expertly attach a set of cabinets where once a shelf of Justin's soccer and baseball trophies had sat. Pictures of Jennifer at homecoming and college graduation, Jessica dressed in an array of dance costumes, and Justin posing with various sports teams used to hang on that wall. Now the photographs awaited places in the scrapbooks Brenda was planning to create. The cabinets would hold glue sticks, fancy-edged scissors, photo corners, blank paper, stickers, beads, wire, pliers, tweezers, trims, tiny paint bottles, and every other implement and embellishment Brenda had gradually collected over the years while building dollhouses, creating necklaces and tiaras, or putting together the elaborate birthday parties her kids had always enjoyed.

Setting the last screw in place, Nick opened and closed each of the cabinet doors and then ran his hand over the desktop to sweep away the sawdust. "There you go," he said, giving Brenda a broad smile. "Two down and one to go. I still think we should have painted the potting area when we did the other walls, but let's see how that green looks now."

As jovial as always, he hooked his tools into the sueded leather belt at his waist as he sauntered over to the two paint cans by the door. "I don't think this shade you chose is going to be too dark, Miz Brenda," he said. "I really don't. Not with all the light coming in through that sliding door. Are you planning to hang curtains over it?"

"No, just blinds I can pull up."

"That's great. You can have the fresh air through the screen if you want it. And in the fall and winter, you'll be able to get a nice view of the lake through the trees. I'm a summer man myself, but there's something to be said for winter. Not so many leaves. You can see things better."

He lifted a can of paint and turned to survey her. "Something wrong? You look wore out."

Brenda smiled. "I'm not tired. I guess I'm just sorry to see this project come to an end. It's been so much fun."

"We're not done yet, girl!" Nick held up the paint. "How about you do the cuttin' in on that wall while I start the potting bench?

When you told me you wanted a sink with running water, that threw me for a loop. I've got to figure out how to tie into your plumbing without tearing up the floor."

Brenda shook her head. "Nick, you know I can't cut in. You'll have to brush next to the ceiling and the doorframe; then I'll roll on the rest of the paint — like always. I know we're going to lay down a vinyl floor, but I don't even trust myself with the baseboard."

"For an artist of your caliber, cuttin' in is like shooting fish in a barrel," he said. "Come over here and stir up this paint. When you get ready to start, use my good brush. You've got everything taped off anyhow. There's no way you'll mess it up."

Squaring her shoulders, Brenda took the paint can and knelt near the stirring sticks. Nick exited through the sliding doors into the backyard as she used a flathead screwdriver to pry off the paint lid. Why did the man never have a negative thing to say about her? To Nick LeClair, she was an artist. She had chosen the perfect paint colors for the walls. She could sew like Betsy Ross. Her garden beds looked as neat as a new pin. Her chocolate cake was delicious. He enjoyed hearing her sing along with the country songs on his radio. Lately, Nick had even started complimenting her looks — saying how much he preferred a blonde to a brunette and that he had always liked short hair on a woman.

With Nick around, Brenda felt like she could do anything. He treated her with respect and admiration. And he made her feel pretty. He never spoke of his wife, so she had no idea how he felt about the second woman he had married. But Nick loved his grandkids, and Brenda enjoyed hearing his stories of their antics. In fact, there was hardly a minute of the day that she didn't feel upbeat and excited.

Except at night. That's when Steve trudged into the house after dark, spoke a couple of words of greeting to his wife, and turned on the television. As usual, he rarely ate dinner at home and offered up not one interesting piece of information about his own life or kind query about hers. In fact, Brenda doubted that Steve had seen the basement since the day she proposed the remodeling project. He never asked her about it. If they spoke at all, it was to discuss the kids — which one had called or e-mailed, what time of day they planned to arrive for spring break — that sort of thing.

As she poured paint into a smaller bowl, Brenda thought back over the years of her marriage. How few couples had stayed together as long as she and Steve had — nearly twenty-five years! For the most part, their life together had been good. Sure, they had weathered some rough spells when Steve's income didn't quite match their needs or when one child or another was ill. Brenda's mother had been sick for three years before finally dying, and Justin got kicked off the baseball team his senior year for drinking at a party down by the lake. If she really worked at it, Brenda could dredge up plenty of problems that she and Steve had endured. But through it all, they had been loyal to each other, honored their faith, adored the children, and enjoyed a lot of happy times.

Nick LeClair had told Brenda he liked winter because the trees shed their leaves and the view was better. As she climbed onto a ladder to start painting the corner next to the ceiling, Brenda decided she could not agree with him on that. Life with Steve had come to feel like an endless winter. Bitterness and hurt filled her heart every time she thought of the way her husband had rejected her in favor of his work.

Drawing the paintbrush along the line of tape protecting the ceiling, she tried to find reasons for hope, joy, and optimism. The last thing she wanted was to leave the man who had fathered her children and built a marriage with her. But how much more of this discouraging emptiness and cold climate could she take?

At the thought of the chilly atmosphere her children might observe between their parents when they came home for spring break, Brenda's hand clenched, and the paintbrush veered upward.

"Oh no!" she cried out. A blotch of green marred the white ceiling. "I knew I couldn't do this! I just can't seem to . . . to do anything right. . . ."

Tears sprang to her eyes as Nick slid open the glass door and leaned into the basement. "Whoa, Nellie! What's going on in here?"

"Look what I did to the ceiling! It's green. I never should have tried —"

"I thought you'd fallen off the ladder, girl. That paint is nothing to worry about. Come on down, and let me take care of it for you."

He tugged a damp rag from the back pocket of his jeans and took Brenda's place on the ladder. In moments, the blob of latex paint had vanished, and the white ceiling looked as good as ever. Brushing away tears, Brenda sniffled as he climbed back down and handed her the brush.

"Are you crying?" he asked. "Over a little paint on the ceiling?"

"It's just that the kids are coming home for spring break, and —"

"We'll have everything done but the floor, girl. You don't need to worry. This basement is going to look really nice, and you can show off your slipcovers and your crafts and all the amazing things you do. Those kids will be pleased as punch . . . you watch."

She bent her head, pressed her lips together, and did her best to keep from bursting into tears again. Nick stood two steps in front of her and hooked his hands into his back pockets. She could see the paint-splattered toes of his work boots, and she wished he would just go back outside. Or paint the wall for her. Or something.

"Come here, girl," he said, taking her hand. "I'm going to show you how to cut in a wall. Then you won't have any more green paint where you don't want it, and your kids will be so proud of you they'll just about bust."

At that, she nearly sobbed out loud. Who had ever been proud of her? All her adult life, Brenda had tried her best to be a good wife and mother and daughter, doing everything just right for her husband and children and parents. They had accepted her labors as her expected contribution to the family. Rightly so. But once — just once — couldn't someone be proud of her?

When Brenda had been a child, her father was so cold and distant that she came to expect nothing but the gruffest of greetings from him. Her mother had found fault with almost everything Brenda did, no matter how hard she tried to please. Like her parents, Steve barely acknowledged the lifestyle his wife had created for him and their family, though she knew he had come to rely on her to keep things running at a high level. But *proud* of her? Never a word.

As Nick led her to the corner of the basement, Brenda brushed her cheek with the back of her hand. She couldn't let him see her break down like this. He was just a hired handyman, after all — a remodeler, a simple craftsman. He didn't owe her the slightest bit of kindness or sympathy.

"Now then," he said, taking the brush to demonstrate, "you want to dip the tips of the bristles down into the paint. Not the whole brush — otherwise you'll wind up with a mess clear onto the handle and all over your fingers. Okay, now take the brush and press it right up against the wall. See how it flattens out? The bristles make a clean line that's so pretty it looks like you used a ruler. Now, I'm going to paint a strip on the wall, and then I want you to do the same thing."

Sniffling, she watched as he dragged the damp bristles down the wall in a perfectly straight stroke. He gave her the brush. "Your turn, Miz Brenda."

She glanced into his eyes and saw deep caring written in the pools of blue. "I'll try," she said softly. Following his instructions, she painted a second green swath on the wall.

"Perfect. Now then, move over into the corner and line those bristles up. There you go. That's it." He watched her paint for a moment, then put out his arm. "Now hold on a minute. When your brush starts to run dry, you need to slide the bristles up and away from the wall like this."

Nick's hand covered hers, and with gentle pressure he illustrated how to paint a corner, lift away the brush, dip it back into the paint, and then start again.

Brenda held her breath as his warm fingers gripped hers. She could feel the calluses on the inside of his palm grazing against her knuckles. He smelled like the outdoors, like paint, like freshly cut wood, like soda, hot dogs, and mustard. His flannel shirtsleeve touched the bare skin on her arm. She shivered.

"Okay," she whispered.

"Okay?" He didn't move for a moment, standing behind her, his arm against hers, their hands entwined. She could hear his breath in her ear, slow and labored.

And then he released her, backed away, and stepped toward the sliding door. "I'd better get to building that potting bench," he said.

As the door shut, Brenda closed her eyes and let out a breath. She realized she was trembling.

CHAPTER SEVEN

"That makes me as mad as a wet hen." Esther Moore carried her purse from the cashier's desk toward the tearoom alcove. "I won't let it happen, and neither will Charlie."

"Hold on, Esther," Patsy said, following. "You jerked off your cape, and now you've got hair on the back of your shirt. Let me brush it off." It was the day before Good Friday, and Patsy was glad she'd decided to close the shop tomorrow. She'd enjoy the break.

"Oh, leave it be," Esther said. "I'll throw this blouse in the washer tonight anyhow. Look, there's Ashley Hanes in the corner." She paused and whispered to Patsy, "I bet Ashley didn't sign it, did she? Young people today never do get involved with politics."

Patsy sighed as Esther marched over to the table where Ashley was reading the latest hair magazine. One of her friends was getting married in two months, she had told Patsy. Ashley wanted her long red tresses styled into a fancy updo. As matron of honor, she would get to wear a different color gown than the other bridesmaids, and she wanted to look extra special.

"Ashley, did you sign the petition on Patsy's desk?" Esther demanded. "We don't have even half the signatures we need to keep that place from moving in next door. They're going to carry adult movies, Charlie tells me, and those awful magazines."

Looking up, Ashley glanced at Patsy and then back at Esther. "I don't know what you're talking about, Mrs. Moore."

"About the new store! Patsy, bring that petition over here, and let's get this young lady to sign it."

Patsy knew Esther meant well, but she sure could get bossy. Ever since Pete Roberts's visit to the salon the other evening, it seemed to Patsy like the video-rental store was all anyone could talk about. Not a single person who entered Just As I Am had a positive word for the prospects of a place like that in Tranquility. It would drive down property values. It would ruin the area's quaint, peaceful reputation. It would bring in all kinds of unwanted strangers.

The men who sat in Patsy's chair to get

their hair trimmed remained mostly taciturn on the subject. They thought it was a bad idea, most of them muttered, but America *was* a free country after all. You ought to have the right to start up a business if you could afford to, no matter what. That's what made this nation great — free enterprise. Of course, none of *them* would patronize a store like that, they insisted. Still, you couldn't deny that a successful business of any sort helped the tax base.

"Now then," Esther said, snatching the petition from Patsy and slapping it down on the tea table in front of Ashley. "You just sign that right this instant, sweetie. We're trying to keep an X-rated movie-rental store out of the strip mall, and we need all the help we can get. You ought to bring your friends in here and have them put their signatures on this petition. Pete Roberts wrote it out, and I never saw a better one. As soon as we get enough names to make our point, he and Charlie are taking it to the mall's landlord. And if that doesn't work, they'll go straight to the county commission!"

Ashley set aside her hairstyle magazine and studied the paper. "Brad told me about this," she said in a low voice. "He's not opposed to the store, Mrs. Moore. My husband thinks people ought to be able to do whatever they want in the privacy of their own home."

"That store won't be private!" Esther exclaimed. "It'll be right smack-dab next door to Patsy's!"

"Well . . ." Ashley looked down the list of names. "Brad and I are . . . we're trying to see eye to eye on things, you know? Last weekend we took our boat out on the lake and talked a lot. We want to support each other. I trust Brad, and I know how much he loves me, so a store like this wouldn't be a problem for us. We just want to do all we can to keep from getting into any disagreements. I'd hate to do something if we weren't of the same mind about it."

"Now you listen to me, Mrs. Bradley Hanes. You two might be as chirpy as a pair of nesting robins in the springtime, but there are other people at this lake who need to be protected from temptation. Do you want your husband's friends to sneak over to Tranquility and rent those movies? Or buy those trashy magazines?"

Ashley paled. "I guess not."

"Then sign!" Esther presented the younger woman with a pen. "Hurry up. Here comes Kim Finley. I bet she's waiting for her kids to get off the school bus. We'll have to get her name on here too."

As Patsy watched, Ashley scribbled her signature at the bottom of the list. Esther set her purse down on top of Ashley's magazine and beckoned to Kim. As the three women settled in together and began to carry cups of tea and orange–poppy seed muffins to the table, Patsy returned to her station.

Her next client, a regular cut and perm, was coming through the front door, and she couldn't keep from worrying that Pete would start up some kind of engine in the adjoining room at Rods-n-Ends. It seemed like every time the alcove filled with people chatting and sipping afternoon tea, a thunderous buzz suddenly shattered the mood, drowned the music on the sound system, and rattled the cups on the counter.

No matter how cordial Pete had been the other day, he didn't take Patsy's objections to his machine repairs seriously. She was glad she hadn't gone out to dinner with him. That would have complicated everything and made it uncomfortable for her to protest the hullabaloo he caused. It was just about time for another confrontation. She could feel it building inside her.

As she worked with her customer — sliding small sheets of thin paper over clumps of hair, rolling each section onto a tiny plastic curler, and then wedging a strip of cotton around the woman's face to protect her from the harsh chemicals in the perm solution — Patsy concentrated on the CD she had slipped into the sound system at lunchtime. It was the group Color of Mercy, three lake-area women with voices like angels. Their melodic music and Christian lyrics helped Patsy stay calm and keep her focus in the right place.

At this moment, her brain felt like a Missouri tornado whirling with sand, stones, and broken branches. All she could think about was pornography shops. Chain saws. Bossy women. Weed whackers. X-rated videos. *Trouble.* There was always something brewing at the lake, and it wasn't necessarily Patsy's chamomile tea.

Steve Hansen would be walking through the salon door in ten minutes. He had made an appointment to get a haircut right before his two college kids came home for spring break. Even though they had always been friendly, nowadays Patsy hardly knew how to talk to him.

Steve was as nice as nice could be, of course. Handsome too. Smart, funny, successful, determined. All the things that made a woman sit up and take notice of a man. But people never saw the Hansens together these days, not even at church. Steve still went every Sunday, but Brenda had stopped attending.

There was talk — terrible, gossipy, whispered talk — that Brenda was involved with Nick LeClair of A-1 Remodeling Services, the fellow working on the Hansens' basement. Patsy didn't believe it for a minute. Brenda had been too good a mother, too loyal a wife, too faithful a Christian to fall into a trap like that. But what *was* going on over there at the pretty house on Sunnyslope Lane in Deepwater Cove?

As she began coating her client's curlers with perm solution, Patsy heard the bell over the front door jangle. Sure enough, in walked Steve Hansen, as professional, polite, and good-looking as if he'd just stepped in off a big-city street. A man like him could probably make a killing in New York or Chicago. People said Steve's real-estate agency was raking in the dough. With a husband like that, what on earth would make Brenda look to a handyman for comfort?

"I'll be with you in five minutes, Steve," Patsy sang out, doing her best to keep the concern from her voice. "I've got to get Opal under the dryer, and then you can come on over."

Steve nodded, making his way toward the row of seats against the wall in the waiting area. Men, Patsy had noticed, tended to sit on the edge of the chairs or pace back and forth while they waited their turn. Something about the smell of gels and mousses, the whirr of hair dryers, the rows of cosmetics, and the ladies' magazines made them antsy.

Steve Hansen was no different. He picked up a magazine and then set it down again. He walked to the window and pretended to take interest in the goings-on in the strip mall's parking lot.

And then Esther Moore corralled him. "Steve Hansen, the very fellow we've been talking about!" she exclaimed, slipping her arm through his. "You're the man of the hour. Bet you didn't know that! Come on over here and tell us what's going on."

Patsy watched as Steve mustered an uncomfortable grin. "Hey, Esther," he greeted the white-haired woman. "I've got an appointment for a trim in just a minute."

"Oh, Patsy will allow you time for a little visit with the girls. You know Kim Finley and Ashley Hanes, of course. We were discussing this petition that Pete Roberts has put out. Sit down here and give us an update."

Steve perched on a chair and folded his hands on the tabletop. "Not much to report, ladies. We've got to get enough names on the petition to make the strip mall's owner sit up and take notice. If he realizes how much opposition there is, maybe he'll choose to rent out the space to someone else."

"Who wants it? Have you got any nibbles?" Esther asked. "Charlie says nobody has even looked at the place in a couple of years."

"I don't handle any rentals, Esther," Steve said. "But I think Charlie's right. Tranquility is out of the way, and people tend to have a hard time making a business successful in such a small community."

"There's the whole population on the west side of the lake," Kim spoke up. "I can think of a lot of stores we need. Some fast-food places would help out a lot. With Derek and me both working, there's not much time for us to sit down at a regular home-style restaurant."

"And it's such a pain to cook a whole meal, you know?" Ashley said, giving her long auburn hair a flip over her shoulder. "I get sick of trying to think of stuff to make, especially since I've usually gone to the country club by the time Brad gets home for supper. I'll leave him a casserole in the refrigerator, and he'll gripe because he has to heat it up. Brad burns everything — even in the microwave. And then I come home to an awful mess. If we had a fast-food restaurant here on the strip, then Brad and I could meet for a quick bite before I head for work."

"I'm afraid it's not as easy as you might think to attract a chain restaurant," Steve told the women as Patsy stepped over to let him know her station was free. "The owners do all kinds of feasibility studies before they'll license a franchise. They check out the population size, the busiest months and the most active times of day, the cost of transporting raw materials — the whole nine yards. Chances aren't good that a small strip mall in a resort community this isolated is going to attract a fast-food place."

"I just don't think I can take it if that video store moves in," Patsy said, sinking into a chair for a moment. It felt good to get off her feet, and even with a short break, she would still have enough time to cut Steve's hair and finish the perm. "A town named Tranquility is supposed to be peaceful. Well, let me tell you, it's getting to be a real nightmare around here. Kids race their cars ninety-to-nothing up and down the highway. The bar down the way makes me nervous to drive home at night. Pete Roberts is still raising a ruckus with his small-engine repairs next door. And the tattoo place brings in the motorcycle crowd and the Party Cove kids."

"Oh, don't get started on Party Cove," Kim exclaimed, referring to a favorite hangout for young adults at the lake. "That's about all Derek talks about when he gets home from work. The Water Patrol has their hands full every summer trying to control that place."

On summer weekends, visitors drifted into Anderson Hollow and tethered hundreds of runabouts, pontoon boats, Jet Skis, and other craft together to form a several-acre patch that was nothing more than one huge party. The chosen playground was awash in alcohol, drugs, loud music, and anything else people could dream up as girls in bikinis crossed from boat to boat while young men hooted and whistled. Party Cove was a nightmare for the State Water Patrol and lake-area police and sheriff departments. But other than issuing countless citations for underage drinking, boating while intoxicated, and public indecency, once a group moved into a location, authorities could do little to dislodge them.

"An adult-video store would just ruin the atmosphere here at Tranquility," Patsy continued, deciding to have her say. "I've done my best to draw a quiet, polite clientele to Just As I Am. The tearoom is a place where a person can relax and get her thoughts in order. I want to have a godly influence on people, Steve, and if my customers have to walk through a bunch of seedy, google-eyed pornography users, well, I'll lose my business and my ministry."

"I'm doing my best to keep the store out, Patsy," he said gently. "But I don't imagine their patrons will be as bad as you think. Folks don't want to be seen at an adult-video place, so they'll probably duck in and out as quickly as they can."

"But my business is mostly women!" she said, heating up. "Most women want nothing to do with those kinds of videos and magazines. The girls who do that trashy stuff are airbrushed and implanted and liposuctioned and everything else to make them fit an image. Real women want to be loved and cherished, not treated like some kind of object."

"Patsy is exactly right," Esther spoke up. "We like to be listened to — not ogled. When I'm talking, Charlie knows he had better perk up and pay attention to me. Even if he disagrees with me, he takes the time to really hear what I'm telling him."

"Are you ladies still talking about the video store, or is this Marriage 101?" Steve asked.

"Both!" Esther said. "You're influential, and we want you to know how we women feel. I've been around a lot of years, most of them married. My husband has learned that he had better listen — and listen good — if he wants me to feel any affection for him. And that's all I have to say on *that* subject."

"A wife can't live up to images in those videos," Kim said. "What attracts me to my husband and makes me want to please him is when he helps me."

Ashley sighed. "Brad hardly lifts a finger around our house. He can build a house, hang drywall, shingle a roof, and attach siding, but he claims he can't figure out the dishwasher."

"Oh, my stars and garters," Patsy exclaimed. "Send him over here, and I'll teach that young man a thing or two. I've got the salon's dishwasher going half the day. And the washer and dryer run nonstop too."

Kim nodded. "I love it when Derek does his part to make the family run smoothly. When I walk in the door after work, right away he'll say, 'What can I do to help you, Kim?' "

"Now *that's* a man!" Esther said firmly.

"Hold on a minute," Steve said. "I thought we were talking about the women in adult videos."

"But don't you see, those aren't real women," Kim said. "If a man wants a real woman to meet his needs, he has to do his part. Derek is always trying to figure out how to be a better husband."

"How did you get so lucky?" Ashley asked.

"Well, I think he may believe he's competing with my ex-husband, but as far as I'm concerned there's no contest. Of course we've had our ups and downs, but overall Derek is amazing."

"A man with that kind of attitude isn't going to be patronizing an adult-video store," Patsy said, returning to the matter at hand. "If we can keep good, wholesome businesses in this area, it will help our property values, Steve. Keep things in their proper place, I say. Look at Bagnell Dam. The strip there reminds me of a carnival midway. Bumper cars, arcades, fudge makers, tattoo parlors, hippie nostalgia shops, bungee-jumping towers, car shows. None of that is my cup of tea, though I know it brings in tourists. But this town is called

Tranquility! It just makes me so upset!"

At that moment, the roar of a lawn mower blasted through the wall that separated Just As I Am from Rods-n-Ends. Patsy clenched her teeth as the teacups began dancing across the table. Outside the salon's front window, the school bus rattled to a stop and kids poured out onto the parking lot. In a moment, the door flew open and Kim Finley's daughter, Lydia, raced toward the alcove, her cheeks red and her dark braids flying.

"Mommy!" she cried out over the lawn mower. "Luke got sick at school, and the lady at your office said you were helping with a surgery, and so Daddy came to get him!"

"Joe picked him up? But it's not his day!" Kim exclaimed, standing so suddenly her chair fell over backward. "If I've told that man once, I've told him a hundred times — he cannot see you two unless it's his day."

"But, Mommy, Luke is sick!"

Grabbing her daughter's hand, Kim Finley fumbled for her cell phone as she hurried toward the door. Ashley covered her ears to block the growl of the lawn mower, and Esther rolled her eyes as she shook her head.

"Well, Steve," Patsy said. She focused on

the Just As I Am sign painted over the cash-register desk and blew out a breath. "Come on, honey. It's your turn."

Brenda sat on the end of her bed and stared down at the cat lying on the floor between her feet. Nick LeClair had gone home for the evening and wouldn't be back for two weeks. Another project had come up, and since it overlapped with the kids' spring break, Brenda had urged him to accept it. Then when he came back, he would lay the vinyl floor in the basement, set up the potting bench he'd been building, and leave to start another job he had waiting for him at a house in Camdenton.

All that morning, Brenda had painted the basement walls the way Nick had taught her — cutting in at the edges and then using the roller for the middle. In the afternoon, she prepared two of her family's favorite casseroles and refrigerated them. When Justin and Jessica came home on Saturday to start their vacation, Brenda wanted to have everything ready so she could spend as much time with her kids as possible. They would have their picnic day on the lake, a chick-flick afternoon for herself and Jessica, a trip to the outlet mall in Osage Beach to shop for spring clothes, and several ventures to favorite local restaurants.

Setting her palms on her knees now, she gazed at her wedding ring, tainted with green latex paint. As she studied the gold band, she recalled the moment that morning when Nick's hand had covered hers and his deep voice murmured near her ear. Even now, the thought of his breath on her cheek made her shiver.

How could she have let herself stumble into such a trap? Brenda shook her head. As if under a spell, she had stopped being angry with Steve and convinced herself that his behavior toward her no longer mattered. No longer resenting him or feeling hurt by his abandonment, she had simply become indifferent, erased him from her heart — as though she had hit the Delete button on her computer and blipped him out of her existence.

As if by the same magic, Nick LeClair had ceased being a handyman, the twice-married owner of A-1 Remodeling, and a grandfather of two. He was Brenda's confidant. Her closest friend. Funny, interesting, complimentary, he grew into the person she looked forward to seeing every morning. She valued his opinions. She sought his ideas.

An invisible line had been drawn in front

of Brenda the moment she married Steve Hansen. But at some point in the past few weeks, she had stepped over it without even realizing what she'd done. Nick had suddenly begun to change from a rangy, paint-splattered construction worker into a handsome, desirable man. In his presence, she felt young and silly. She even giggled. When he flirted with her and teased her, she flirted right back.

Nick's blue eyes had burned into her mind, and she saw them as clearly as a pair of sapphires as she labored over her turkey-tetrazzini and broccoli-chicken casseroles. Their conversations replayed in her mind from the moment she awoke alone in the morning until she finally fell asleep at night in her cold bed beside her silent, distant husband.

"Brenda?" Steve's voice suddenly filled the master bedroom, startling her into a guilty flush. "Are you all right?"

She lifted her head and tried to look at the man she had married so many years before. She recognized his familiar shape in the doorway, but where was Steve? What had become of the boyish athlete who had swept her off her feet? Why did she suddenly long to run away from this stranger in her bedroom, run down the road and through the woods and into a pair of arms that smelled like warm flannel and fresh-cut pine?

"I'm fine," she managed. "Fine. Really."

As she pictured herself standing inside Nick's embrace, Brenda's pretend world suddenly crashed before her like a Christmas ornament shattering on the floor. As she imagined herself racing toward Nick, she pictured his wife opening the door of their mobile home. His grandchildren would be seated around the dinner table. He would look quizzically at Brenda and ask why she had come and what on earth she was doing on his doorstep. Clueless, he would recall only that he had showed her how to paint corners that morning. He would be dumbfounded if she told him she had made up her mind to escape to a cabin in Colorado and that she wanted him to go with her so they could live together happily ever after.

People didn't do ridiculous things like that. Nick wouldn't want such a life. Neither would Brenda. She had a husband, three children, a nice home, and a neighborhood. She was a Christian and went to church and had taught Vacation Bible School every summer for fifteen years.

"What are you thinking about?" Steve

asked, taking a step closer to the bed.

"Vacation Bible School."

"Are you planning to help out again this summer?"

She stared at him, blinking. Noah's ark. Daniel in the lions' den. The Ten Commandments. All her life, Brenda had known the stories, the rules, the morals and codes of the Christian faith. As a little girl in St. Louis, she had realized that lying to her parents and slapping her little sister were sins. Not only had she hurt her family, but her behavior had displeased God, too. Filled with remorse, she had repented, given control of her life to Jesus, and been baptized. Her own children had grown up with Christ at the center of their world — so much so that Jennifer was now in Africa doing missionary work, teaching people about God, and leading them away from evil and toward the light.

"Brenda?" Steve asked again. He looked down at her, concern etched on his face. "Are you sure you feel okay? You look pale."

"I'm not going to teach Vacation Bible School this year," she said. "You know I'm not going to church anymore."

"How come, Brenda?" He sat down beside her on the end of the bed. "What's wrong?

you?"

"I'm not sure where God is these days. I don't know who I am anymore. I'm so tired of everything . . . the past, the way I used to be, my old way of thinking."

"I liked the old you," Steve said. "You were happy and busy. We used to do things together."

"That's over now, isn't it?"

"What? No, nothing's different. God is still right here with us. We're married. We have this house with the basement all fixed up. The kids are coming home tomorrow. We've got money and friends and our church. Things are good."

"Really?" She looked into his dark brown eyes. "But you're not here anymore . . . here in this marriage. And neither am I."

"That's ridiculous, Brenda. Of course I'm here. I'm sitting right beside you on our bed. I come home every night, and if you'd stop feeling so hostile toward me, we could love each other and get back to normal and be happy again. I don't exactly know how to say this, honey, but you've got some kind of a problem. I'm not sure what's going on, but why don't you go talk to Pastor Andrew? Maybe he could recommend a counselor or a doctor. Ever since Jennifer left for Africa and Justin and Jessica went off to college, you've been acting . . . well, different."

"So *I'm* the one with the problem?"

"That's how it looks to me. I sure don't have any problems. I'd be fine if you could just stop giving me those icy stares all the time. I love what I'm doing, and the prospects are incredible. My agency is busy seven days a week, and houses are moving so fast I can hardly keep up. I'm thinking of expanding into commercial real estate. And in fact, I have an idea I wanted to talk to you about . . . but I don't even want to broach the subject unless you can hear me out without getting mad."

Brenda moistened her lips. Mad? How could she be angry at someone who didn't even exist?

Steve was sitting there beside her, so familiar and yet so irrelevant. He was talking, but she couldn't concentrate on the flow of his words. She could no longer make him matter.

It had nothing to do with the kids leaving home or Nick LeClair murmuring in her ear. It was Steve. He had walked away, and finally — after crying and raging and hurting for weeks on end — finally Brenda had shut the door behind him . . . and locked it.

"You can say whatever you want," she told

him. "I won't get mad."

"Well, it's about the strip mall at Tranquility." He practically jumped off the bed and began to pace around the room. "I'm sure you've heard that someone wants to put in an adult-video rental store. Patsy's beside herself over it, and Pete drew up a petition to protest it. He's got enough names to make a strong case to the landlord. Dr. Hedges is furious. He's threatening to move his business. Parking is limited at the mall, and Dr. Hedges doesn't want his chiropractic patients having to leave their cars in front of a pornography shop. So there's a good possibility that we can put a stop to this thing just by pressuring the owner. But, Brenda, I've been thinking about . . . well, about buying the strip mall."

"Oh," she said, her voice flat.

"It would mean we'd have to go into debt for a while, but I think we could swing it. The kids' college costs are covered, and you and I both have new cars. With the basement almost finished and that cost budgeted in, we don't need to fix anything else around here."

"Except our marriage," she put in.

"What?" He shook his head. "Listen, our marriage is fine. Something's wrong with *you* — probably just a midlife thing. I've asked you to go see Pastor Andrew. Please do that. If anyone can help you, Brenda, it's him."

"I see."

"What I'm trying to get across is that I'm pretty sure I can rent out every space in the mall — to good people. It won't be easy, and I've never done anything like this before. There's a possibility that we could take a financial hit. But you know how hard I work and how much I believe in the future of the lake. So this could be a great thing for us. We might even make a lot of money, Brenda. A *lot.* What do you think?"

She picked at the green paint on her wedding ring. "I don't know. I'd have to —"

"Hang on. I've got a call coming in." He reached for his cell phone. "It's Justin," he mouthed to Brenda as he glanced at the caller ID and took the call.

"Hey, bud," Steve said into the phone. "We're looking forward to seeing you on Saturday. Everything okay down there?" He paused and glanced at Brenda. "Your mom's right here. Do you want to talk to her? . . . Okay, well, just tell me about it, then."

Falling silent for some time, Steve alternated between studying his wife and facing the bank of bedroom windows that overlooked the lake. "Yes, I hear you, but . . .

Justin, you know what that's going to mean. . . . Well, I can't stop you, but I wish you'd think about how this will affect your mother and me. What about Jessica?" He paused. "Are you serious? Is there any possibility you might have mentioned this before now? . . . All right. . . . No, I'm not going to argue with you — just be careful. We love you, Son. Bye now."

Steve's jaw tightened as he shook his head. He let out a deep breath. "Justin has decided to drive down to Padre Island with a bunch of friends for the entire spring break," he told Brenda. "He's got the money, and he's twenty-one, and there's not a thing we can do about it. They came up with the plan last night, and they're heading out tomorrow morning."

Feeling as though she might suddenly be sick, Brenda sat with her mouth open.

"Jessica's still coming home on Saturday, though. She asked Justin to let us know that she'll be with us through the Easter church service, but that afternoon she's heading south. Her new boyfriend's family owns a cabin on Table Rock Lake, and they've invited her to join them. Josh's dad teaches religion classes at Southwest Baptist University, and Jessica told Justin to assure us that they'll be chaperoned and everything will be all right."

"But that's just two days," Brenda said. "Twenty-four hours with only one of our children."

Steve pushed his hands into the pockets of his slacks and stared at his wife. "They're not children anymore, Brenda," he said gently. "They're all grown up. You have to accept that. You're on your own."

She stood and stepped toward the bathroom to put on her pajamas. "I know," she said. "I figured that out."

CHAPTER EIGHT

"Well, look at you, Miss Jessica Hansen," Patsy exclaimed as the young woman and her mother walked through the door of Just As I Am. "Aren't you the belle of the ball, the homecoming queen, the sweetheart of Lake of the Ozarks! You get more beautiful every time I see you. I bet those boys at Missouri State are tripping over their own feet to get dates with you!"

Patsy had been cutting Jessica's hair since she was eight years old. The two were close friends, and Jessica had always openly shared with Patsy the details of her many activities and feelings. Patsy was eager to catch up with her now that she'd been away from home for several months.

Jessica laughed. "You're my biggest fan, Patsy. All I am in the beauty department, I owe to you."

"Now, that's quite a compliment! You and your mom make yourselves at home, and

I'll be with you in a minute. From here, it looks like all you'll need is a little trim." Patsy squirted a mist of hair spray over her seated customer's perfect coif. "How are you getting along these days, Brenda? Seen anything of Cody?"

Mother and daughter, so alike in size and appearance, settled into chairs in the waiting area. Both in blue jeans and simple, solid-colored tops, they might be sisters except for the age difference. Even that wasn't easy to spot, Patsy realized. Jessica had matured over the months of her freshman year at MSU. Her face and figure were transforming from teenage gangliness into full-fledged, curvaceous womanhood. Brenda Hansen, who lately appeared to be shedding pounds like a molting hen, had always been lovely. She looked much younger than her forty-five years, and it was no wonder she had managed to catch such a handsome husband.

Brenda spoke up. "Pete Roberts told me he saw someone rooting around in the Dumpster behind the Italian restaurant the other day. He thought it might be Cody, but when Pete got close, the man ran off into the woods."

Patsy finished with her client and began the endless sweeping and tidying that the law required to keep her salon in business. As she bent to brush the hair into a dustpan, she said a little prayer for Cody. Wherever he was, the poor man no doubt needed help and protection. The memory of Cody running out of her salon brought Pete Roberts to mind for the hundredth time that day, and Patsy struggled to keep her focus on godliness and peace.

For the past three days, the man had been repairing another chain saw next door. Every time her salon got quiet enough for the music to drift through the room and the tinkle of teacups to be heard, that blasted machine started up — ripping away the silence and ending the peaceful mood she worked so hard to create. She had only a few more hours to go before shutting down for the Easter weekend, but Patsy felt sure that if she heard that whining buzz one more time, she might launch herself right through the dividing wall and whack her neighbor over the head with one of his fishing rods.

"Come on over here, Miss Jessica," she called. "I'm ready for you now."

When the young woman and her mother looked up from their magazines, Patsy felt like she was staring at identical twins. But as Jessica approached, Patsy noted a major difference. Brenda Hansen's face was solemn, her shoulders slightly slumped, and her green eyes empty — almost dead looking.

Jessica — with her long blonde hair, white teeth, dimples, and sparkling emerald eyes — reminded Patsy of a fresh spring daffodil. Where the mother might be a dormant limb fallen from a winter-blasted tree, the daughter shone in full bloom.

What on earth had happened to Brenda? Patsy patted the seat of her chair and fastened a cape around Jessica's neck. In truth, this was the Hansen family's business, and no one else had a right to pry. Yet the changes in Brenda startled and concerned Patsy.

Could the rumors she'd been hearing be true? Were Steve and Brenda having marital problems? Had Brenda been spending too much time with the handyman who had worked on her basement? Might Steve be carrying on with a client or another real-estate agent? People had whispered damaging, almost cruel things about the Hansens, and Patsy did her best to divert the conversation to other topics. But if everyone had noticed that something was wrong at the house in Deepwater Cove, should Patsy turn a blind eye to it? Was there any way

she could help or make a positive difference? Or would that be interfering?

"Follow me over to the sink and let me
wash you up, sweetie," she told Jessica. "My
goodness, this hair is thicker than ever. You
must be eating right. And I'd guess you're
happy, too."

"You can tell that from my hair?" Jessica
asked as they walked to the row of black
sinks along a wall. "That's weird, Patsy."

"Looking at a person's hair is almost like
gazing into a crystal ball. If they're not eating right or sick or stressed out or unhappy,
you can tell by what their hair is doing.
People lose hair or it gets thin and brittle
when things aren't going well. Sometimes
it's aging or a bad dye job. But I can usually
tell a lot just by putting my fingers into a
client's hair."

Jessica's face reflected serenity as she
leaned back in the sink while Patsy ran a
stream of warm water over her long blonde
tresses. "Oh, that feels good," the younger
woman sighed. "There are all kinds of
salons near campus, but I told Mom I didn't
want to let anyone touch my hair but Patsy
Pringle."

"Well, you just made this gal's day." Patsy
worked the shampoo through Jessica's hair.
"You're so grown-up now. One of these days

I'll have been here so long, I'll start seeing grandkids of clients I've worked on since they were children themselves."

"Maybe not. Dad told me you've got a secret admirer," Jessica said. "You might be having kids and grandkids of your own one of these days."

"Lord, have mercy — if your dad is referring to Pete Roberts, you can tell him there's not a chance in the world that'll happen. The man takes delight in ruffling my feathers. You just wait. Any minute now he'll start up a chain saw or a weed whacker and scare us all out of our wits."

"Why don't you go next door and ask him to be quiet?"

"I've been over there about fifty times, yelling at him till I'm blue in the face. It doesn't do a bit of good. He's making money by repairing those machines, and he isn't about to take *my* customers into account."

"Yelling? You?" Jessica's green eyes opened wide as Patsy rinsed the shampoo from her hair. "You're always so nice."

"Not with him. He's a mean old billy goat, and I don't care if we do butt heads."

"Maybe you ought to sweet-talk him instead."

"Pete Roberts?"

"Yes, Pete Roberts!" Jessica grinned as Patsy wrapped a towel around her hair and led her back to the station. "Ask him nicely, Patsy. Remember what you always used to tell me when I would complain about how mean my big brother was to me? You'd remind me of the Bible verse where a man asked Jesus how many times a person ought to forgive someone who had done him wrong. The man asked if seven times was enough. But Jesus said to forgive him seventy times seven. And you said that was how many times I ought to forgive Justin. Now it's your turn. Go next door, forgive Pete Roberts, and be as sweet as molasses to him."

Patsy rolled her eyes as she worked a comb through Jessica's wet hair. "Wouldn't you know it? My wise advice has come back to haunt me."

"I'm full of good ideas," Jessica declared. "I'm actually very mature for my age."

"You are? Says who?"

"Josh. He's my boyfriend."

"I thought you were dating Darrell Dugan from over in Osage Beach."

"Oh, that was ages ago. Darrell and I broke up after we both went off to college. He's at St. Louis University, you know, and it's such a long drive down to Springfield.

He came to see me a few times, or we met at the lake, but I could tell his heart wasn't in it. After a while, we just said thanks for the memories. By then I had met Josh."

Patsy was used to hearing such confessions from her customers, and usually she just kept her mouth shut. But with Jessica, she knew it would be okay to ask for more details. "So this new fellow . . . is it true love?"

Jessica flushed a pretty pink. "I think it might be. He's wonderful. Josh is a premed major, and when he gets his MD, he wants to do inner-city medical work. What a great Christian he is, Patsy. I'm telling you, he's really an inspiration to me. Sometimes I just listen to him, and I think . . . *wow.* I've never met anyone like that. He's so deep, you know? He's very smart, and he loves to read, and he ponders everything just like a philosopher. His dad is a pastor. Tomorrow after church I'm driving down to Table Rock Lake to meet his parents and spend the week with them. I'm really nervous, but I can't wait."

Patsy had begun trimming off about an inch of blonde hair, but she paused mid-snip. "You're leaving Deepwater Cove *tomorrow?*"

"Yeah." Jessica lowered her voice. "Mom

is upset that I won't be staying for the whole break, but I can't help wanting to be with Josh instead of my parents. Mom thinks all us kids still consider the lake house our home — even Jennifer. You should hear what Mom had planned for Justin and me to do this week. A picnic on the boat. Grilling hot dogs. Shopping at the outlet mall — well, that wouldn't have been so bad. But the rest of it is boring. I mean, I feel like I *need* to be with Josh, you know? We're still at the place where we're getting to know each other. And I don't want to sit around at home with no friends and nothing to do but grill hot dogs or work on some dumb craft project or jigsaw puzzle Mom comes up with. Several of my friends are even going back to the dorm so they won't have to spend all that time around their parents."

"What about your brother?"

"Justin warned me not to plan to stay home the entire time, because he's been through it before. He said Mom gets all sentimental and wants to do family things together. A bunch of his friends figured out that they had better come up with a plan or they'd be stuck with their families for a week. So the minute the last class got out yesterday, they headed for Padre Island."

"Justin went all the way to Texas?" Patsy

had to pause her scissors again. "I've heard the spring-break parties there can get wild. Are you sure going someplace like that was a good idea?"

"It's a terrible idea, but that's Justin. Mom and Dad have no inkling how their dearly beloved son behaves at college. He caused them a little trouble in high school with his drinking, but nowadays he parties all the time. I honestly don't know how he keeps his grades up. I thought about telling on him, but I've decided to keep quiet. It's Justin's business how he spends his time, and if he blows it, Mom and Dad will find out anyway."

Patsy glanced across the room at Brenda, who was immersed in a decorating magazine. "Your mother must be very disappointed not to have either of you home all this week."

"She's been a total grouch ever since I got home. She keeps holding her head like she's got a migraine or something. I don't know what's going on with her. I'm just glad I'm getting out of the house tomorrow."

"Could your mom be sick?"

"She never gets migraines. She hasn't said anything to me about feeling sick, and neither has Dad. He's hardly home, but who can blame him? Mom rarely says a word to him, and when she does, he snaps back at her. If I didn't know them better, I'd think they were having trouble in their marriage. But not my mom and dad. You know them. They've always been happy together. It's strange to watch my parents these days, Patsy. It kind of scares me."

Measuring the ends of Jessica's hair to make sure they were even, Patsy tried to think what to say next. She was certainly no psychologist, but she did care deeply about the Hansens. "Have you talked to your mother about what's bothering her?"

"Sure. She says she's disappointed in Justin and me for abandoning the family. But what does she think she's been working toward all these years? Everything in Mom's life has been geared to shaping us into capable, independent adults. And she has. Jennifer is living in Africa and having a blast doing her missionary thing. Justin . . . well, he's making his own choices and somehow getting through college too. I've got a full, busy life outside of Deepwater Cove. I don't know why Mom isn't thrilled to death. She succeeded! We grew up, and we're turning out to be pretty awesome. But instead of being glad, she goes around grumbling and pouting. Plus, she's acting so weird about the basement."

"The basement?"

"At first, she didn't want me to see it. She said she'd packed away all the pictures and trophies, and she was afraid it would upset me. Like I care? I mean, what's the big deal about whether or not my seventh-grade volleyball-team picture is hanging on the wall? Or those three rows of all our school photos? Who cares?"

"Evidently your mother does."

"But last summer she made a big deal about how she was excited that I was finally going off to college so she would have time to do her own things. She said she wanted to become a decorator and sell painted furniture . . . stuff like that. She knew this time was coming."

"But I guess she still wasn't ready for it," Patsy murmured. "She misses you kids."

"I know, but honestly, how many years can a girl take tap dancing and ballet? And who gives a rip about Justin's football helmet? Mom had it mounted on a special shelf with framed newspaper clippings — and his only years on the football team were in junior high! Anyway, the basement looks totally wonderful. She hired some guy to paint it in different shades of green, and now she has a place to sew and do crafts and work on her potted plants. I don't know what the big deal was, but the minute we got downstairs to look at the basement, Mom burst into tears. She started saying she was sorry, and she didn't know what she was doing. I told her to just forget it. The whole room looks great, and now she has something to work on that's all her own."

"She must be struggling a lot more than people realize."

"You can say that again. She sat down on a paint can and cried for about ten minutes straight, saying 'Why, oh why, oh why?' It freaked me out bad. Dad was at work, so I went upstairs and made her a cup of tea. Then she calmed down and that was that. But I'm telling you, Patsy. It was bizarre."

They fell silent as Patsy worked the blow-dryer through Jessica's long hair, brushing the golden locks until they gleamed. All the while, she gazed across the room at Brenda Hansen and tried to make sense of the things Jessica had told her.

A lot of issues worried Patsy these days. Pete with his chain saws and weed whackers. The adult-movie store. And the usual batch of irritants — having to sweep and tidy after every client, suddenly discovering that she was out of Earl Grey tea, cutting someone's hair too short or not short enough. But of all the troubles that weighed on her heart, Patsy realized she had begun to worry about one more than any other. . . .

Brenda Hansen was sitting across the room, dabbing the corners of her eyes with a wadded tissue, and looking for all the world like a woman hovering right on the verge of hopelessness.

Steve couldn't resist taking his daughter's hand as they strolled down to the lake after the Easter service and lunch on Sunday. Jessica had always been the baby of the family. No matter how tall she grew or what amazing things she accomplished, he could hardly see or think about his youngest child without reliving the memory of a pudgy, pink-skinned infant with a wide toothless smile and a round head topped by silky blonde wisps of hair. He knew he would do anything in the world to protect her and make her happy. Anything.

"Have you caught many fish lately, Dad?" Jessica asked as they stepped onto the long community dock that served Deepwater Cove. "I remember our crappie nights when Mom would fry up a mess of fish and make hush puppies and coleslaw, and you would play tag with us kids in the yard. That was fun."

Steve smiled at the memory. "Believe it or not, I haven't been down to the lake but once this year," he said. "I miss fishing, but with just your mom and me to eat them, it's hardly worth the trouble."

"I always thought you enjoyed heading out into the lake in your johnboat. You said it relaxed you, and we loved crappie night. I bet Mom misses that. She says you never come home for dinner."

"Now, that's not right." He scowled, wondering what else Brenda had told their daughter. "I come home when I can. Working in real estate is very different from selling auto parts at a nine-to-five store. This job demands a lot of hours and an irregular schedule. One of the reasons I've had so much success is the time I spend on my clients."

"Mom says people are talking about you being voted Realtor of the Year."

"That's possible. Your ol' dad has accomplished more than anyone would have thought possible for a boy with no college and a blue-collar upbringing. Did Mom tell you I keep a standing reservation at the country club?"

"No, she just said you come home very late every night."

"That's because I break bread with the

buyers and sellers who have the greatest potential to bring a profit to my agency. It gives us a chance to talk things over. Provides them with a higher level of trust in me. And if they're on the fence about a decision, it allows me time to use my powers of persuasion."

"Why don't you take Mom with you to dinner?" Jessica asked. She settled cross-legged at the end of the dock. "She would enjoy eating out, and maybe she could help you with your business."

"Your mother wouldn't want to eat at the country club, Jessica. She's a homebody. You can see that by what she's put all her time and energy into lately — the basement project. Mom likes to sew and do crafts and keep the garden tidy, not hobnob with clients. Besides, I couldn't write off her meals. You have to think about tax deductions all the time in this business. Otherwise your overhead can run you into the ground."

Steve hunkered down beside his daughter. Jessica's long blonde hair lifted in the breeze and blew back from her beautiful face and slender neck. What a gift she was. Their oldest, Jennifer, had always been driven — the number-one child, eager to please, hard on herself and others for not meeting her high expectations. And, ever since she was twelve years old, determined to do missions work in a foreign country. Justin was the family clown. Goofy, not ambitious enough to please his parents, getting into a little trouble now and then, but, all in all, a lot of fun to be around.

And then there was Jessica. Daddy's girl. As a toddler in her pink-flannel footed pajamas, she had loved climbing into Steve's lap and snuggling up to him while he read the newspaper or watched TV. She clearly adored her father, clung to his leg when she was afraid, and called out for him at the first sign of trouble.

Steve couldn't deny that a few years back he'd had trouble accepting her budding interest in boys — and he had wanted to knock the block off the first fellow who broke her tender heart. But he had learned to let Jessica go, little by little, into her adult world. Of the three Hansen children, Steve expected she would probably turn out the happiest and most loving.

In that way, she was like her mother. Or at least, she was like her mother *used* to be. Jessica had that same gentle, caring spirit that had so captivated Steve when he first met Brenda. Where had it gone? What had happened to his happy, delightful wife?

"Dad," Jessica asked, propping her chin

on her knees, "are you angry that I'm going to spend the week with Josh and his family?"

"I'd love to have you at home, honey. But, no, I'm not mad. I understand how you feel about him, and it's important that you get to know his parents — especially if there's going to be any future for the two of you."

"Mom is livid. She doesn't say much, but I can tell by looking at her face. She hardly gave me a hug when I got home, and now she won't meet my eyes when I try to tell her something. It's like she's so angry that she can't even look at me."

"She's not angry, sweetie. Your mother is just having a hard time adjusting to the empty nest," Steve said. "At least, I think that's what it is."

"I thought she might be missing us kids, but the longer I'm around her, the less sure I feel about it. I'm confused by how she's acting. Look what she did to the basement. If she was grieving for us, she would have kept all that junk on the walls, and she'd be calling us every day and e-mailing all the time. I mean, I'm glad she gets to do what she wants with the basement, but it feels kind of like *she's* the one who has gone away. It's almost as though she erased Jennifer, Justin, and me. The old basement wasn't important . . . not really. What bothers me is Mom's attitude. I mean, she painted the dining-room chairs and made new slipcovers for the sofas. Now the basement is green, and the TV and sectional are gone. The house hardly looks the same as when we lived there — yet she's upset that we don't come home more often. I can't figure out what's gotten into Mom."

Steve let out a breath and studied the lake. People in Missouri loved to say that if you didn't like the weather, stick around, because it would soon change. But this Easter Sunday had been perfect at sunrise, through lunch, and now in the early afternoon as Steve sat on the dock with his daughter. A shade of deep teal, the water sparkled and lapped at the sides of the pleasure boats and pontoons in their slips. Occasionally in the distance, a fish broke the surface, leaping in an arc of silver before gliding back down into the cool depths. Bass, crappie, paddlefish, sunfish, catfish, and several other species thrived in the many coves and inlets of the winding lake.

Lake of the Ozarks was becoming a major holiday destination for the Midwest. Fishermen raced about in their glittery bass boats or set out trotlines. Jet Skis and all manner of other craft cut through the waves, towing wakeboards, inner tubes, and just about anything else that would float. As spring warmed into summer, the whole place came to life. Shops bustled, restaurants had lines of people waiting outside their doors, and the real-estate market heated up with the temperature.

"Mom's doing good things to the house," Steve told his daughter. "I've looked at hundreds of homes, and I can assure you I wouldn't want to move anywhere else. Deepwater Cove was the perfect place to raise you kids. Your mom and I have been happy together here. We've got a good church and lots of nice neighbors and plenty of friends. Mom is just doing what it takes to adjust to the changes in her life, that's all. She'll be fine the next time you see her."

Jessica's green eyes were solemn as she faced him. "Are you sure, Dad? Are you guys okay? Because I've hardly been home, and it's like you two are always snapping at each other."

Steve's heart sank as he gazed into the perfect face of his beloved daughter. How could he tell her that there were problems between himself and her mother?

"We're a little tense," he said finally. "Your mom was disappointed not to have you and

Justin here for the holiday. And she's been kind of testy with me lately."

"Testy? How come?"

"I really don't know. I can't think of anything I'm doing to upset her. I'm bringing in good money, paying for you kids to go to college, setting up retirement accounts — the whole nine yards. She did a fantastic job raising her children, and now she's got a work space geared to give her plenty to do with her time. But . . . well, she's struggling."

"Why? Is it because you're always gone?"

"I'm not *always* gone, honey. Did your mother tell you that?"

"Actually, I haven't seen much of you since I came home. You got in late last night, and then we had church this morning, and this is the first time we've really talked." She paused and studied the rumpled water for a moment. "You know, Dad, maybe Mom misses you."

Steve shook his head in frustration. "She does complain about that. But there's no other way to do my job, and I'm not giving that up just so I can sit at home and watch TV with your mother."

"I think she's lonely."

"Well, I've told her to go talk to Pastor Andrew at church. He'll have some good local resources to help her through this — counselors, doctors, whatever she needs."

"Maybe she needs *you,* Dad."

"Jessica, honey, I haven't gone anywhere. I'm right beside your mother in our bed every night, and I'm right there in the house when we get up in the morning. If you want to know the truth, I think it might have something to do with the change of life."

"Dad, she's forty-five."

"It can happen that early. I read up on it online the other day. A lot of the symptoms sound like your mother. Mood swings, irritability, depression — that kind of thing. I'm thinking a doctor could give her some sort of a pill."

Jessica slid her feet out of her sandals and dipped her toes in the water. They fell silent, listening to the cries of the gulls and watching the ravens soar overhead.

Finally Jessica spoke again. "Dad, I think I might want to marry Josh," she said in a hushed voice. "I love him. And he says he loves me. I realize we haven't been dating long, but some things you just *know.* All my life, I said I wanted to have a marriage like you and mom had. But what I'm seeing now scares me. I don't ever want to end up angry and hurt and depressed."

"Marriage has its ups and downs, Jessica.

You know that. Things can't be rosy all the time. The feeling of being in love lasts awhile, but then it fades. What you're left with is the commitment you've made to each other. Sometimes, when troubles crop up, that's about all you've got. You remember that you made a vow before God, and you stick with it. Eventually, things sort themselves out, and the marriage gets better again. Once in a while, you even get back to that rosy feeling. You realize how much you love the person you married, and you can't imagine why God chose to bless you so richly."

"And at other times, you want to throw her in the lake?"

Steve chuckled. "No, you just bear it. You plow through the days, one after the other, until everything resolves itself."

"So things always do work out?" Her voice sounded so fragile, as if she needed reassurance from her daddy that life would somehow be beautiful, no matter what.

"Things don't always work out," he told her honestly. "You know there are plenty of divorces in this world. Christians and non-Christians alike have trouble keeping their relationships going. There's no magic wand, Jessica. But if you remember your vow, if you keep your focus on Christ, and if you just stand firm through the storms, you'll make it."

"I think there's more to it than that," Jessica said, standing suddenly and dusting off the back of her jeans. "Mom used to tell me that marriage took work. But you're saying it just takes endurance. Well, I'm with Mom. I love you, Dad, but you had better start doing your part to put this relationship back together. If you don't, then Jennifer, Justin, and I will be like all the other kids who leave home and their parents suddenly get divorced."

"Divorced? Now, Jessica —"

"That's right, Dad," she cut in, her voice suddenly harsh. "If you guys don't fix this, then one of these days, you'll go one way and Mom will go another, and it will be just like what happened to my roommate, Chrissie. She asked her parents why they got divorced, and they told her they stopped loving each other. They said maybe they never should have gotten married in the first place." By now, tears were trickling down Jessica's cheeks. "And you know what Chrissie said? She said she feels like if her parents made a mistake in getting married, then that makes *her* a mistake. I don't want to be a mistake, Dad! I want you and Mom to stop yelling at each other and do what it takes to love each other again."

"Jessica, honey, you're overreacting." He reached for his daughter as she darted past him and jogged down the dock toward shore. He called after her. "Mom and I are fine. We really are fine!"

"Then take *her* to the country club for dinner once in a while!" she yelled back over her shoulder.

Steve watched as his daughter threw open the front door of the house and ran inside. He stood and hurried down the dock. But before he could get back to his own yard, Jessica emerged again, threw a bag into her car, and climbed in.

Brenda appeared on the porch, her face ashen. "Jessica, wait!" she called. "Honey, come back! What's the matter, sweetheart?"

Steve stared after his daughter as her car backed out onto the road and spun off toward the highway. Looking toward the house, he met Brenda's icy glare. Her eyes narrowed for a moment; then she turned on her heel and stormed back inside.

CHAPTER NINE

After church, Patsy Pringle usually joined a group of families who were headed to a local restaurant. She had always been welcomed as part of the LAMB Chapel mix, and she didn't mind being a solo act. With the large number of people, she just blended in, sitting by a child or with one of her clients from Just As I Am.

But Easter was different. Most people went home or to Grandma's house for roast chicken or baked ham, mashed potatoes and gravy, green beans cooked with bacon, and gelatin salads loaded with fruit cocktail. Patsy remembered the days when her own family had gathered around the dinner table on a Sunday after church for a big homemade meal. Being the youngest, she had enjoyed the chatter and storytelling, the aroma of good Southern-style food, and the feel of Mama's starched white napkin on her lap.

But then Daddy had died, the kids moved away, and Patsy was left to tend a woman who didn't remember ever having children. When Alzheimer's disease finally took Mama, Patsy was long past the stage of pining for a big family meal. She was doing her best just to pay the utility bills and keep groceries on the table.

Though she was in a lot better shape financially now, Patsy had no desire to cook a large Sunday dinner just for herself. So she joined the group from church. And on Easter, Thanksgiving, and Christmas, she had learned to enjoy eating by herself at a restaurant. She usually took a book and read while she ate.

She didn't think about it much anymore, which was why the arrival of Pete Roberts at Aunt Mamie's Good Food in Camdenton that Sunday just about shocked the pants off her. He had been at church, of course. Even the folks who claimed to be Christians but didn't show a shred of evidence to prove it went to church on Christmas and Easter.

Pete had been attending ever since he moved to the lake area, and Patsy had surreptitiously noted where he sat. After church, she usually said hello to him and moved on to join her dinner companions.

But today he showed up at Aunt Mamie's not five minutes behind her.

Having just been seated in a booth inside the nearly empty restaurant, Patsy was reaching for her menu when she saw the front door open and Pete Roberts step inside. He looked around, spotted her, smiled, and made straight for her booth.

"Looks like we're in the same boat," he said, taking off his cap to reveal a head of thick brown hair. "Mind if I join you, Patsy?"

Well, she *did* mind. She was right at the most exciting point in her novel, and she had planned on eating a quiet, leisurely meal while she read.

"Have a seat," she told Pete, putting on her polite voice. She almost asked him if he'd brought a chain saw along to destroy the atmosphere at Aunt Mamie's Good Food, but she managed to keep her mouth shut.

"What did you think of the church service?" he asked, sliding into the booth. "I think Pastor Andrew gives a good sermon. We never went to church when I was a boy, and I only went a couple of times with my first wife. But when I moved to the lake, everyone was talking about LAMB Chapel and how friendly it was, so I decided to visit

— seeing as how I'm working on changing my life and all. Sure enough, I liked it a lot. I'm even thinking about giving the Sunday morning Bible study a try."

Patsy hadn't heard Pete say so much all at one time before, and for a moment, she just stared at him. Once again, it startled her a little bit to discover what a nice-looking face appeared to be hidden under that big beard and mop of shaggy hair. He had kind eyes and a friendly smile, and for some reason, she couldn't quite summon up all the anger and frustration she wanted to pour out on him.

"You never went to church as a boy?" she asked. "Where did you grow up?"

"Halfway. It's down south near Bolivar. I always said that was a fitting place for me to come from. Halfway. I'm halfway smart, halfway decent-looking, halfway polite, and halfway civilized. The other half ain't so good."

Patsy laughed. "I guess it all depends on which part is winning out."

"For most of my life, the bad half won. But like I told you, I quit drinking a few years ago, and that set me to working on myself. I think the better half might be coming close to taking over."

"And which half is it that keeps starting

up his chain saws and weed whackers next door to my salon, making an infernal racket?"

"Does it bother you that much?"

"How many times do I have to tell you?" she asked, leaning across the table. "Are you halfway deaf, too?"

At that, Pete threw back his head and gave a hearty guffaw. "All right, all right. I'll have you know I've been working on a solution. Since I'm only halfway smart, it's taken me a while. But I'm about there."

"I sure hope so." Patsy studied the menu a moment as their waitress brought ice water and napkin-wrapped silverware.

"I'll have the roast-beef dinner, please," she told the young woman. "And no dessert. Just a cup of hot tea at the end."

"Sounds good," Pete said. "I'll have the same. Only I want a slice of that pecan pie in your display case."

When the waitress left their table, Patsy realized she was now going to have to be alone with Pete Roberts for a good hour. She had already blurted out her annoyance about the noise he made next door, and she couldn't think of another subject she cared to talk to him about.

How long had it been since she'd gone out on a date or even been seated across from a man at a restaurant? The only thing in her life was Just As I Am, and how interesting could that be to a bait-and-tackle-shop owner? Still, she did talk to men while cutting their hair, and she ought to be able to think of something to say.

"Do you like marigolds?" Pete asked before she could come up with a question of her own.

"Marigolds? Well . . . no, to be honest; I think they stink."

"I agree. Good. We won't have any marigolds, then. How do you feel about petunias?"

"What are you talking about, Pete?"

"I thought I'd build some flower boxes for the window fronts of all the stores on the strip. But I want to be the one who chooses the plants and keeps the weeds out, the dirt damp, and the flowers deadheaded. I was thinking about using reds and yellows with a little bit of orange thrown in. What would you say to that?"

"Did you talk to the landlord about putting up flower boxes?"

"Yep, I called on him for that purpose. But then, of course, I worked in a few questions and thoughts about the adult-video store. Between you and me, Patsy, I think we've got enough signatures on our petitions now to make him think twice. Trouble is, he's determined to rent the space, and he's got a fish on his hook. So if we don't come up with another person to fill that slot, we'll probably get stuck with a pornography shop."

"I can't think of anyone who's looking for space in Tranquility. It's just not a hot spot for the tourist trade like Osage Beach. Even Camdenton has a lot to offer."

"I figure if I dress up the front with my flower boxes, that ought to attract attention. The parking area gets a lot of sun, so I'm considering geraniums, petunias, gerbera daisies, and blanketflowers. How does that sound?"

Patsy struggled to hide her surprise that this shaggy sheepdog of a man with grease under his fingernails was interested in flower gardening. She smiled as best she could. "That sounds really nice, Pete."

"I'll probably put in some small mums," he continued. "That way when fall comes, the boxes will still look pretty. And then we can set out pansies for the winter. There's nothing like a bed of yellow pansies to draw the eye."

"Pansies in winter? I didn't know any flower could survive a Missouri freeze."

"Oh, sure. People always make a mistake

and plant their pansies in the spring. When the first heat of summer hits, those poor pansies just wither right up and die. Pansies love the cold. You need to put them in your flower beds in early fall. Unless there's a hard freeze that lasts for several weeks, they'll just zip right on through winter and into early spring, smiling up just as sweet as you please."

As the waitress brought their lunches, Patsy leaned back against the booth and tried to figure out Pete Roberts. Before she could ask him more about Halfway or flower boxes or his idea for solving the chain-saw problem, he announced that he would pray. Patsy tried to keep her face straight as he blurted out a few awkward sentences thanking God for Easter, asking that children find plenty of colored eggs in their yards, and blessing the meal to the nourishment of their bodies. Finally he added, "And thank You, dear God, for Patsy Pringle . . . my friend. Amen."

"I like that hair color you've got on today, by the way," he said as they began eating. "Brown. It looks real good on you."

"It's ash-blonde," she told him.

"Well, whatever it is, I think it suits you. Must be close to your natural shade."

"I hardly recall. I like trying different

things. One time I even got another of the stylists to do extensions on me. You should have seen me walking around with black hair halfway down my back. Finally someone told me that if I would paint my fingernails black and put on some dark eyeliner, I'd look like one of those Goths. I could have just about died. I had been fancying myself as a Mexican senorita or an Italian countess. A Satan worshiper! You never saw anyone get their hair changed as fast as I did. Before the day was over, I had a halo of blonde curls."

Pete smiled. "I never think much about my looks, but I guess that's a big deal for women."

"I see it as a ministry. Fixing people up helps them feel better about themselves, and then they can go out and do a good job at whatever the Lord has given them to do. I guess you've noticed the pamphlets by my cash register and the music I play. My goal is to bring glory to the Lord all day long."

He scratched at his beard for a moment. "I don't guess I've ever thought about it one way or the other. I'm just trying to make a living."

"That's important, of course, but God wants a lot more from believers. We're supposed to reach out to people, share with them, help them, make a difference in their lives. That's the kind of thing that builds treasure in heaven."

"Do you really believe what Pastor Andrew said this morning — that those Roman soldiers killed Jesus, and then He woke up from being dead?"

Patsy looked up in surprise. "Of course I do. It's written right there in the Bible, plain as day."

"But who says the Bible is right?"

"If you'd go to Bible study on Sunday mornings, you'd get the answers you're looking for. There are people who have proved the historical facts. And the rest of it you have to take on faith."

"Faith is tricky business. I think I've only got it partly figured out."

"Well, Mr. Halfway, you'd better get it *all* figured out, or one day you'll check out of this life, and then where will you be?"

"You trying to scare me into heaven, Miss Patsy Pringle?"

"I'm telling you the truth, that's all. What we do on this earth doesn't mean squat unless we do it for God. And our goal ought to be that when we die, He'll look us square in the eye and say, 'Well done, thou good and faithful servant.' "

Pete studied her long enough that Patsy

began to feel uncomfortable. "You really are something, aren't you?" he said finally. "You're a Christian, you own your own business, you've got about a bazillion friends and customers. You must be really happy."

"I'd be happier if a certain someone would quit revving up chain saws next door." She looked away, instantly regretting the way she had snapped that out.

"Listen, please don't get the idea that I'm perfect, Pete," she said in a softer voice. "I've had my problems through the years. I've made my share of mistakes. But am I happy? You bet. I've got a joy, anyway — 'joy, joy, joy, joy down in my heart,' as the song says. There'll be days when I'm blue or angry or frustrated. Days when it seems like nothing's going right. Sometimes I feel lonely, or I might wish my life had taken a different turn or two. But when you've got the Holy Spirit living in your heart, Pete, you know for sure that God is walking with you. He's beside you and in you and all around you. And that's what I call joy."

"I never met anybody like you," Pete said, shaking his head. "I mean that. You just buffalo me, Patsy."

"Because I change my hair all the time?"

"That's part of it. Mostly it's just . . . well, just because."

"Don't you dare put me on some kind of pedestal, or you'll get to see me fall flat on my face."

"All right, I won't put you on a pedestal — if you won't leave me in the long drop under the outhouse."

"What a thing to say! Especially while we're eating Easter dinner. Good grief, Pete Roberts, are you just full of bad manners?"

His mouth tipped up into a slow grin. "Aw, only about halfway."

Brenda was pulling weeds from the flower bed in front of her porch early Tuesday afternoon when Ashley Hanes drove down Sunnyslope Lane in her golf cart. Coming to a stop, she put the vehicle in reverse and backed into the Hansens' driveway. Brenda got to her feet and brushed her hands on her jeans to dust off the heavy Missouri clay.

"Hey, Mrs. Hansen," Ashley called as she stepped out of the cart and started across the lawn. "Is Jessica home? I haven't seen her since church on Sunday. I'd like to catch up on things. So much has been going on in my life, and I'm sure she has stuff to tell about college too."

The girls were the same age and had been friends since elementary school. But while Jessica had chosen to go off to college, Ash-

221

ley had elected to marry Brad Hanes. That made the two young women about as different as night and day — not that they had ever been very much alike.

Jessica wore a cool blonde loveliness that both attracted young men and frightened them off. Like her older sister, she had a fierce moral code and a strong faith. Brenda wondered if this Josh fellow knew exactly how stubborn, determined, and single-minded his girlfriend could be.

Ashley, on the other hand, was attractive in a funky, bohemian, almost garish way. She wore her auburn hair long and rumpled, her necklines cut way too low, her gathered gauze skirts slung down on her hips, and beads of every color imaginable layered around her neck. She and Brad had made no secret of the fact that they were living together even before they got married. The arrangement didn't seem to bother Ashley's parents, either, when Brenda visited with them at the ice-cream-and-sandwich shop they owned in Camdenton. The little place was always on the verge of closing its doors, and Brenda had heard that Ashley gave her parents part of her paycheck every week.

From Jessica's point of view, Ashley was smart and talented — but she didn't try very hard in school, and she had barely managed to graduate. Her whole focus had been Brad and her job at the country club. Those left little time for friends or extracurricular activities, let alone schoolwork.

Brenda tried to stifle a sigh at the memory of her daughter's hasty departure from Deepwater Cove. "Jessica left on Sunday after church," she told Ashley. "She has a new boyfriend whose family wanted to meet her. She's spending the rest of her break down near Branson at Table Rock Lake."

"No way." Ashley's face fell. "That's a rip-off to you and Steve. Is she coming back before school starts up again?"

Brenda couldn't help but notice that Ashley had referred to Steve by his first name. Somehow that rankled.

"I doubt it," Brenda said. "She plans to stay with Josh and his family the whole week. We were disappointed, of course, but we understand. Evidently this young man is very special to her."

"More special than Darrell Dugan? That's hard to believe. He was the catch of Camdenton High. Not that I noticed him much. Brad's three years older than me, you know. Every day when he was done with his construction job and I got out of school, I spent most of my time with him and his buddies instead of hanging out with the high school crowd."

Brenda smiled, sat down on the porch step, and patted a place for Ashley. The young woman settled down beside her. Wearing a pair of green shorts, she stretched out long legs as bare as her midriff and shoulders. Tiny straps held up her skimpy pink top. The usual stack of multihued beads covered Ashley's collarbone and neck.

"Nice day to be outside," she remarked to Brenda. "I don't have to go into work until four. I was really hoping to talk to Jessica."

"I know she would have enjoyed visiting with you."

"I wanted to tell her how good Brad and I are doing. Did you see my engagement ring?"

Only about fifty times, Brenda wanted to say. But she admired the sparkly diamond all over again as Ashley turned it one way and another.

"Did you know Brad has a new truck?" Ashley asked. "He bought it a few weeks ago. It's red."

"I'll bet that's helpful for carrying firewood and moving furniture," Brenda remarked. "I always kind of wanted a truck myself."

Ashley laughed. "I can't see you driving a

truck, Mrs. Hansen. That would be too weird."

"You can call me Brenda. After all, we're both married women now, aren't we?"

Even as she said the words, Brenda could think of Ashley only as a gap-toothed first grader with long red pigtails and dirty jeans. She realized she probably remembered her own children that way most of the time too. Scraped knees, braids, braces, sunburns. So hard to imagine them all grown up and on their own.

"Yeah, I guess you could say I'm an adult," Ashley said. "I can't get into bars yet, though. Not that it matters, of course. It's just that Brad likes to toss back a few beers with the construction crew after work. They go over to Larry's Lake Lounge, you know — in Tranquility? But I'm not old enough to get in. There's other girls in the bar, and that really bugs me. I can't wait until I'm twenty-one, but it seems like forever. It's hard to sit around by yourself all day, don't you think?"

"I do. It gets lonely."

"Guys are lucky. After work they get to go hang out somewhere cool — like Brad at the Lounge, and Steve at the country club. I know Brad looks at the girls in the bar, and Steve's always eating dinner with his rich, beautiful, la-di-da clients. I always admired you whenever I came over to hang out with Jessica. I mean, you can cook, you keep your house so pretty, you sew and paint, and you fix your flower beds all nice. You have this great husband and three awesome kids. If I were you, I'd be so happy. Sometimes it seems like Brad and I hardly see each other. That really ticks me off. I mean, I thought when we got married, it would be even more awesome than before. Like we would be together all the time, you know? But Brad is so busy building houses, and then I'm gone at night. I hate it. I'd quit the country club, but I make really good money, and Brad wants me to keep my job."

Brenda's brain had snagged on one thing in Ashley's long rant: *"Steve's always eating dinner with his rich, beautiful, la-di-da clients."*

Of course, these were business appointments, as Steve had told Brenda. But they included women. Could some of these clients be unattached women? Dining alone with her husband?

Brenda had always envisioned Steve seated at the country club with a married couple. A man and wife. Perhaps even a couple of kids. Steve would regale them with the advantages of buying property at the lake.

He would modestly note how successful his agency had become and how happy his clients were. They would eat dinner together, shake hands, and part congenially with a plan for a future meeting. Then Steve would come home to Brenda.

It never occurred to her that he might be with a single woman. That they might sit long hours in the dim light of the country-club dining room. Perhaps dance together. Laugh and tell stories and feel attracted to each other.

Guilt seeped into Brenda's worries as she suddenly realized that the emotion she was ascribing to Steve could fit her feelings for Nick LeClair. She had spent hours alone with him. They had shared memories and emotions. And, yes, Brenda felt attracted to him. More than she should. She had prayed for that feeling to go away, but lately it seemed God had taken a vacation from the heart of Brenda Hansen.

Probably He had vanished because she had stopped going to church and never read her Bible anymore. Despite years of faithful obedience and dedication to her faith, she could no longer bring herself to spend her time that way. God seemed far away and silent these days. Her prayers had changed too. Once she had been filled to the brim with gratitude and joy. After Steve slowly started abandoning her and then the kids left, she offered up heart-wrenching pleas for God's help and comfort. Despite all her agony and tears, nothing in her life had changed for the better. Now, when she thought about praying at all, her efforts at communication were simply grumpy, matter-of-fact requests for God's protection over her children. Brenda wasn't sure she even believed in prayer anymore.

About the time Nick began work on the basement, Brenda realized she had come to resent spending her Sundays listening to stories and sermons she'd heard since she was a child. So she just stayed home, even though it made Steve mad. He said if they didn't go to church together, it affected their standing in the community. She told him if it was that important, he could go stand in the community by himself.

"Brad doesn't like the fact that I give part of my paycheck to my parents," Ashley was saying when Brenda focused in again on the talkative young woman. "He thinks they should make their own way, and we shouldn't have to support them. But my folks did so much for me, you know? I mean, they paid for me to go to basketball camp and do beadwork and even get a car.

None of that was easy on them. They work hard for every penny. The restaurant doesn't bring in as much income as people think, and when I was growing up, we always barely got by from week to week. I bet you're enjoying all that money Steve is raking in. I heard over at Just As I Am that you've remodeled your whole basement."

"Nearly," Brenda told her. "We still have to lay the vinyl flooring and install a potting bench to store my gardening tools and bags of peat. That will happen next week."

"You must be so proud of your husband — all the money he makes and how smart and cool he is. I mean, he's really pretty handsome for an older guy, if you know what I'm saying. Not that you two are old or anything, but Steve is nice-looking and polite and generous. You're working with A-1 Remodeling, aren't you?"

"Yes, and they're doing a great job."

"Nick LeClair is kind of cute, don't you think?"

A prickle ran up Brenda's spine, but she shrugged as if the name meant nothing. "I suppose so. Nick is nice, and he works hard. He's married, you know. He has a couple of kids and even grandkids. I think he loves his family a lot."

"You could hardly call Nick LeClair married," Ashley said. She lifted her hair off the back of her neck to feel the cool breeze from the lake. "His wife left him months ago. Maybe a year."

"Are you serious?"

"Yeah. I know it's true, too, because Brad is good friends with Nick and Nelda Le-Clair's son, Leland. Brad and Leland are both in construction, so they hang out together at the Lounge after work. Leland told Brad that his parents were fighting like cats and dogs, until one day she up and called the sheriff on him."

"Oh no." Brenda was torn between her curiosity and the realization that she was encouraging Ashley to cross the line from friendly conversation to outright gossip. But since the girl seemed eager to talk . . . "What had he done?"

"She claimed Nick popped her, but he didn't. See, Nelda had a meth lab set up in a little shed back in the woods behind their house, and he didn't like it. Then she got it in her mind that he was cheating on her, which he might have been — nobody knows. The sheriff hauled Nick off to jail, and while he was gone, Nelda packed up his clothes and stuff and threw it on the lawn. He went over there and got it the next day, took it to an old single-wide trailer on his brother's property, and he and Nelda haven't been together since."

"My goodness," Brenda said, unable to reconcile the picture Ashley portrayed with the kind, gentle, supportive man with whom she had painted her basement.

"I'll give Nick one thing," Ashley went on. "He could have told the cops about the meth lab, but he didn't. That probably would have landed Nelda up at the women's prison at Vandalia, but then there wouldn't have been anyone to look after the grand-kids. Their no-good daughter is a tramp, and she lives in Texas somewhere. Leland isn't married, and he works all day like Brad. So he sure couldn't take care of the grandkids. We thought it was pretty good-hearted of Nick not to rat out Nelda, when he could have gotten revenge on her so eas-ily. He must have been tempted, but he didn't do it."

"That's quite a story," Brenda said. "I'm surprised Nick never mentioned any of it to me."

"What man wants to admit that his meth-cooking wife sent him to jail and then kicked him out of the house? It's not really something you can brag about."

"I guess not." Brenda rubbed her temples. "Wow."

"Anyhow, I'm glad you hired Nick. He's supposed to be a good handyman."

"You'll have to come over and see the basement when he's finished. You won't recognize it. The TV and sectional sofa are gone, all the pictures and plaques are in storage, and the LEGOs went off to the elementary school in Camdenton."

"I'd love to see it. And I'll bring over my beads to show you. Did I tell you I'm starting a bead business? I used to think about going to college and then teaching kindergarten. But we don't have that kind of money right now. So I've got another idea. See this necklace, right here?" She pointed to one of the many strands. "I made these beads. Made 'em out of this kind of clay you can bake in the oven. One of the regulars at the country club asked me where I got them — and what do you know? She bought two strands for fifty bucks! That put me into business. Brad thinks it's dumb to bake beads instead of pork chops and beans in our oven. But I'm going to give it a try."

"I'd love to see your beads," Brenda said as Ashley stood. She rose to join the younger woman and knitted her fingers tightly together. Swallowing hard, she took a deep breath before plunging ahead. "Um, Ashley, you mentioned something earlier about

Steve at the country club?"

"He's a good tipper; I'll give him that. I'm glad he's over there nearly every evening. We all fight over who gets to wait on him."

"About these people he takes to dinner. Are they ever women by themselves?"

"Once in a while. They're those types with fancy leather shoes and matching purses and way too much French perfume. You know the kind I'm talking about. We get a lot of them at the club, especially in the summer when the Kansas City and St. Louis crowds swarm in."

"Isn't he usually with couples? Or families?"

"Oh, sure. Or with men by themselves. Steve does a good job schmoozing rich people like that. But he's just a regular guy, even though he does throw money around. I still can't see Steve as anything but Jessica's dad, heading off to mow the lawn in his sneakers, shorts, and an old ragged T-shirt. You should be grateful, Mrs. Hansen. At least he's not hanging out at the Lounge after work. That really bugs me. You'd think a husband would be eager to get home to his wife. But not Brad. He'd rather drink a few beers with the same people he's been working with all day than come home and see his wife for a few minutes before I head off to work."

Giving her long hair another flip, she rolled her eyes. "Oh well. One of these days I'll get pregnant, and then Brad will want to get home to be with the kids." As she spoke the final few words, Ashley gasped and covered her mouth with her hand. "I wasn't supposed to tell anyone that we're trying to have a baby. Don't tell, Mrs. Hansen! Promise?"

"I promise."

Ashley let out a deep breath. "Whew! Tell Jessica hi for me the next time you see her."

"I'll do that," Brenda called as the young woman strolled back to her golf cart. "And thanks . . . thanks for stopping by. It was nice to have company."

CHAPTER TEN

Patsy had just finished painting blonde highlights on one of her regulars when the pounding began. Alarmed, she glanced across the salon at the tea area. Sure enough, the entire wall was shuddering, the pictures of cottages and flower gardens were sliding cock-eyed, and Patsy's customers clenched their cups as they stared open-mouthed at the crack slowly running down the corner of the room near the dessert counter.

"What now?" Patsy muttered.

Ever since Easter, she had allowed pleasant thoughts of Pete Roberts to infiltrate her mind. At Aunt Mamie's Good Food, he had been polite. Funny. Even gentlemanly — insisting on paying for Patsy's meal and then opening her car door for her. She decided she had misjudged the man, and he really was just a good ol' boy trying to get along the best he knew how. He meant well, and the occasional chain-saw and weed-whacker incidents could be forgiven.

Now this.

She led her customer to a dryer to set the highlights. Then she signaled the other stylists that she was going next door. These days, it had become almost a routine. The noise would begin, everyone in the salon would jump half out of their skins, and then Patsy would head over to Rods-n-Ends to give Pete Roberts a piece of her mind. By the time she got back to work, things usually had quieted down. Until the next incident.

As she hurried along the sidewalk, Patsy noted the nearly completed flower boxes that Pete had brought over the other day. At the time, she had been delighted. He told her he was going to line them with a special black fabric that would keep the dirt in but let the water drain out. Then he planned to fill them with his specially blended soil mixture. And finally, he would plant the flowers. He had asked Patsy if she would like to accompany him to a couple of nurseries the following Sunday afternoon, and she said she would enjoy an outing like that.

Not anymore. She rolled up her sleeves, pushed open the tackle shop's door, and stared at a pile of lumber on the floor. Wearing a pair of faded overalls, Pete stood high on a ladder as he attempted to set a stud in place against the wall. He had a mouthful of long screws. Hammers and drills hung from loops on his tool belt, and sweat ran down his temples into his beard.

"Pete Roberts!" Patsy called to him. "What on earth are you up to now?"

Pete glanced at her, then spat the screws into his hand. "Oh, hey, Patsy. I'm building you and me a soundproof wall. I got the instructions from a guy at the home-improvement warehouse over in Osage Beach. He said once this wall is up, you won't hardly hear a thing coming from my side."

She didn't know whether to be angry or grateful. "Are you aware that my drywall is cracking?" she asked. "Right in the corner."

"No kidding? I hoped I could get this frame up without having to touch your wall." He scratched his beard for a moment. "Well, if you can hold on till I get things done over here, then I'll come next door and fix your place."

"The wall is *cracking,* Pete. That's not just a simple patch, you know."

"Hey, you're blonder than you were at lunch the other day." Pete began climbing down the ladder. He tugged a blue bandana from his pocket and rubbed it over his damp face. Then he stuffed it back into his pocket. "It's hot enough to fry bacon up there near the ceiling. Feels like summer. I think I liked that ashy color better, by the way. Looked more natural on you. Blonde is good, but it can tend to make a woman a little brassy, if you know what I mean. 'Specially if she gets to curling and spraying it till it's so stiff it would crack like an egg if you touched it."

"Yeah, well, you don't sweat much for a fat man —" Patsy caught herself and threw up her arms. "Truce, Pete. I'm glad you're soundproofing the wall. But are you sure you got good advice at the home-improvement store? It's like an earthquake next door. My pictures are hanging all whoppy-jawed, and that crack has me worried."

"Is it running straight up and down or side to side?"

"It's vertical — right next to the corner."

"That means it's the tape the builders used on the Sheetrock seam. No problem. I can glue that back down, spackle it, and give it a little paint touch-up. Nobody'll know the difference. Hey, how do you like the idea of yellow for those flower boxes? I'm talking bright yellow, like a sunflower."

"It would attract attention."

"That's the idea. We need to get more people coming to the mall at Tranquility. Did you notice that the For Rent sign is gone from the window on that space next to yours? I have a bad feeling we're going to get stuck with the video store nobody wants."

"Didn't you give the landlord all those petitions people signed?"

"I did, but he threw them in the trash can while I was standing there talking to him. Said they weren't legal, and he didn't much care what the community thought. Did a lot of swearing and cussing at me too. Threatened to shut down Rods-n-Ends and throw me out on my ear, but I don't believe a word of it. He's just blowing smoke. This place needs all the renters it can get, and I pay my bills on time."

He let out a deep breath. "If you ask me, Patsy, this is war. Only I don't have a clue how to fight it. We have no weapons and no soldiers, and our battle plan just went into the Dumpster."

"Well, rats," Patsy said, hands on her hips. "That makes me madder than you putting cracks in my walls."

"So you're not upset about that anymore?"

"Looks like I'm stuck with you, Pete —

unless the landlord figures out some way to run you off."

"He won't. After he bellyached over the petitions for a while, I asked permission to put in the flower boxes and build the sound-proof wall, and he said okay."

"Then I guess I can keep on putting up with you." Patsy shook her head and started for the door. "You know, you'd be a lot less sweaty if you shaved off that beard and got a haircut."

"I think I look sort of handsome, myself," Pete replied.

"If you can call a sheepdog handsome."

Leaving him chuckling, Patsy set out for Just As I Am once again. It seemed like she never made much headway with Pete, but maybe this new wall would help. In the meantime, she was going to have to listen to him screwing in the studs, stapling down the insulation, and then hanging more Sheetrock. The whole situation was enough to make her wonder: *Why me, Lord?*

Brenda Hansen had just sat down at a table with Ashley Hanes, Kim Finley, and Esther Moore when the pounding started up again next door. Discouraged by persistent cold spring rain that had put her gardening on hold, Brenda had decided to drive to Tranquility this Friday afternoon and have a cup of tea at Just As I Am. She hadn't bargained on Pete Roberts causing another ruckus.

"I swear that man is going to drive poor Patsy clean out of her wits," Esther predicted, leaning across the table toward the other three women. "The minute Pete starts tinkering with an engine, Patsy works up a head of steam, marches over to Rods-n-Ends, and reads him the riot act. I never knew such animosity since the Hatfields and McCoys."

"Maybe it's not what you think, Mrs. Moore." Ashley laid her hands on the table, displaying her new French manicure and diamond engagement ring. "One of my girlfriends is a waitress at Aunt Mamie's Good Food, and she said she saw Patsy Pringle having Easter lunch there with a *man.*"

"A man!" Esther sat up straight.

"It could have been anyone," Kim Finley said. "Patsy has lots of male clients. She's got plenty of friends who might go out to lunch with her."

Kim had told the group of women she was waiting for the school bus to drop kids off in front of the Tranquility strip mall. That morning she had promised to buy her twins ice-cream sandwiches at Pete's and then walk by the lake with them. The weather had put an end to that plan. Now, she told the ladies, she would have to drive Luke and Lydia home in the pouring rain and find something to keep them busy while she fixed supper.

"My friend said the man with Patsy was a big burly guy with a beard," Ashley spoke up. "I think it was Pete Roberts who took her to Easter lunch. I'll bet they have something going on, and they just don't want people to know."

"Well, if they're lovebirds, how come she went running out of here the minute he started pounding just now?" Esther asked.

"Maybe it's just a good excuse to see him," Brenda offered. "Could be his ruckuses have become kind of like a signal between them."

Kim chuckled. "I remember Derek used to come over to the dentist's office in Osage Beach to get his teeth cleaned or check up on a possible cavity about every three or four days," she said. "I thought the poor man must have the worst teeth of anyone in the entire Water Patrol. It turned out he had a bad case of lovesickness. I never would have figured it out if the dentist hadn't told me point-blank that Derek's teeth were perfect."

"That sounds like Brad stopping by my parents' restaurant to get an ice-cream cone every day after school," Ashley said. "I was working there, of course. I always served him, and we would talk a little bit, but Brad was so popular and three grades ahead of me that I never gave it much thought. I couldn't believe he was still wanting his regular chocolate cone even in December. Finally he got up the guts to ask me out, and that was the end of his ice-cream habit."

"People will do about anything if they're in love," Esther agreed. "I tried out for the cheerleading squad just so I could meet Charlie Moore, the best-looking boy in school. He was on the football team, you know. Well, I was the smallest of all the cheerleaders, so of course I got thrown around the most — picked up, twirled, flipped through the air. I'm telling you, no gal ever went through as much as I did trying to get the attention of a boy. But it worked. I got my Charlie, bless his pea-pickin' heart. I could just about choke that man sometimes, but I wouldn't trade him for a million dollars."

As the women chatted, Brenda pursed her lips, recalling how often during the past week she had fought herself to keep from picking up the phone and dialing A-1

Remodeling. With Justin in Texas, Jessica at Table Rock Lake, and Steve selling real estate as usual, Brenda knew she had a good excuse to call Nick back to work. Every day she felt exactly as she had before Nick and his paint-splattered blue jeans stepped into her life. Alone. With a dial of his number, she could have him in the basement again — installing the potting sink and laying the vinyl.

But then what? Soon he would go off to work on his next project, and she would be stuck sewing sofa pillows for a husband who would never even notice them. Lately, every time Brenda thought of Steve, she recalled Ashley Hanes's casual statement about his country club dinners. Sometimes with women. Single women. La-di-da women with matching shoes and purses . . . and French perfume.

How could it possibly be fair for a man to expect his wife to sit at home waiting for him while he entertained other women at expensive dinners? What if Steve was having an affair? Even an emotional attraction to someone would mean a deep betrayal of their marriage vows.

But wasn't that what Brenda was feeling for Nick LeClair? Didn't she think about the man day and night, wondering what he was doing, remembering funny things he had said? All the details Ashley had given about Nick's wife and their separation had added more kindling to the fire inside Brenda's heart. She could hardly wait until Monday morning, when Nick's pickup would pull into the driveway and he would knock on her front door.

"Shh, here she comes," Esther said, elbowing Brenda. She winked at Ashley. "Maybe we can get something out of her."

"Well, I just want you ladies to know that our troubles are almost over," Patsy announced as she approached their table in the tearoom. "That awful pounding you hear is Pete Roberts building us a soundproof wall. It'll take him a few days, but he's got all the supplies and the directions. He's putting up the framework right now. Before long, we'll have peace and quiet again."

"You won't know what to do with yourself," Esther quipped. "You've been getting so much exercise running over there all the time."

A slight pink stain crept across Patsy's cheeks. "Don't worry about that. I'll be glad to have things back to normal. The salon was going along so smoothly until Pete moved in."

"Sometimes change can be good for a woman," Kim spoke up. "We get so used to our routines. I think it's been kind of interesting around here lately with Rods-n-Ends next door. Derek is thrilled to have the gas station open again. He says he won't buy his minnows anywhere else. I noticed Pete has built you a nice flower box."

Kim rarely offered her opinion, and Brenda had to smile at the slight teasing note to her voice.

"He's built one for every store in the mall," Patsy clarified. "Planning to paint them bright yellow to draw attention, so we can get more business. But if you ladies are looking for some change around Tranquility, I'm afraid we're about to get it. The bad kind. Pete tells me the mall's landlord threw our petitions in the trash."

"He did not!" Esther exclaimed. "Why, that just burns me up!"

"Oh no." Kim's shoulders sank. "I can't let Lydia and Luke get off the bus in front of a store like that. What if they see something in the window?"

"You can bet they will," Ashley said. "Those video people are going to be advertising their stuff just like everyone else here at the lake. The swimming-suit people, the tattoo people, the T-shirt people — folks

246

would put their products right out on the street if the county would let them. My dad bought a great big plastic ice-cream cone and a hot dog that looked so real you could almost eat it. He put them in the window of the restaurant so they could get attention from all the people walking up and down the strip in Lake Ozark."

"But there ought to be something decent people can do about a trashy video shop," Esther said. "We shouldn't have to put up with indecency."

"And what about getting places we *do* want?" Ashley asked. "We need another restaurant. That way Brad could meet me for an early supper, and he wouldn't spend so much time at the Lake Lounge."

"You need to get that husband of yours out of the bar," Esther said firmly. "You keep moaning about it, honey, but that's not getting you anywhere."

"Well, what am I supposed to do? How do you get a man to spend more time at home?"

"Give him a project! That's what I used to do with Charlie. I told him I wanted a porch swing to rock my babies on, and we were too poor to buy one. So he came home every day after driving his mail route and worked on that swing."

"You can't give your husband a project if he can afford to buy everything you could want," Brenda said in a low voice. "Especially if most of his work is done in the afternoons and evenings."

The women stared at her in silence for a moment, and Brenda felt sure she had said too much. She gave her tea a stir and tried to figure out how to leave without making it look like she was running away. What if these ladies knew what Ashley had said so openly the other day? What if everyone thought Steve was staying out every night because he was involved with another woman? Brenda felt foolish and vulnerable suddenly, and she couldn't think of any way to rectify what she had let slip.

And then sweet, quiet Kim spoke. "We should help each other with things like Brenda is talking about," she said firmly. "We all live close together in Deepwater Cove, and we see each other nearly every day. We don't want our children exposed to this video store. We do want our husbands to come home to us in the evenings. We want good marriages and happy homes and strong friendships. So . . . why don't we just . . . just help each other?"

"How?" Ashley asked. "I'm not even twenty years old yet. I don't know how to do anything but wait on tables and bead necklaces. I sure don't have any advice for you guys."

"Could you invite Brenda and Steve to your house for dinner some night when you and Brad are both off work?"

"I guess so. Brad says I make really awesome fried chicken."

"And maybe you and Brad could help Brenda with one of her garden projects," Kim went on. "If we met here at Patsy's shop now and then, we could put our heads together and work out our problems."

"Like a ladies' society!" Esther crowed. "That's the best idea I've heard in ages. We'll call it The Ladies' Club, and we'll get together on . . . Tuesdays."

"The dentist's office closes early on Wednesdays and Fridays," Kim said. "I try to meet the school bus at four when it stops at the mall."

"Wednesdays, then." Esther looked around at the others. "What do you say, Patsy? May we have our club meetings here on Wednesdays?"

"Be my guests," Patsy said. "Only I want to be a member too."

"That's okay with me, but let's call it something besides The Ladies' Club," Ashley said. "It sounds . . . old. Like we're a bunch of old folks."

"I *am* old," Esther said. "Suits me just fine."

"How about the Tea Ladies' Club?" Kim offered. "We'll call ourselves the TLC, because that's what we're here for — lots of tender loving care."

"Well, now, isn't that just about the cleverest thing you ever heard?" Esther announced to the group. "We are the founding members of the TLC — Patsy Pringle, Ashley Hanes, Kim Finley, Brenda Hansen, and me, Esther Moore. Five of us. We'll meet right here next Wednesday afternoon at three o'clock to discuss our progress and help each other figure out how to handle problems. In the meantime, Ashley, you invite the Hansens over for fried chicken. Brenda, you give Brad a job in your yard building a wishing well or some such thing so he'll stay out of the bar. And Kim and I will put our heads together on what to do about that blasted video store."

Brenda felt silly and excited all at the same time. She hadn't been in a club since elementary school when she and a group of girlfriends had formed a secret We Hate Boys club. That had lasted about a week until one of the members decided she liked Timmy, who lived down at the end of the cul-de-sac. The group disbanded. In high school, Brenda had belonged to the school choir and the Spanish club, but those weren't social organizations. The whole idea of the TLC seemed childish — and at the same time fun.

Despite her dark mood and troubled heart, Brenda couldn't help but enjoy the company of Ashley, Kim, and Esther. Of course, Patsy always lifted Brenda's spirits, and she kept the salon a quiet, wholesome place where it was hard to grumble or tell nasty stories about other people. Regular tea meetings might actually be sort of enjoyable. Even helpful.

Was it possible that Ashley really would invite Brenda and Steve over for fried chicken? They were old enough to be her parents. And should Brenda really ask Brad Hanes for help in her garden? She needed a bridge built over the drainage ditch at the edge of the yard, but she had been toying with asking Nick LeClair to take on the job.

"How about some Sunday evening?" Ashley asked, turning to Brenda. "I know you guys usually go to church, but that's the only time Brad and I are both off at night. I could fix my fried chicken and some mashed potatoes."

Brenda studied the young woman's warm

brown eyes and saw in them a reflection of her own frustration and loneliness. "That sounds wonderful, Ashley," she said. "How about if I bring my chocolate cake?"

"Oh, that reminds me!" Esther cut in. "Charlie was making the rounds on his golf cart the other evening, and he swears he saw that backward boy . . . what was his name, Brenda? The homeless fellow who liked chocolate cake and slept on your porch swing?"

"Cody?"

"That's him. Charlie said he saw Cody down by the lake, poking around on the dock. Charlie was about to run him off, but then he realized who it was and decided to leave him be. Figured he was probably looking for something to eat."

"Oh, great," Ashley said. "If that guy starts hanging around the neighborhood again, Brad is going to get so ticked off. He doesn't want anyone touching his truck."

"But this is just the kind of thing the TLC can take on," Kim insisted. "If Cody comes into Deepwater Cove again, instead of being upset about him, let's figure out how to help. Brenda wasn't scared of him, were you?"

"Not at all. Cody's like a child. In fact, I hope he does come back."

"I'm not sure I'm going to be the best person to have in this club of yours," Ashley murmured. "I work a lot of hours, and Brad has strong ideas about things, and . . . well . . . maybe you guys should go on without me."

"No ma'am," Patsy said firmly. "You have every bit as much right to share your ideas and opinions as anyone else, Ashley Hanes. I'm going to clear my schedule for next Wednesday at three, and I want to hear about Ashley's supper and Brenda's yard project and Kim's and Esther's efforts to keep that video store out of Tranquility."

"What about you?" Ashley asked. "What are you going to do for the TLC?"

"I'm going to donate tea and goodies for everyone who comes to the club meeting." She smiled and gave one of her highlighted curls a twirl. "Well, Kim, I see the school bus coming up the highway. Ashley, your nails are dry, so you don't have to keep 'em spread-eagled on the table that way. Esther, it's been good to see you today. Brenda, don't be a stranger. And now I need to get back to my perm."

As the women stood to leave, Brenda felt the first wave of peace and fulfillment she had experienced in months. For one whole hour, she had not mourned her children, gotten angry with her husband, or been tempted toward another man. Instead, she had been sent on a mission — one that might help a young friend. And she had been given hope that she and Steve might enjoy an evening out together. Cody possibly could return, and the basement would become her sanctuary for sewing and potting plants. Maybe Ashley would come over and make necklaces in the craft area. Or Kim could bring the twins by to play in the big backyard Brenda kept so perfectly manicured.

As she walked out of Just As I Am into the gentle spring rain, waved good-bye to the other members of the TLC, and climbed into her car, Brenda decided she didn't need Nick LeClair to fill the empty place in her heart. She had friends, hobbies, and now even a tea club.

Maybe God had been listening to her prayers last fall when she had felt so alone and had cried out to Him in anguish. Maybe He was with her now, in the cold, stony silences when she couldn't even bring herself to pray. Maybe — just maybe — things were going to be all right after all.

CHAPTER ELEVEN

Steve took off his shoes and crept through the house, hoping he wouldn't wake Brenda. Ever since Jessica had left to spend spring break with her boyfriend at Table Rock Lake, Brenda had resumed her bleak outlook. Steve was about ready to call that handyman from A-1 Remodeling back to work. At least with Nick LeClair in the basement, Brenda had something to keep herself busy, and she wasn't quite so resentful when Steve had to work late.

Tonight had been one of those evenings when dinner at the country club just seemed to go on and on. He had tried several times to leave politely, but his client had come all the way from St. Louis to look at luxury lakefront homes, and she viewed the dinner as a way to evaluate each house room by room. Even so, Steve might have found a way to escape her, but this woman had been different. She promised not only a lucrative sale, but the possibility of a whole new venture for Steve.

If things at home had been normal, he would have loved to climb into bed, snuggle up next to Brenda, and tell her all about it. Before all this moodiness came over her, she used to kiss his neck and undo his tie and sit on his lap while he told her about his day. Steve had loved that. He would have done just about anything to feel his wife cuddling in his arms and kissing him.

As Steve had suggested, Brenda had gone to visit Pastor Andrew, but she hadn't changed a bit for the better. Pastor Andrew recommended that she and Steve come in for some joint counseling . . . just to tweak their marriage back into shape after such significant life changes as Steve's new line of work and the kids going off to college. But Steve had wanted nothing to do with that, especially since he felt sure Brenda was the cause of their problems. He told her to go to the doctor, and after that, they would talk about what to do next.

The Hansens' family doctor had run some blood tests, asked Brenda a bunch of questions, and determined that she probably wasn't yet starting the change of life. That sent Steve's primary theory right down the drain. Fit, healthy, and active, Brenda appeared to be in great physical shape, the doctor had told her. He acknowledged that she might be struggling to adjust to the absence of her children, and he suggested a mild antidepressant. Brenda had turned him down. She wasn't depressed, she had assured him. Just fed up.

So the Hansens were back to being two icebergs in bed, barely speaking in the morning, rarely calling by phone during the day, and almost never seeing each other at night. It reminded Steve of a scene in *The Lion, the Witch and the Wardrobe,* a book he had listened to Brenda read time and again to the children. The wicked, icy White Witch of Narnia had turned a faun and several other characters into stone. That's exactly how the Hansen house felt, Steve thought as he tiptoed toward the master bedroom. Like Narnia, where it was always winter but never Christmas. And no promise of a thaw.

Drinking down a deep breath for fortitude, he slowly pushed open the bedroom door, praying it wouldn't squeak. As he inched into the room, he noticed that Brenda's light was on. Propped up on a stack of pillows, she looked at him over the edge of an open book.

"It's nearly two," she said.

Steve raked his fingers through his hair

and dropped his shoes on the floor. "I know, I know. I'm sorry. I figured you'd be asleep by now."

"Where have you been?" Her voice was clipped, the words tight, as if struggling to emerge from a heart that was frozen solid.

"I was at the country club," he said. "I had a client who wanted to —"

"What's her name?"

Steve sat gingerly on the end of his side of the bed. "Uh . . . Mrs. Patterson. Jacqueline Patterson."

"Was her husband with her?"

"She's divorced. But, Brenda, don't get the wrong idea here. Jackie has four grown children, and —"

"Oh, it's Jackie? I thought you said Jacqueline."

"Jackie is what she prefers to be called. See, the deal is that she wants a lakefront home with room for her kids — and then the grandkids when they come along. So I spent most of the day driving her around —"

"And then you took her out to dinner. Until two in the morning."

Steve could see where this was going, and he suddenly felt hot and uncomfortable. He loosened his tie, unbuttoned his collar, and ran a finger around the back of his neck. An eight o'clock meeting in the morning meant that he wouldn't get much sleep tonight, and the last thing he wanted to do with his few hours of downtime was argue with Brenda.

Steve decided the best thing to do was end this nonsense and hit the hay. Brenda was acting strange, as usual, and he didn't know how much longer he could take it. Pastor Andrew and the doctor had been of little help, and Steve couldn't figure out where to turn next. If his wife didn't get her head on straight pretty soon, he felt like he might explode. It was bad enough to be carrying around a briefcase filled with more projects than one man could manage. But then to come home at night and get the Spanish Inquisition . . .

"Listen," he said firmly. "Jackie Patterson is a wealthy woman from St. Louis. She wants to invest in a large lake house, and I intend to be the agent who finds one for her. But Jackie is different from most of my clients. She's got a head for business, and she knows what to do with her money. We had a long talk not only about houses but about other things."

"Oh, really?" Brenda said, snapping her book shut. "You know, *I* had some things to tell you tonight, Steve. Things that are important and interesting to me. I had hoped to talk to you about my life and some exciting news that I have to share. But I guess Jackie Patterson and her money and her head for business were more attractive to you."

"It's not that way, Brenda!" He stood, wanting to flee. "You make it sound like I'm having an illicit relationship with the woman."

"You're having an affair."

"I am not!"

"Yes, you are. If it's not Jackie Patterson or someone else, it's certainly your job. You love it. You nurture it. You'd do anything for it. You would sacrifice your marriage for it, wouldn't you? I may only be good at choosing the right shades of green for a basement wall, but I'm not stupid. It hardly even matters whether there's a woman involved, Steve. You've left me. You replaced your wife and our relationship with a real-estate agency, a precious bank account, and a bunch of rich clients."

"I have *not* done that, and frankly I'm too exhausted to sit around here and get yelled at by you. I'll sleep in Justin's room."

"You do, Steve Hansen, and you won't ever get back into this bed. If you care about me at all anymore, you have to show it. You have to fight for me. If you aren't willing to do that, then I don't see how we can go on."

"What are you saying? You want a divorce?"

"I don't want a divorce. I would never want that. But who can live in a marriage that's only a mirage? Every time I think I see hope ahead, I reach out . . . but there's nothing to touch. We used to love each other, Steve. We used to enjoy spending time together. We would sit together and rock for hours on the porch swing or play half the day in the lake with the kids. You took time to ask me about what I had been doing, and at night you were always right here in bed beside me. But now your time belongs to someone else. All you want to do is be with your mistress."

"Brenda, would you stop saying that? There's no mistress, and I'm not having an affair. How can you even think I've abandoned our marriage in favor of my job? Lots of people work hard, long hours. I'm one of them, and it feels good. For once in my life, I'm proud of myself. People admire and respect me. I'm accomplishing important things, and I like that a lot. I'm finally a success . . . but you've put me in the doghouse for it. You won't touch me. You treat me as though I've got some kind of disease. If I even get near, you run in the opposite direction. We have no love life. We might as well be strangers. Tonight when I came into the house, I thought how nice it would be to hold you in my arms and tell you about everything that's going on at the office. But then you started in on this ridiculous nonsense about an affair. All you ever do is attack me . . . that, or shun me."

"What wife would want to wait up until two in the morning while her husband spends his entire day with another woman? You can't expect me to feel tender toward you if you treat me like that."

"Like what?" Steve yanked off his tie. "I'm not treating you like anything. You're the same wife I've been married to all these years, and I'm not doing anything different toward you. It's not me who's different — it's you. I don't freeze you out every time you come near. I don't make accusations about you having an affair with someone. I just do my work and try to be a good man. Why does that make you so angry?"

Brenda flopped back on the pillow and shut her eyes. Steve could tell she was trying not to cry. Her chin quivered and her nose began to turn pink. If she hadn't just insulted him, he might go over and try to comfort her. But he couldn't trust Brenda anymore. What if he attempted a touch of tenderness and she lashed out at him again? He honestly didn't know what to do with her, and he was so worn-out from working all day and then trying to shore up his collapsing marriage that he just couldn't think straight.

"Listen, honey," he said in the most gentle voice he could muster. "I love you. I do. I always have, and I always will. I don't know what the problem is, but if I could fix it, I would."

She covered her eyes with her hands, pressing back tears. "Here's the problem," she told him, a sob echoing in her throat. "You don't need me anymore. My husband doesn't have time for me."

Steve glanced at the clock through bleary eyes. He shook his head and groaned. "For pete's sake, Brenda, how can you even say that? We live in the same house. We have three great kids together. We've been married nearly twenty-five years. How much more of me can you possibly want?"

"Minutes," she said. "Hours."

"You've had me nearly half an hour tonight, and all you've done is yell at me and accuse me. Look, I've got a meeting at the title company at eight, and I need to do some prep work in the office before that. I don't know how to do this marriage any better than I'm doing it, all right? I'm a good man. I'm being the best person I know how to be. And if that's not enough for you, then . . . well, then I guess it's up to you. Decide what you want, and let me know."

With that, he stood and walked into the bathroom. He could hardly believe the words Brenda had been throwing around. *Affair. Divorce.* Surely things couldn't be that bad between them.

As he brushed his teeth, Steve thought about Jackie Patterson and her interest in putting seed money into his agency. Jackie thought Steve ought to purchase property as well as move into the commercial side of the real-estate market. She saw the big picture, and she made Steve feel as though he was capable of accomplishing anything he set his mind to.

Brenda was right about one thing. He didn't enjoy spending time with his wife. Why should he? A woman like Jackie Patterson was interesting, supportive, and intelligent. Even though she was older than he, she was very attractive. If she reached out to him, he might find it hard to hold back.

Steve felt sure he would keep his marriage vows to Brenda, but she wasn't making it easy with all her whining and complaining.

Each day that passed, he found it more and more difficult to keep his mind from wandering where it shouldn't go. So he focused on his business instead. And then, when he couldn't postpone it any longer, he finally drove home to the frozen wasteland of Narnia.

Stripped down to his boxers, Steve stepped into the bedroom. As he climbed under the covers, he noticed that Brenda's light was off. He reached over, hoping for at least a touch, but her side of the bed was empty.

"Brenda?" he murmured.

Glancing down the hall, he spotted the light on in Jennifer's old room. So Brenda was the one who had left their marriage bed after all. He thought about mustering the energy to get up and walk down there and try once again to fix the tangled mess of their relationship. Laying his head back on the pillow, Steve closed his eyes. And that's when he realized this was the first peaceful moment he'd had in his own home in a very long time.

"I reckon that basement of yours ought to be about done by now," Pete Roberts said early Monday afternoon. He slipped two rotisserie hot dogs into a paper sack, dropped in some packets of mustard and ketchup, and stuffed a handful of napkins on top. "I guess I'll have to start cutting back on how much I order from my food and condiment supplier. You and Nick Le-Clair have been keeping me in the hot-dog business for quite a while."

Brenda smiled at the bearded man as she took the sack. "Don't cut your order too low. Summer's almost here, and that means your traffic should pick up a lot."

"I hope you're right. It was pretty dead around here last week. Spent most of my time building that soundproof wall between here and the salon."

"Does it work?"

"No idea. I'm waiting for a leaf-blower or chain-saw repair to come in. That'll really put it to the test."

"Poor Patsy. Pete, you have to know that you've just about driven that lady out of her mind."

"Aw, she loves coming over here and getting up on her high horse about all the noise. You'd think she was a schoolmarm the way she goes to pointing here and there, chewing me up one side and down the other, and threatening to call in the law. We have a good time."

Brenda had to laugh. "I think she might

see it a little differently."

"Don't let her fool you. Patsy's sweet on me; that's for sure."

"Sweet on you? Pete, can I be honest?"

"Sure. I can take it."

"I've known Patsy a long time, and she is awfully persnickety about certain things. The truth is, Pete, half the time you smell like catfish bait, and the other half you smell like engine grease. If you want Patsy to be sweet on you, you'll have to do a little better on your grooming."

"You really think she cares about a thing like how a man smells? Especially one as big and tough as me?"

Again, Brenda chuckled. "Just go next door and you'll see what Patsy Pringle likes best in a man. Nothing puts a smile on her face like a client with a nice close haircut, a clean shave, and maybe even a little cologne. As for herself, she always wears pretty dresses and skirts, and she's got the nicest shoes of anyone in Tranquility. Her makeup is always perfect, and her hair —"

"Yeah, about that hair . . . one day it's black, the next it's red, brown, or polka-dot. Who knows what's coming at you? I keep waiting for plaid."

"My point is that Patsy enjoys looking nice and making the world around her a pretty place. She's the first one to give out compliments. You should have heard her going on about my daughter Jessica when she was home. Has Patsy ever said anything nice about you, Pete?"

He scrunched up his nose and searched the upper corner of the room as if that might help him remember. "Come to think of it . . . not exactly. But looks aren't all there is to a man. I've got everything else a fellow could need — loyalty, good deeds, a kind heart, and enough money to treat a woman to a nice restaurant dinner every once in a while. I don't drink, smoke, or cuss . . . well, I hardly ever cuss. And I've been going to church, too."

"Good for you. Maybe you're just the kind of man Patsy needs."

" 'Course I am. I just have to prove it to her. Give me a little time, and you'll see. She'll come around."

"All right. I'll be watching." Brenda straightened her purse strap and turned to go.

"Say, Steve was in here bright and early this morning," Pete called after her. "Told me he has a long day ahead."

"As always." Brenda rolled her eyes and pushed open the door to Rods-n-Ends as she waved good-bye to Pete. The morning after her last fight with Steve, she'd woken to an empty house. They had barely spoken since. Brenda had left him a voice mail to tell him about the invitation to have dinner with Ashley and Brad Hanes on Sunday evening, but Steve called back to say he couldn't go. He needed to prepare for an early meeting on Monday morning and would be working in the office until late Sunday night.

As she drove toward Deepwater Cove, Brenda sensed the pain in her heart growing more intense and heavy as the days passed. She had told Steve point-blank what the problem was between them: she wanted them to spend more time together. But he had flatly turned her down. He believed the fact that he had married her, fathered their children, and provided for her to be sufficient. Why should he give her anything else, especially his valuable time?

The more Brenda thought about it, the more she wondered what more she could do to make Steve want to be with her. The answer was always *nothing*.

She could never compete with the wealthy, attractive women whose company her husband enjoyed every day. They wore the latest fashions and hairstyles, they mingled with the kinds of upper-class people Steve would love to sign on as new clients, and no doubt they had hundreds of interesting things to say. After all, what did they talk about but real estate? Steve's favorite subject.

Brenda knew almost nothing about the property market and how it worked — and in truth, she didn't care to learn. She rarely enjoyed dressing up in fancy clothes. She preferred the jeans, sneakers, and T-shirts she wore almost every day. She got a haircut when she noticed the ends getting scraggly. And the topics she most enjoyed discussing were the differences between annuals and perennials, the techniques of painting plaid on a chair, or the skill it took to bake her well-loved chocolate cake.

The truth was obvious. To Steve, she was boring. Plain. Dull. No wonder he preferred to spend time working in his office or driving clients from house to house around the lake.

As she pulled into the garage of her house in Deepwater Cove, Brenda allowed a horrible thought to creep into her mind for the third time that day. More and more now, she caught herself pondering it. Turning it over one way and then another. Wondering what it would be like.

Divorce.

She imagined herself telling Steve their marriage was hopelessly dead, asking him to move out of the house, dividing up their belongings and their money, sitting the children down and breaking the news. Oh, it was too awful to even contemplate. But she did.

She imagined the peace of a life without a husband whose apathy toward her ate at her heart and twisted her stomach into knots. She imagined inviting friends over to the house, weeding in her garden, perhaps sewing a wedding dress for Jessica or Jennifer. At night, she could sleep without hearing Steve snore or having him wrestle the covers away from her. She could open the windows and blow away the dusty bleakness of their marriage. She would start afresh. Be her own person, not some barnacle attached to someone else's speedboat.

And then she thought of all the negatives. The kids would be crushed if their parents separated after so many years together. God would be disappointed in Brenda — surely He already was disgusted with her for entertaining such thoughts. Actually going through with it would be even worse.

How could she hold her head up in town if she had tossed out a marriage just because her husband wasn't paying enough attention to her? It sounded so selfish. So petty. No one would understand the pain and emptiness she felt every time she reflected on her current life and the many long, lonely years to come.

Brenda gathered her purse and the sack of hot dogs and climbed out of her car. There was no way to turn. No path out of the impossible nightmare in which she found herself.

If she stayed with Steve, she would spend the rest of her life playing second fiddle to his career, his goals, and all the interesting people in his life. She would be the little wife at home, sewing pillows and planting petunias. Even if she did one day manage to start an interior-decorating business, they would have nothing in common. She would do her work while he immersed himself more and more deeply in his separate world.

But if she left him, she could never forgive herself for hurting her children and making a public issue of something many people would consider trivial. She would toss out all the years she and Steve had spent together as if they had been irrelevant. They hadn't, though. She and Steve once shared a good life — mostly happy and definitely united in the effort to raise their children and build a strong home.

Brenda knew she still loved Steve, but her emotion was based more on what had happened between them in the past than on how she felt about him now. These days her husband brought little but hurt, doubt, even fear into her heart. What desire could he possibly have toward her? She was nothing but a body in his bed at night. In truth, he could replace her with someone else and hardly know the difference.

What hope was there? How could she ever get out of this black coffin with its nailed-down lid and suffocating lack of air? Brenda wanted to cry, but she couldn't summon up enough emotion toward her husband to shed even a single tear.

On entering the house, she heard Nick LeClair working downstairs. As usual, he had his radio tuned to a country-music station, and he was whistling along with a favorite song. Brenda listened to him for a moment as she laid her purse on the table in the foyer. Then she stepped into the kitchen, took a plate from the cupboard, and poured him a glass of soda, no ice. She slid the two hot dogs onto the plate and squirted mustard along the length of each.

It felt so routine now, doing these small things for Nick. As though they had fallen into a comfortable pattern that might go on and on forever.

But today it would end. Nick was already laying the vinyl on the floor, Brenda reminded herself as she carried his plate down the steps. He would install the potting bench next and finally hook up the sink. And then he would be gone.

Perhaps by the end of the day, he would have completed all his work, and they would never see each other again. She couldn't even ask Nick to build a bridge over her ditch. He had another remodeling project waiting for him, and besides, she had promised Ashley Hanes to ask for Brad's help.

As Brenda stepped onto the cool concrete floor, Nick looked up, spotted her, and smiled. "There you are!" he said, his blue eyes warm. "I thought I might have lost you, girl. You were gone a long time."

"It took me a while to find the right parts in the plumbing section of the hardware store," she told him as she set the plate and soda on the sewing table in the corner where he usually ate. "I had to get help with the elbows."

"Something wrong with your elbows?" He chuckled as he dropped a hammer into its loop on his leather tool belt. Moving toward her, he took her arm and pretended to examine it. "Looks like a mighty fine elbow to me. Best I've seen in a long while, in fact."

Brenda tried to calm her heartbeat as his hand moved up and down her bare arm. She knew it was wrong to be so near him. To let him touch her. To welcome his compliments. Yet she ached with a yearning for more as his words swirled through her and his warm fingers stroked her skin.

"Not *my* elbows." She managed a smile. "Those PVC ones you wanted for the sink. I've got them in a paper sack upstairs. Here's your lunch."

He released her arm and studied the plate. "Hot dogs and mustard," he said. "It'll be hard to get used to making my own peanut-butter-and-jelly sandwiches again."

"I guess your wife . . ." She pressed her lips together and looked away. "Well, there's nothing wrong with a good PBJ."

"My wife left me," he said, his focus still on the plate. "You probably know that by now. Folks around here talk. Nelda's got the grandkids with her, but I see them a lot. It's not too bad."

"I'm sorry. You were married a long time."

"A good while, yeah."

"What happened, Nick?"

"Nelda had some problems, and so did I. We got to where we couldn't work things out. It was just . . . you know . . . arguing and fussing all the time."

"I know," Brenda said softly.

He turned one of the hot dogs perpendicular to the other on the plate. "I figure we'll probably get divorced. Nothing to keep us together any longer. I've got a mobile home on my brother's land. It's not much, but it does me fine. My son, Leland, stays there most of the time too. He works construction like me; only he's with a contractor. My daughter went off someplace and left her kids behind. We think she might be in California, but really it's anybody's guess. Drugs, you know? I don't hold with drugs. They never did anybody a bit of good. I won't take so much as an aspirin."

"What about all those bones you broke in your rodeo days?"

"Nope. Not even an aspirin. Just wrapped up those broken bones and let 'em set. They healed pretty good. I don't have much to complain about."

Brenda watched him align the second hot dog with the first. "You're a good man, Nick," she said. "I'm glad you worked on my basement."

Blazing blue, his eyes focused on hers. "You're a lot better than me, girl. Smarter. Richer. Educated. Classy. Listen, before I get done here, I've got to tell you . . . I want to say . . ."

She swallowed as he hung his head and pushed his hands into his back pockets.

"Well, I'm glad too," he said. "Glad I worked here with you. Glad I got to know you. Most jobs, I just show up and do the work. But I looked forward to —"

"Me too," she cut in. "I was always happy when I heard your truck."

"Brenda . . ." He reached up and ran his callused finger along a row of tiny embroidered roses on the sleeve of her T-shirt. "I would never hurt you."

"I know that." She was trembling as his hand slipped around her back and pressed her toward him. She shook her head. "Nick, you shouldn't."

"Just let me hold you, girl," he murmured, pulling her close and wrapping his arms around her. "I can't leave this place unless I hold you just once . . . but I'm scared if I do, I'll never be able to let you go."

"This is wrong, Nick. I know it is, but it feels so wonderful." She slid her hands around him and rested her cheek against his firm shoulder. "I don't see what we can ever do."

"Let me kiss you, Brenda. Just that much."

"Nick, I —"

The basement's sliding door scraped open. "Hi, I'm Cody!" a cheerful voice announced. "Wow, hot dogs! I love hot dogs!"

CHAPTER TWELVE

"I see you!" Cody stumbled into the basement as Brenda pushed out of Nick's arms and hugged herself in dismay. The young man grinned and lifted a grimy hand to wave at her. Cody looked ten times worse than a few weeks before. His beard had grown longer and was now tangled in with his long brown hair. Littered with leaves and burrs, his hair had begun coiling into naturally matted dreadlocks. Sunburned, filthy, smelling like the inside of a trash barrel, he wore rags that barely hung together on his skinny frame. His teeth were brown.

"I see you, Brenda," he said, smiling happily, "and I've been looking hard to find you. Here you are! Your house is right where it used to be, but I couldn't see it for a long time."

"Now, listen here, fella." Nick LeClair squared his shoulders and took a protective step in front of Brenda. "You can't just go barging into a person's house like that. Who do you think you are?"

"Hi, I'm Cody. Who do you think *you* are?"

Realizing she was suddenly trembling, Brenda laid a hand on Nick's arm. "Nick, this is Cody," she murmured. "It's all right. I know him."

"Who do you think you are, fella?" His eyes on the other man, Cody repeated the words in his usual cheerful voice.

Brenda spoke up quickly. "This is the man who painted the basement, Cody. He's my helper."

"How old is he?"

"Older than you," she said. "Cody, let me take you upstairs to the kitchen and make you a sandwich. I bet you're hungry."

"Those hot dogs look good. I love hot dogs."

"They belong to Nick."

"Nick." Cody's brows drew together as he studied the handyman. "Brenda is my friend, Nick. She makes me soup and sandwiches and chocolate cake. She's a Christian, because my daddy said anyone would give you food, but only a Christian would give you chocolate cake."

"Come on, Cody. Please." Brenda knotted her fingers together as she spoke, stunned that she had been caught in Nick's arms and fearful that Cody might mention it to someone. If she could get him upstairs, maybe a big plate of food would make him forget what he had seen. She unlocked her fingers, took his thin wrist, and began to pull him toward the staircase.

"Nick, are you a Christian?" Cody asked as he shuffled backward.

"I reckon so. . . . Brenda, listen —"

"No," she blurted out, glancing over her shoulder at him. "Just finish up, Nick. Finish the basement and go. I'm sorry. I'm so sorry."

"Brenda . . ."

"Hurry, Cody. Let's go see what we can find for you to eat. I know I have some roast beef in the freezer, and we'll make you a big sandwich."

"I love chocolate cake. Triangles are okay, but I like squares better."

"I don't have any chocolate cake," she muttered, tugging him up the last couple of steps.

Brenda felt tears welling up in her eyes as if a flood had suddenly broken through a dam. What on earth had she just done? Why had she ever gone into that basement alone with Nick in the first place? Had she purposely lured him into her arms this afternoon? Or had he seduced her? What kind of a man was he really — sincere, honest, and truly attracted to her . . . or a Romeo who would pick up any woman he could?

Oh, why had she let herself do something so wrong and stupid? What if Steve found out? What if Cody told on her . . . or what if Nick said something?

On the other hand, why did she even care what her husband thought? She had just been considering how it would feel to divorce Steve. But did she really want that? What if Steve informed the kids that their mother had been unfaithful?

Adultery. That awful word.

She hadn't given in to infidelity — at least not physically. But wasn't there a Bible verse about adultery in your mind . . . looking at someone with lust . . . sinning with the heart? She couldn't even think straight! What was Nick doing now in the basement? Would he come upstairs? What would she say if he did? How could she possibly make everything feel all right again?

"I see you, Brenda," Cody said. He was moving along behind her slowly. "I see you, and you're my friend. You look just the same as you did that night when it was raining. Remember? I thought Jesus was in the basement, but it was just me in the glass door, huh?"

"Yes, that was it." Brushing a tear from her cheek, Brenda opened the freezer door and took out a chunk of roast beef she had cooked in preparation for her kids' aborted spring-break visit.

"Maybe Nick was in the basement that night," Cody suggested. "Do you think Nick looks like Jesus?"

"No, absolutely not. Listen, Cody, please forget about him, okay? Nick is just the man who fixed up the basement. You never saw him before, and you won't ever see him again."

"I don't think Nick is like Jesus, because he didn't share his hot dogs with me. Jesus shared five loaves and two fishes with a multitude, and a multitude means lots and lots of people. 'And he commanded the multitude to sit down on the grass, and took the five loaves, and the two fishes, and looking up to heaven, he blessed, and brake, and gave the loaves to his disciples, and the disciples to the multitude. And they did all eat, and were filled.' Matthew 14:19–20. My daddy learned me that one when it was snowing outside and we didn't have any groceries. And my daddy said Jesus always shared His food."

Brenda couldn't bring herself to respond. Hands shaking, she cut several slices from a loaf of French bread while the plastic container of roast beef defrosted in the microwave oven. Why had she let Nick touch her? Oh, it had felt so good to be held again . . . sweet words whispered against her cheek . . . words of desire.

She would have kissed him. There was no way she could deny it. But how had she let it come to that? She barely knew the man.

"I went with you to get a haircut," Cody was saying. "Then a really loud noise started near us, and I thought it was coming after me. I ran down in the woods and climbed a tree. I went real high up . . . so high I got myself scared to deaf. I could hear you calling me, but I was too scared to come down. I thought I might fall out of the tree or that noise might start again."

Brenda tried to concentrate on Cody as she spread mayonnaise on the bread and took a handful of potato chips from a bag. Had he actually observed her in Nick's arms? Might he ever blurt out that information in front of Steve? Or anyone? She longed to hustle Cody out the door and tell him to never come back. But he was rambling so happily now, as if he had found peace at last.

"I never thought I would see you again, Brenda," he said. "But I to see you now — I sure do. After I climbed down from the tree, I looked for you everywhere, up and down the lake and in the woods and on the roads. I searched just the way I searched for my daddy, even though he already had told me he was never coming back. I searched for him a long time, but he was telling me the truth. 'You're twenty-one now, Cody. Time to make your way.' That's what my daddy said. I thought it would be the same with you, and you were never coming back. But here you are, and how about that?"

She pushed a plate toward the young man as he perched on a stool at the kitchen counter. "Here, Cody. Eat this, and then you can go sit on the porch swing."

"Okay. But it's not night yet, Brenda. I don't go to sleep until it gets dark." He bit into the sandwich, closed his eyes, and chewed blissfully.

"You look like you haven't been eating much," Brenda observed, her heart softening toward Cody as she watched him. "You're very thin."

"I found a restaurant where they throw out French fries and onion rings. Sometime you can get pizza there too. I stayed awhile, but then they ran me off. People don't like me to eat out of their trash. I learned that a long time ago. But sometimes that's all you can find. Trash-can food is not as good as soup and sandwiches and chocolate cake, like you gave me. It's cold and sometimes it stinks. But I learned you have to make your way. That's what my daddy told me to do, and I do it."

Unable to stop her tears and her trembling hands, Brenda worked for a while in the kitchen — washing dishes that were already clean, wiping the counter until it shone, polishing the window over the sink. Cody devoured three large roast-beef sandwiches and most of the potato chips from the bag. He drank two glasses of iced tea, ate seven peanut-butter cookies, and burped loudly at least three times.

Downstairs, the sound of Nick LeClair's country-music station kept Brenda in knots. She blotted her eyes and blew her nose, but the tears just wouldn't stop. As she cried, she began to realize that it wasn't only Steve and Nick and Cody who had filled her heart to overflowing with remorse, fear, sorrow, pain, and a hundred other jumbled emotions. It was Jennifer so far away in Africa and Justin and Jessica at college. It was the boxes of trophies stashed in the garage, the sewing table in the green basement, the plaid chairs in the dining room. It was the memory of sitting beside her mother on a hard wooden pew, reciting verses of Scripture at Vacation Bible School, watching her father pass the offering plate from one row of churchgoers to another. Her parents, her children, her husband — all the victories and all the mistakes. And God, too. She had lost God, and He had let her go.

Brenda sagged onto another stool as she thought of her flower beds, still unplanted. Her hair, shaggy on the ends. Cody needing help. How could she ever summon the energy to do anything again? Hope, joy, and dreams had all fled, washed away in the flood of her tears.

"You are the best friend I ever had," Cody announced as he swallowed the last of the cookies. Bread crumbs were scattered across his beard and hanging from the damp ends of his mustache. "You're just like Jesus, because you share."

Brenda couldn't bring herself to face him. She sprayed her flour, coffee, and tea canisters with disinfectant cleanser and began to wipe them with a paper towel. How would she ever get him out of her house? Why wouldn't he just go away again and leave her alone?

"I believe I will sit outside on your porch

swing after all," Cody announced. "I like it there. That's where I slept when I stayed with you, before I ran into the woods and climbed that tree."

"What a great idea," Brenda said, sniffling again. "I'll get you a pillow and some blankets."

Cody followed her onto the porch and watched in silence as she spread the bedding for him. He sat on the swing for a moment, and then he put his head on the pillow and smiled at her.

"I don't think I'll lose you again, Brenda," he said in a low voice. He reached up and touched her damp cheek with his dirty fingers. "I see you, and you see me. Now we can be together . . . like before. You're crying, because you're happy that I came back. My daddy used to tell me he was crying because he was happy. He said he was happy to have me. And now you have me. So I think I might go to sleep right here for a little while."

Brenda pulled the blanket up over his shoulder and patted his arm. "Rest now, Cody. You just rest."

Steve couldn't believe his eyes as his car pulled up to the garage of the house in Deepwater Cove. *The bum was back.* The

288

familiar shape, covered in blue blankets, reclined on the porch swing as if he belonged there. This was not a complication he needed, especially with so much on the line right now. No doubt he would have to take time to talk this over with Brenda, but he certainly couldn't afford any delays today.

Heading home early, Steve had decided to shower and change clothes after a round of golf with a client that afternoon. Though he enjoyed wearing jeans and an old T-shirt, dinner at the country club required a pair of nice slacks and a white shirt. Sometimes he would do without a tie, but not if he was about to close a deal.

The afternoon on the golf course had been hotter than he had expected, Steve thought as he drove into the garage and let the door down behind him. He always carried a change of clothes in his gym bag, but tonight was special. Jackie Patterson had been working with her attorneys in St. Louis, and she'd called earlier in the day to say she had put together a deal she thought Steve would find attractive. Nervous, excited — and at the same time irked that the homeless guy was back — he pushed open the door to the kitchen.

Brenda's voice carried in from the foyer.

"No!" she was saying to someone. She sounded agitated, almost frantic. "Not now . . . I mean . . . not ever. Just go, okay?"

Steve stepped around the corner into the entrance hall and saw his wife standing with the handyman from A-1 Remodeling. She was clutching her purse to her stomach and pushing on his arm. Steve couldn't remember the guy's name, but he had one hand on Brenda's shoulder and a worried expression on his face.

"Honey?" Concern sweeping through him, Steve moved into view. "Is something wrong?"

Brenda and the man both gasped audibly as they turned to stare at him. And what he saw written on their faces was guilt. Plain as day. Absolute, undeniable guilt.

Steve gazed at the two of them as thoughts and images he couldn't accept whipped through his mind. His wife and this man . . . *together?* Impossible. No. Not Brenda.

He glanced at her disheveled hair and swollen eyelids. Was she crying? angry? afraid? Now he focused on the handyman — his paint-spattered jeans and work boots, his faded T-shirt and blue eyes.

"Brenda?" It was all Steve could bring out of his throat.

"Nick is leaving," she fumbled out. "He's

done. Finished downstairs."

"Is something the matter here?" Steve asked again. "I heard you talking to him. You sounded upset, and you told him no. What was that about?"

There was a moment of awkward silence. Then the handyman spoke up. "She said no, because . . . because, see, I was asking her for more work. But she's done with me. We're finished."

"There's a bridge," Brenda said, overlapping Nick's words as she faced her husband. "The drainage ditch in the front yard needs a bridge, remember? I promised Brad Hanes could build it."

"Ashley's husband? I thought Brad did major construction projects. Houses and offices."

"Yes, but . . ." Brenda moistened her lips. "But Ashley and I agreed at the tea club. It was a trade. The Sunday night supper and the bridge."

Steve tried to force down the terrible certainty that something had gone badly wrong in his house. "Brenda, I don't understand what you're talking about."

"Nick can't build the bridge," she said, "because Brad is going to do it."

"She paid me already," the handyman told

Steve. "So we're all settled up. I'd better get going."

"I wrote a check." She turned to the man who stood awkwardly in the foyer. "Well, thanks again, Nick. You did a good job."

Nick tipped the brim of his ball cap. "Thank you, Brenda . . . and you, too, Steve. Glad I could help out here. If you need any other small jobs done, give me a holler."

Before Steve could say anything else, Nick left the house, shutting the door behind him. Brenda turned immediately and fled toward the master bedroom.

Unable to make himself move, Steve tried to digest what he had seen and heard. The brief scene in the foyer had looked like something out of one of Brenda's chick flicks . . . a movie where everyone ended up in tears. Inside the Hansens' house stood a man with his hand wrapped around a woman's arm. The woman was rejecting him in an anguished, heart-wrenching tone. But the woman was Brenda . . . Steve's wife. And the man — Nick, the remodeler — had on a greasy baseball cap and paint-covered jeans and a ratty T-shirt. He was no romantic hero, and yet Steve had seen Nick touching Brenda. All that . . . plus a homeless kid lay asleep outside on the porch swing. And there had been something about a bridge and a Sunday night dinner and a tea club, and none of it made sense.

Suddenly aware of the passing time, Steve shook himself back to awareness and hurried down the hall. He found Brenda in the master bathroom with the door shut, and it sounded like she was sick . . . or was she crying?

He knocked on the door. "Brenda?"

Nothing like this had ever happened before. For so many years, Brenda had always been the same — blonde and sweet and gentle, loving toward the children and her husband as she puttered away in the kitchen or garden. What had happened?

"Brenda, it's me. What's going on in there?"

"I'm fine." The words were barely audible.

"I need to take a shower and change clothes before my dinner. Are you planning to be in there awhile?"

Silence. He rubbed his eyes and tried to think what to do. Somehow things at home were coming apart at the seams. In his business world, he neatly stitched up deals almost every day. But here, in Deepwater Cove, great rips had been torn in the fabric of his life. The stuffing he had relied on to cushion him from hardships and trials had burst out and was floating away like feathers in the wind. He didn't even know how to begin to catch it.

"Are you upset?" he asked. "I saw the kid on the porch swing. Did he say something to you?"

"No." Brenda opened the bathroom door and shouldered her way into the bedroom, head low and hair covering her face. "Go ahead and take your shower."

Steve hesitated in the doorway. "Brenda, something's wrong. I can tell you're not feeling well. Is it that man? That A-1 guy . . . Nick? Did he do something?"

"Just take your shower and go to the club," Brenda replied. Like the last brown, dead leaf of winter, she drifted down onto the bedroom's bay-window seat and turned her face toward the evening sky. Propping her arms on the sill, she pressed her cheek against the glass pane.

Steve glanced at his watch. Jackie Patterson would be arriving at the club any minute now. She would walk into the dining room, and the hostess would seat her at Steve's reserved table. Ashley Hanes or one of the other waitresses would ask if she wanted a drink. And then she would wait.

He rubbed his hand around the back of his neck. "Brenda, I'm supposed to be at

the club in ten minutes. I've got an important dinner."

"Go ahead," she said. Her voice was flat.

"But something's going on here at the
house. You have to talk to me." He walked
toward the window seat. "I've never seen
you this way. What happened?"

"Go to the club."

"I'm serious, Brenda. Is it the kid on the
porch? What's his name?"

"Cody. He's fine."

"Did Nick do something that upset you?
He was . . . he was touching you. Holding
your arm."

She closed her eyes. "Please go away,
Steve. I don't need you. I don't need anyone."

"What is that supposed to mean?"

"It means I'm fine. Go away."

Steve's cell phone vibrated. That would be
Jackie calling to find out where he was. He
decided to ignore her for a moment. Frustration built in his chest like steam in a
sauna. How could Brenda do this? She was
just sitting there like a lump. A few minutes
ago, she had been so agitated, nearly in
tears, pleading with the handyman. Now
she slumped on the window seat like an old
coat someone had cast aside.

"Brenda, please talk to me," he demanded.

"I mean it. I want to know why that man had his hand on your arm."

She said nothing. As if she were dead.

Lifting his phone, Steve glanced at the ID. As expected, it had been Jackie Patterson. He punched in her number. Jackie's voice came on the line.

"Hey there," he said, forcing cheer into his tone. "Listen, Jackie, I'm running a few minutes late. My wife is . . . she's not feeling well."

"Oh, why didn't you call me sooner?" Jackie asked. "Now here I am at the table all by myself."

"I just got home from the golf course to take a quick shower, and . . ."

How could he even begin to explain this thing he didn't understand himself? Steve dropped into a chair. A photograph of his three children in a soft silver frame sat beside a stack of books on the nearby table. He focused on each of their faces. Beautiful, serene Jennifer. His little missionary-in-training. Goofy Justin, always up to something. And Jessica. So sweet. So loving.

As Jackie Patterson continued venting her displeasure on the phone, Steve thought back to his last conversation with his youngest child. *"You know, Dad, maybe Mom* misses you," Jessica had said. *"I think she's lonely."*

He had argued his case, of course, righteously defending himself against Jessica's nonsensical theory. And then she had told him that what she was seeing in her parents' marriage frightened her. *"I don't ever want to end up angry and hurt and depressed,"* she had informed her father.

Was that how Brenda felt? Steve studied his wife now, her face pressed against the window pane and her swollen eyes shut tight.

"So things always do work out?" Jessica had wanted to know. When he couldn't assure her of the one thing she most wanted to believe at this time in her life, his daughter had expressed her fear that her parents might divorce. Steve had done his best to convince Jessica that his relationship with Brenda was fine, but his precious little girl had run away shouting at him. Her words had seemed silly at the time — trite and impractical, he had thought. *"Then take her to the country club for dinner!"* Jessica had yelled at him.

"And I have the proposal here for you to look over," Jackie Patterson was saying. "The lawyers spent a great deal of time on it, and this is really the best night for me,

Steve. I simply have to be back in St. Louis by noon tomorrow for a luncheon."

"All right," he told her. "Can you give me a few minutes? I need to take care of a couple of things first."

"I guess I'll nurse my drink and hope I see someone I recognize."

"I'm sure you will." Steve said his good-bye and put away his phone.

He studied the huddled shape on the window seat, certain no good could come of the impulse that had trickled into his brain as his real-estate client chattered away. It wasn't smart. It was a bad business move. It might cause him to lose everything he had been hoping for and dreaming of all these months.

But each time he tried to make himself stand, ignore his wife, and walk to the bathroom, he saw his daughter's earnest face. For so many weeks, Steve had hoped for some solution to Brenda's problem. He'd prayed for it. Nothing he had done made any difference. So maybe it was time for drastic measures.

"Brenda," he said, rising, "I want you to put on a dress and brush your hair while I change into a clean shirt and tie."

Bleary-eyed, she turned to him. Her nose was red, and her hands trembled. "What?"

she whispered.

"Get dressed," he repeated. "We're going to have dinner at the country club with one of my clients. And I won't take no for an answer."

CHAPTER THIRTEEN

Brenda followed two paces behind Steve as they entered the dimly lit dining room at the country club. A dark green, richly patterned carpet covered the floor all the way to the cherry-paneled walls hung with gold-framed copies of vintage golf, hunting, and boating prints. The tables, each covered in a round green cloth topped by a square white one, held small candle lamps and elegantly folded napkins. The service staff wore various versions of tuxedos — black jackets, white shirts, bow ties, and black slacks. Some of the serving girls had on skirts and low heels. A mounted deer head with an impressive set of antlers peered out from one end of the room. An elk head gazed impassively from the opposite wall.

Brenda had visited the club many times. Usually it was to take the kids swimming with friends in the Olympic-sized pool or to have lunch in the café with a group of local families after church on Sundays. She could count on one hand the number of evenings she had spent in the formal dining room. That had become Steve's domain.

Getting dressed and applying makeup tonight had been the hardest job Brenda could remember in years. She had begged to be left alone in the house. Steve wouldn't hear of it. He took her by the arms, lifted her off the window seat, and propelled her to the closet.

Feeling as though twenty-pound weights were attached to her wrists and ankles, she had managed to pull a dress from its hanger and onto her body. In the midst of toweling off after a two-minute shower, Steve zipped up Brenda's dress and tossed a pair of her sandals out of the closet. She stepped into them before he led her into the bathroom and put a tube of mascara in her hand.

As Steve drove them to the club, Brenda stared blankly out the window. Her thoughts went around and around, and she began to feel that someone was stirring her brains like a bowl of brownie batter. *Steve is my husband,* the refrain went. *I don't love him. He doesn't love me. I can't divorce him. I don't want to leave him. But I can't live with him. I love Nick. I don't know Nick, so I can't possibly love him. I would be miserable with Nick.*

But Nick cares about me. I betrayed Steve. God hates me. I hate God. I hate Nick. I hate Steve. I hate myself. Over and over, the whispered words ran circles through her mind, until the car pulled into the parking lot of the club.

Now Steve was waving to a woman who sat near a window that looked out onto Lake of the Ozarks. In a daze, Brenda stepped up to the table. The woman, a frosted blonde in her early sixties, held out a hand tipped with manicured nails. She wore a designer suit in coral knit, two ropes of pearls at her neck, and a bracelet watch covered with diamonds. Her smile of perfectly veneered teeth was polite but hardly warm.

"My goodness, Steve!" she exclaimed as she shook Brenda's hand. "This is an unexpected surprise. How nice to meet you, dear. Mrs. Hansen, I want to tell you that your husband treats me like a queen. I wouldn't work with any other real-estate agent at the lake. You must be so proud of him."

"Yes," Brenda mouthed.

As they seated themselves, a server emerged from the shadows. It was Ashley Hanes. She handed out menus and recited the specials for the evening. And then she focused on her customers.

"Mrs. Hansen!" she gasped. "What are you doing here? I mean . . . wow, are you all right?"

"Brenda's not feeling too well tonight," Steve spoke up. "Do you have any hot tea?"

"Sure. I'll bring some right out."

Embarrassed, yet at the same time oddly apathetic, Brenda leaned back in her chair while Steve and Jackie Patterson chatted. Jackie, as it turned out, was not after Steve's heart. Brenda saw that at once. The woman had been dating some man in St. Louis whom she mentioned as regularly as if they were married. And she certainly wasn't flirting now — a demeanor Brenda had learned to recognize in about fourth grade.

But Jackie Patterson *was* on a mission. She spoke with great animation and fervor, punctuating her speech with a firm tap on the back of Steve's hand or an index finger jabbing the table. Brenda found it difficult to listen to the woman. Instead she thought about Cody and how he would wake up on the porch swing and wonder where she had gone. She thought about Nick, his single-wide trailer, his son Leland, and his meth-making wife.

"Nelda had some problems, and so did I," Nick had told Brenda. *"We got to where we*

couldn't work things out." She wondered about those words as she stirred milk and sugar into the tea Ashley had poured. What had been Nick's problems? Ashley once hinted that Nick had "popped" his wife. Could that be true? Was there a violent man hiding behind the kind words and gentle craftsmanship that Brenda had believed characterized Nick?

She recalled the strength with which he had pulled her into his arms. And the way he had faced off with Cody. And then she remembered how his fingers had clamped onto her arm after she'd paid him and asked him to go. Nick had refused to leave the house. He told her he wouldn't go without her. He insisted that she wanted him as much as he wanted her, and then he shook her when she denied him. He shook her . . . and it hurt . . . so maybe he *was* the kind of man who would "pop" his wife.

"I'm going to the restroom," Brenda said, suddenly realizing she felt sick to her stomach. "Excuse me."

She grabbed her purse and made it to the ladies' room without stumbling over her own feet or tripping on a chair leg. Feeling ill and stupid and hopeless, she pulled the stall door shut and sat down on the closed lid of a toilet. She put her head in her hands and stared down at the tile pattern swimming dizzily on the floor.

Where could she go to escape everything? How could she fix this? How could any of it be made right? The tears started again, and she could think of no way to make them stop.

"Hey, Mrs. Hansen?" Ashley's voice echoed in the bathroom. "Are you in here? Steve's worried about you."

"I'm fine." Brenda pressed her damp, swollen eyelids shut with her fingers. "I'll be out in a minute."

"You look really awful," Ashley said. "I can't believe Steve brought you here tonight. You ought to be in bed, and he should have stayed home with you. You need some chicken soup, not dinner at the club. For pete's sake, men are so stupid sometimes."

"I guess he wanted me to come," Brenda said, wiping her eyes with toilet paper. Swallowing at the lump in her throat, she stood, smoothed down her dress, and stepped out of the stall.

Ashley's face registered shock. "You've got mascara all over your cheeks!" she exclaimed. "You've been crying. Oh, my word. We've got to get you cleaned up and taken home."

"No, I . . . I have to be here."

"For what? Jacqueline Patterson? All that woman cares about is pushing Steve into joining her big scheme."

"What?" Brenda muttered. "What scheme?"

"She's got more money than you can shake a stick at, and she wants to buy up a bunch of lake property and get Steve to manage it for her. He doesn't have time for that, not with his agency doing fine as it is."

Brenda stared at Ashley, trying to comprehend the younger woman's words. "Steve is in trouble?" she asked.

Ashley pursed her lips together. Then she leaned over near Brenda's ear and spoke in a low voice. "Well, let's just say Mrs. Patterson has been coming to the country club for years, even while her husband was around and their kids were younger, and she always treated the serving staff like the scum at the bottom of the bucket. She's not friendly the way lake people usually are. Sure, it might be all right for Steve to buy a rental house or two, but not if it means getting tangled in that woman's scheme."

For the first time in days . . . maybe weeks . . . Brenda suddenly saw a view of the world outside herself. And what she saw was Steve Hansen. She saw two things about Steve: First, she had long ago stopped feeling proud and supportive of a man others admired. And second, if he wasn't careful, Steve might become involved in something dangerous. Something that might cost both of them a great deal of money, effort, energy . . . and time. More time than ever.

"Here, we'll have to use soap," Ashley said, dabbing at Brenda's cheeks with a wet paper towel. "You really are a mess. I'm sorry to keep saying it, but I've never seen you look like this. Are you sick, or what?"

Brenda followed the flickering brown eyes of the younger woman, who was doing her best to sponge away smudged mascara and streaked blush. How could Brenda explain something she didn't really understand herself? Could she admit that she had willingly let a man other than Steve hold her? that she had wanted to kiss him? that she had dreamed of abandoning her husband, home, church, even her children's respect, to have an affair with a handyman she barely knew? She might have done it. All of it. If Cody hadn't pushed open the basement door, she might have let every moral restraint snap.

"I heard that homeless guy is back," Ashley said as she lined Brenda's mouth with a stick of lip gloss she had pulled from her apron pocket. "Is he the one who's got you so upset?"

"No, but . . . I don't know what to do with him."

"Well, he's not worth crying about. Take him over to the police station and let them figure it out. Or drop him off on Highway 54 in Osage Beach. It'll take him the rest of the summer to find you again."

"I couldn't do that."

Ashley stood back and eyed Brenda. "You still don't look very good, but I have to get back to my tables."

"Thank you for trying, Ashley."

The young woman fiddled with the stack of black bead necklaces that took the place of her tuxedo tie. Evidently Ashley had been working at the club long enough to break from the dress code.

"You and I are in the club that Mrs. Moore started at Just As I Am," Ashley reminded Brenda. "The Tea Ladies' Club. That means you still owe Brad a job building a bridge over your ditch, and I still owe you and Steve dinner. But the main point of the club is to help each other out, right? So here's the best way I know to help you tonight, Mrs. Hansen. Go out there and tell your husband to take you home *now*."

"Call me Brenda, remember?"

"Brenda. Okay. Listen, my buzzer's gone

off three times while I've been in here with you. I'd better run."

Brenda reached out and touched Ashley's arm. "Thank you," she said. "You've helped me a lot."

A crooked grin brightened Ashley's face. "Really? Cool! Okay, see you, Brenda. And don't forget about that bridge."

As Ashley hurried out of the bathroom, Brenda turned to gaze at herself in the mirror. She really did look awful. Just the thing to convince Steve to take her straight home.

Patsy Pringle had cleared her schedule for most of the afternoon this Wednesday, and she was looking forward to the arrival of the other members of the Tea Ladies' Club. She had filled the urn with fresh water and set out a large variety of tea bags. That morning, she had baked a lemon–poppy seed bread for the group. Now she took it out of the foil wrap, sliced it into sweet, moist portions, and arranged them on a cut-glass plate she had inherited from her grandmother.

This would be the fourth meeting of the club, and Patsy had quickly discovered that the gathering of women was the highlight of her week. Each Wednesday they sat in the tea area, sun streaming through the windows, and chatted in cheerful voices while music played softly in the background. Sometimes the recounting of a story sent everyone into gales of laughter, and other times the whole group ended up in tears.

Every Wednesday afternoon without fail, into the salon marched Ashley Hanes and Kim Finley. Esther Moore was never far behind. In fact, she often showed up first. She considered the club her idea, so she told Patsy she felt responsible for making sure everything was set up. The only member who had failed to reappear for tea at Just As I Am was Brenda Hansen.

Patsy hadn't seen her or heard a peep out of her since the day they had formed the group almost a month ago. This morning on her way to the salon, Patsy had stopped by the Hansen house to leave a little reminder note for Brenda and tell her how much they had missed her. As she stepped onto the porch, the homeless man lifted his head from a pillow on the swing and nearly scared Patsy out of her wits. Once she recovered from the shock of that scarecrow face and ratty hair sticking out in all directions, Patsy asked him about Brenda.

"She makes me sandwiches and soup and chocolate cake," he had said, proudly displaying a cooler filled to the brim with food.

"Brenda is my friend, but she doesn't talk to me anymore. She says she doesn't feel like talking and please leave her alone. So I do. I sit on the swing or wash the windows with the garden hose. I like to keep things span. That's what I used to do for my daddy."

Patsy hadn't known what to say after that, so she tucked the note inside the screen door and drove off. But all day she kept thinking about Brenda Hansen, worrying about her and wondering if there was anything she could do. She worried about the homeless man, too. After dredging around in her brain for a while, she finally remembered that his name was Cody. What on earth would happen to Cody when winter came around again? And why would Brenda cook for the fellow but not talk to him? The whole situation was definitely a matter for prayer.

Which is exactly what Patsy was doing this afternoon as she finished spraying her last client's hairstyle into place and the door opened to admit the main members of the TLC. All except Brenda . . . once again.

Esther bustled everyone into the tea area and began passing around the basket of colorful tea bags. She chose a central table and moved chairs around so that everyone had a place. Kim and Ashley were caught up in discussing the health of Kim's son, the twin who seemed to be having more bad days than good lately. Kim and her husband, Derek, had driven Luke to a doctor in Osage Beach, but so far they weren't sure what was wrong with him. They had been thinking of seeing a specialist in St. Louis.

As the women took their places, Patsy checked out her customer at the cash register and motioned to the other stylists that she would be away from her station for a while. Then she hurried into the tearoom, fixed herself a cup of steaming Darjeeling with plenty of milk and sugar, and took a slice of poppy-seed cake. Her favorite CD by Color of Mercy was playing, and for once she was absolutely certain that Pete Roberts would not interrupt with a leaf blower or chain-saw engine.

As much as Patsy hated to acknowledge anything good about the man, he had done a fantastic job soundproofing the wall between their two stores. Not only that, but he had built the flower boxes, painted them bright yellow, and set them in place on the sidewalk in front of each business in the Tranquility mall. He had asked Patsy if she would consider going to the NASCAR races with him some afternoon, and lo and behold if she hadn't said yes.

"I have a subject to discuss," Esther Moore began when Patsy had seated herself at the table. "I think it's something we can all pitch in on, and if we intend to give each other tender loving care, it's the perfect thing to do."

"Is this about the video store?" Ashley asked. "Because Brad told me to stay out of it. He said this is a free country, and people have a right to do whatever they want as long as it's not hurting anyone."

Patsy had a few words she would like to say to Brad Hanes, but she managed to keep her mouth shut on that account. "It's too late to stop the video store," she told the women. "I saw the new renter over there a couple of days ago. He was painting and working on the light fixtures. He told me he was just waiting for his shelving systems and his product to come in, and he'd be in business."

"Product!" Esther said with a snort. "That makes his trash sound like graham crackers or something!"

"I wonder if the school bus will keep dropping kids off here," Kim mused aloud. "They try to be very careful where they let the children out."

"I'd like to report that Kim and I have

done about all we can think of to keep that business out of Tranquility." Esther was stirring her tea so energetically that it was slopping over the sides into the saucer. "Ashley, how about you and Brenda? Has she asked Brad to build a bridge over her ditch?"

"Not yet. I told you the last time I saw her was at the club that night when she cried her mascara all down her cheeks and Steve finally just took her home. I've thought about knocking on her door when I ride by in my golf cart, but that weird guy is always on her porch. He creeps me out, and Brad doesn't want me talking to him. I called her once or twice too, to try to reschedule our fried-chicken dinner, but she never answers the phone or returns my calls."

"That brings me to the point of today's meeting," Esther announced. "It's Brenda Hansen. She's a founding member of the TLC, remember, and that makes her our responsibility. Something has gotten into that girl, and we need to find out what it is. Not only that, but we've got a duty to help her figure out what to do with that hobo on her porch swing. Charlie tells me he's there night and day, swinging back and forth or eating sandwiches. I hate to say this, but it's almost like the Hansens have a stray dog hanging around."

"A stray dog that needs a bath and a good grooming," Patsy said. "Though I don't think referring to Cody as a dog is going to help matters. He's scary to look at, but he seems nice enough. I've never heard of any problems he's caused in the neighborhood — anything missing or broken — have you?"

The other women shook their heads.

Esther squared her shoulders. "Well, I say we go over there right now. We'll march onto the Hansens' porch and ring their doorbell until Brenda lets us in. Then we'll make her tell us what's wrong, and we'll fix it."

Patsy couldn't help but stare open-mouthed. "We can't just barge into someone else's house and fix their problems. Maybe what's going on is none of our business."

"I'll say this one more time," Esther declared. "Brenda is a bona fide member of the TLC, and that makes her our business. There's trouble at the Hansens' house, and I believe that, as her friends, we need to find out what it is."

"Sounds like prying to me," Kim Finley said. She didn't often speak up, but when she did, it was worth hearing.

Esther was not inclined to listen. "It's not prying. Not when you do it because you care about the person. We love Brenda, and as concerned club members, we need to help her."

"I wouldn't mind going over there," Ashley said. "I've been really worried. I haven't seen Brenda in more than a week, and Steve never mentions her at the club."

"Well, that's two of us," Esther said. "Where do you stand, Patsy? Can you leave the salon for a few minutes in order to help a dear friend?"

Patsy knew her schedule had been cleared for the next two hours, but she tended to side with Kim. Bursting into Brenda's house and demanding to know her problems just didn't feel right. Over the years, Patsy had learned that if people were troubled, they usually booked an appointment and talked things out while she styled their hair. It wasn't in her nature to meddle.

"I don't have any clients for a while," she began, "but I'm not sure —"

"You'll understand how important this is when you get there," Esther assured her. "So, that's three of us. What about you, Kim? Are you with us?"

Kim glanced out the window. "I'm waiting for the school bus, so I only have an hour. I guess I'd agree to it if we only dropped in for a short visit. Maybe we could ask Brenda if we could help her with Cody."

"Now that's more like it," Patsy said. "Let's offer to shave that boy and do something about his hair. I'll take a bag of scissors, shampoo, and such. Then Brenda won't feel like we're being nosy."

"All right," Esther said. "Our stated mission will be to clean up the homeless fellow. But our real efforts will be focused on Brenda. As much as I worry about Cody, it's poor, sweet Brenda who has my heart. We don't have to pry into her private business, but we can at least do our best to help her feel better."

The other women nodded in agreement. Patsy was the first to rise. She stepped to her station, gathered supplies, put them in a bag, and told the other stylists she'd be gone for a while. By the time she was ready, Esther, Kim, and Ashley had finished their cups of tea and eaten the last crumbs of lemon–poppy seed cake. With a prayer for fortitude, Patsy Pringle led the ladies of the TLC out the door of the salon on their first mission of mercy.

CHAPTER FOURTEEN

Brenda sat in the rocking chair in her living room and stared at the family portrait over the sofa. Taken several years ago when LAMB Chapel was putting together a directory of members, the photograph held a prominent place on the wall. Brenda recalled the effort of getting her family ready for the photo sitting — wrangling everyone into color-coordinated outfits, brushing wayward hair, ordering Steve into a coat and tie, and arguing down the children's desire to have Ozzie, the cat, in the picture. All that hubbub, and when they arrived at the church, the Hansens had been an irritable, grumpy bunch. But Brenda had begged for relaxed, happy smiles, and despite everything, she had received her dream portrait in the mail a few weeks later.

What had happened? she wondered as she gazed at the five people posed against a mottled blue background. How had this once-fused unit fissured into fragments that rarely found time to reconnect?

Unable to force herself out of the rocker, Brenda sat for hours. Sometimes she slept. Other times she watched television to blunt the pain. But mostly she just rocked and stared out at the empty, bleak future. No light at the end of the tunnel. No silver lining behind the dark clouds. Nothing enclosing her but four black walls, a black ceiling, and a black floor.

As the days passed, Cody sidled into the house now and then to raid the refrigerator. They rarely spoke. Brenda managed to make him some sandwiches one afternoon. She ate saltine crackers and drank water. She stared. And she rocked.

A knock on the front door startled Brenda from her stupor. She called out to Cody to come in. But instead of the lanky young man, in walked Esther Moore.

"Brenda?" Esther's head of glossy white curls peered into the foyer as the door opened. Her bright blue eyes squinted when she smiled. "How are you feeling today, sweetie pie?"

Unable to think of a response, Brenda stared at the woman. What was Esther doing inside the house? How had that happened? Now she was tiptoeing in like a little pixie bent on mischief.

"Hey, Brenda. What's up?" Ashley Hanes, tall and erect and hair glowing a burnished copper, followed Esther through the door. "I haven't seen you since that night at the country club last week, remember? Are you okay?"

And then Patsy Pringle — today a platinum blonde with bleached eyebrows — stepped inside. "We came over to find out if we could help you with Cody," she told Brenda. "We haven't seen you at our TLC meetings lately, and Ashley told us you hadn't been feeling well. We wondered if you might need something."

Kim Finley entered next, dark-haired and silent, joining the others who stood like a police lineup against the living-room wall. "We don't mean to disturb you if you're not feeling well."

And then Cody walked in and stared at Brenda from the doorway. "Hi, I'm Cody!" he announced, hair and beard surrounding his face like the dusty petals of a roadside sunflower. "Remember me? I thought I saw Jesus in your basement, but it was just me. You said Jesus doesn't live here, but I know you're a Christian because you give me chocolate cake."

Brenda did her best to think of something

to say to the group staring at her as they stood in awkward silence against the wall, but she couldn't. A weight on her chest and heart pressed down so heavily that she could barely breathe. A large, bitter lump in her throat ached with such agony that it stopped any words she might have wanted to speak.

"Would it bother you if we gave Cody a shave and haircut?" Patsy asked. "Because if you'd rather not —"

"He really needs it," Esther cut in. "Wouldn't you agree, Brenda? We'd like to see your new basement too. Could we work on him down there?"

Brenda peered at the women. Cut Cody's hair? Shave him in the basement? She didn't want to think about the basement. Or Cody. Or anything.

"The poor thing doesn't look well at all," Esther said, speaking in a low voice as if Brenda couldn't hear her. "Look at her! She's not even dressed."

Brenda had tried three times to get dressed that morning, but couldn't.

"I had this kind of trouble once," Kim confided to the other women. "Around the time of my divorce. I remember sinking so low I thought I would never see the light of day again — and didn't care to."

Esther shook her head; then she propped

her hands on her hips. "Ladies, we've got to get Brenda up and around before she withers away right in front of us."

"We can't just pick her up," Ashley said.

"Oh yes, we most certainly can!" Esther Moore marched toward the rocker. "Cody, go down to the basement and wait until we get there. Don't you think of running off again, buster."

"My name is Cody," he said. "Who do you think you are?"

Esther visibly bristled for a moment. Then she patted Cody on the shoulder. "I'm Mrs. Moore, and don't you forget it."

"Mrs. Moore," he repeated as he left the room. "Mrs. Moore."

Though Brenda tried to protest, she couldn't fend off the women who surrounded her. They led her to the master bedroom and began doing things to her that she didn't like or want. Kim swabbed her face with a warm, wet washcloth. Patsy ran a brush through her hair. Ashley and Esther pulled off her pajamas and slipped things over and around and up her limp body. A purple blouse took the place of her flannel shirt. A pair of jeans slid up to her waist while flip-flops nudged between her toes and under her feet. Someone popped a piece of peppermint chewing gum into her mouth. Someone else circled her neck with a string of beads. And then the cluster of women propelled her forward toward the bedroom door, out into the hallway, and down the steps to the basement.

"Why, this is simply lovely!" Esther Moore exclaimed. "And, Cody, aren't you a good boy to sit so nice and still right there on the chair?"

Brenda held on to the handrail as she descended the stairs and the basement came into view. She half expected to see Nick Le-Clair standing there in his paint-splattered jeans and ball cap. *"Hey there, girl,"* he would say. He had called several times the first couple of days. Brenda let the answering machine pick up, and then she deleted the messages. After that, he stopped trying to reach her. She missed him. And she resented him.

"Look at these different shades of green!" Ashley said, turning circles in the center of the vinyl floor. "Did you know green is my favorite color? Brad says it's because it goes so great with my hair. Brad loves my red hair, but he hopes we don't have a boy. He thinks red-haired boys are nerds. Oh, I'm not supposed to tell anyone that we're trying to have a baby."

"For pete's sake," Esther snapped. "Brad

Hanes thinks red-haired boys are nerds? That is the biggest heap of foolishness I've heard in a long time, Ashley. And you can tell your husband I said so. Now, Brenda, you sit right here. Patsy, can you work in this light?"

"I'll get a broom," Kim volunteered.

Brenda watched them through a sort of brown haze. Nothing they were doing made sense. Why were they here?

"I'll start with his beard," Patsy declared as she slipped a plastic cape around Cody's neck and shoulders. The women had positioned the young man in the potting area near the sliding glass door and the new sink. Patsy eyed Cody as a sculptor might study a block of marble. "I just love to see a man's face," she said as she walked around him, "especially if he's got a nice, strong jaw. Do you remember if you have a good jawline, Cody?"

"My daddy always helped me shave," he told her. "We had a razor, and we put soap on our faces, and we shaved in a mirror that we hung on a tree. My daddy said a man ought to look good even if he don't have nothing to eat and can't find a job."

"Your daddy was a smart man," Patsy said. "If you don't look good, you don't feel good."

"That's why you put good clothes on Brenda, huh? Because she wore her robe every day, and it made her feel bad to look bad."

"Mostly we just wanted to get her back into the world."

Brenda watched as Patsy snipped off the bushiest part of Cody's long brown beard. She tried to think how long it had been since she'd seen the women who were now bustling around in the basement. First they *ooh*ed and *aah*ed over the sewing area with its long built-in table. Esther said there was a time when she would have given her eyeteeth for a place like that. She had sewn all her curtains as well as most of the kids' clothes on her kitchen table, and she'd had to move the machine whenever mealtime came along or someone had homework to do.

Nick's plate with two hot dogs from Rods-n-Ends always sat on that table, Brenda thought. *A soda. A napkin.* She had walked into his arms right there where Esther Moore was standing. He had pulled her close, and she had felt the strong muscles in his shoulders. She would have kissed him. How could she deny it? How could she live with it? How could she escape it?

"I don't believe this!" Ashley cried out on

spotting the drawers and cubbies in the crafts zone. "This is too awesome, Brenda! You could put different kinds of beads in here, and wire and elastic cording and everything. How come you haven't done anything with it?"

Brenda looked at the neatly ordered area. She couldn't remember why she had wanted it. Nothing creative came to mind now. Beads, wire, elastic cording? What would she do with those things?

"Would you ladies come over here and take a look at what I've just discovered!" Patsy's excitement drew Brenda's focus from the crafts area. "Take a gander at this chin, gals! And how about the jawline? Cody, I have a feeling you might turn out to be quite handsome."

Everyone gathered around as Patsy's razor absorbed the last of Cody's beard. The women were giggling and elbowing each other, and Ashley even reached out and laid her hand on his smooth cheek. Cody looked up at them and gave a wide grin.

"Mercy sakes alive!" Esther gasped, taking a step backward and throwing her hands up in horror. "When was the last time you used a toothbrush, young man?"

"What's a toothbrush?"

"Just as I suspected. And of course he

can't have been to the dentist." She turned to Brenda. "Have you thought of making a dental appointment for this boy?"

Brenda couldn't think of a response. She didn't want to remember dental appointments, because that made her think of her children. She had betrayed them by longing for a man other than their father. She didn't want to be in the basement, because that reminded her of Nick. She hated the purple blouse, because Steve had bought it for her years ago when he went to an auto-parts convention in Arizona. And that was a faraway time when she and her husband had held each other and loved each other and felt so happy to see each other again.

"I'll help you out," someone said, slipping an arm around Brenda. It was Kim Finley. "I can talk to the dentist I work for. He makes exceptions for special cases, and I'm sure he'll be happy to clean Cody's teeth and check him over."

Brenda leaned her head against Kim's shoulder. "Thank you," she whispered.

"Do you have any idea what's making you sad, Brenda?" Kim spoke in a low voice. "Don't tell me what it is. Just nod if you know."

Brenda thought about Steve and her children and Nick. All the lost things. All the emptiness. All the shame. She nodded.

"Is there one thing I can do to make it better?" Kim asked.

"No, because my kids . . ." Despite the lump in her throat, she had managed to say it — the loss that had started it all, the empty hole into which she had poured a terrible mess of sin and failure. And now tears welled again in her eyes.

Kim's arm tightened around her. "Your children are not gone," she whispered. "You still have your memories of Jennifer, Justin, and Jessica. And they'll always have part of you with them — your love, the things you've taught them, the memories you made together as a family. They're turning into adults, but that doesn't mean they've cut all ties with you, Brenda. Right now they're trying out their wings. They'll come back to the nest now and then to reconnect with you. And you know why? Because they love you. They always will."

Brenda tried to gulp down the flood of emotion inside her, but she couldn't. Instead she surrendered to it and let Kim hold her close as she wept. In a moment, she heard voices around them. *What's wrong? Is she all right? Why is she crying?* And Kim was mouthing the word again. *"Kids. She misses her children."*

After what seemed like a long time, the racking sobs began to subside, and Brenda heard the scraping sound of boxes being pulled from under the stairs. Hammers pounding in nails. Chatter and exclamations. Then Kim was drawing away, saying she had to go back to the salon to meet the school bus.

Brenda nodded, empty-armed. For a while, she could only look down at the flip-flops on her feet. She recalled that the shoes had belonged to Jennifer and then to Jessica. And now, worn-out and thin, they were hers.

"Look at this!" Ashley called out. "Patsy, you did Jessica's hair in this picture, didn't you?"

Brenda managed to blink away enough tears to find that the women had been unpacking her storage coolers and that photographs of her three children now covered the wall of the sewing area. There was Jennifer leading a Bible study group on a mission trip to Atlanta. Justin, standing tall with his soccer teammates. Jessica, riding her tricycle. The three of them, bobbing up and down in the country-club swimming pool. Jennifer, wearing the uniform for her first job — working at the concession stand of the outlet mall's theater in Osage Beach. Justin, proudly displaying a stringer of crappie that he and Steve had caught in the lake. And Jessica —

"I have to admit," Patsy said as she cradled the framed photograph, "this style I created for Jessica when she won homecoming queen was one of the best updos in my entire career. See how the curls fall so soft and pretty around her forehead and temples?"

"You had the perfect model," Esther murmured.

Patsy nodded. "I don't imagine you could find a prettier young lady than Jessica Hansen. She is pure peaches and cream. The boy who marries her —"

"It's the garage door opening!" Ashley shrieked as a grinding noise echoed through the basement. "Steve must be home — and we need to get out of here. Hurry up and hang that picture, Mrs. Moore. And, Patsy, how fast can you buzz Cody's head?"

"Quick as a wink!"

Something was up, and Steve didn't like the look of it. As his car pulled up the incline of Sunnyslope Lane in Deepwater Cove, he recognized the string of vehicles lined up in front of his house. Esther Moore's Lincoln, a virtually pristine relic of the 1980s, was parked on the street near the driveway. The battered Honda that Ashley Hanes had been tooling around in since her sophomore year in high school sat right behind it. Patsy Pringle's pretty blue Chevy came next. And Kim Finley's minivan had passed Steve's car on his way into the neighborhood.

Having some visitors might be all right, Steve had decided at first. He was so concerned about Brenda that he had taken to dropping by the house two or three times a day to check on her. She just sat in the living-room rocker and barely spoke to him. When he sat down beside her, took her hand, or tried to say something to her, she turned her head away and began to cry. Steve had never known what to do with Brenda's tears. In the past, he'd always pulled her into his arms and held her until whatever had upset her came spilling out. But now she pushed him away and refused to utter a word.

If some of Brenda's friends had come over to cheer her up, that couldn't hurt. But then Steve noticed that Cody's familiar lanky figure with its bushy, knotted hair no longer occupied the porch swing. The idea that the young man might be inside the Hansen house tied an instant knot in Steve's stomach. He didn't want to kick the kid out, but he had tolerated just about as much as any man could be expected to endure.

As Steve stepped into the kitchen, Esther Moore's head popped up in the stairwell that led to the basement. "Hey there, Steve! Welcome home! Have we got some surprises for you!"

Suppressing the urge to growl, he set his briefcase on the table in the foyer. "Hello, Esther," he replied. "How is Brenda this afternoon? I called earlier, but she didn't answer."

"That was probably because we were keeping her busy. Get yourself down here and see what the TLC has been up to today!"

What on earth was the woman babbling about now? Esther and Charlie Moore kept their fingers right on the pulse of the neighborhood, and most of the time Steve didn't know who or what they were talking about when they shared some juicy tidbit of gossip. He had no idea what the TLC was, but if anyone had upset Brenda any further, he wouldn't stand for it.

He was halfway down the staircase when he heard Patsy Pringle cry out.

"Oh, my stars and garters! Oh, Lord, have mercy! *Lice.* Girls, he's got lice. Everybody back off now. Just back away slowly and let me deal with this."

Holding his breath, Steve stepped into the basement to find a beardless fellow who slightly resembled Cody perched on a chair.

With fear in his eyes, the young man blinked back tears as he stared at Brenda. "What's a lice?" he asked her. "Is it gonna kill me?"

Brenda was sitting across from Cody. For the first time in more than a week, she was dressed in jeans and a blouse and looked halfway normal. Her face was pale as she brushed her damp cheeks.

"Lice won't kill you," Patsy told Cody, patting his shoulder. "Sit still. Don't move a muscle. Ladies, we've got to get something to debug this boy. And I mean *quick*."

Ashley and Esther were pressed back into the farthest corner of the basement, holding hands and looking for all the world like they might be sick. Cody's lower lip trembled. Steve stared for a moment, realizing for the first time that the kid actually *had* a lower lip.

And then Cody let out a yowl.

"Stop!" Brenda said suddenly. She rose from her chair and held her hands toward the young man. "Stay, Cody. It's all right. I promise. It's me, Brenda. I'm here with you, and everything will be okay. There's just a little bug in your hair. A few little bugs. You don't need to be scared."

"Okay," Cody said with a nod. He sniffled. "I'm not scared of bugs. Sometimes I eat bugs."

"I bet you do when you're really hungry." Brenda nodded at him. "Lice are small, and they can't hurt you. They just make your head itchy. Patsy and I will get rid of them for you."

"Okay," he said again.

Brenda turned to Steve and spoke in a calm but decisive voice. "Look on the bottom shelf of the closet in the girls' bathroom," she ordered. "Grab everything you can find."

Then she told the other women, "Justin brought lice home from the nap-time mats in kindergarten, and Jessica got them from her T-ball helmet. I have everything we need. The stuff is old, but it's probably better than nothing."

"We'll use whatever you have, and then I'll bring more later," Patsy said. "Oops, there's a flea!" she exclaimed, taking a small jump backward. "Fleas and lice. What next?"

"Scabies, I'll bet," Esther offered from the far corner of the basement. "We used to get 'em when we were kids. Awful, just awful!"

"It's all right, Cody," Brenda was cooing as Steve hurried up the stairs. "You'll be fine in just a minute. Patsy, can you shave his head first? And then we'll put on the medicine."

Steve rooted through the closet in the master bedroom. Nothing. Not a thing that looked like it might treat lice. His heart racing at the very idea of the parasites even now scattering on their six tiny legs throughout his house, Steve suddenly remembered that Brenda had told him to look in the girls' bathroom. Why didn't he listen to her better? He was going to have to start concentrating on something besides real-estate contracts if this kind of thing kept happening.

The stash of lice treatments was right there on the lowest shelf of the smaller bathroom, just as Brenda had said. He gathered up a few more items that looked helpful — triple antibiotic cream, alcohol, hydrogen peroxide, anti-itch treatment. Throwing everything into a basket from which he had dumped a bunch of ribbons and hair clips, he raced back down the stairs.

"Can lice jump?" Ashley was whimpering from the back corner. "I feel like they're all over me. I'm just itching something crazy!"

"That's an old wives' tale," Patsy said.

"Lice don't jump — they crawl from one host to another. They're just little parasites, not Godzilla. Everybody's going to be okay, including Cody. Steve, fetch us some plastic bags, would you, hon?"

While Patsy and Brenda worked on Cody, Steve ran back up the stairs and grabbed a handful of grocery sacks from the pantry. At least he knew where his wife kept *those*. Fleas, lice, scabies. This was not good, he thought as he took the steps two at a time back down to the basement.

"Good," Patsy said, handing a bag to Brenda. "Put all the hair in this, and we'll give it a good spraying before we burn it. Sweep all those snippings from the floor, too, Steve. That'll take care of anything that might have been in the beard."

As obedient as a child, Steve swept the masses of knotted hair into a pile on his basement floor and dumped it into a bag. The last he recalled, the floor had been plain, painted concrete. Had this new gray-green, stone-patterned vinyl been part of Brenda's rehab project? If so, she had chosen well.

Standing, he took in the green walls, the new tables, the shelving systems, the sink, and the photographs of the children hanging on the walls. This was nice. Very nice.

No wonder Brenda had been so eager to work on it — running back and forth into town to buy supplies each day, as Pete Roberts had told Steve. She and that LeClair fellow had accomplished a small miracle together.

Steve's last memory of the basement involved seven or eight teenagers eating pizza while they reclined on the sagging blue sectional sofa and watched television. Pizza boxes, tennis shoes, backpacks, textbooks, and empty soda cans had littered the concrete floor. The walls had held a jumble of framed pictures, trophies, award ribbons, and original child-created artwork. Now the room was transformed. Perfect. Something you could show off in a magazine.

Even Cody, face and head now totally buzzed and tears streaming from his eyes, came across as something new and better. Patsy had begun rubbing some sort of cream onto his shiny head, and Brenda was dusting his neck with powder. As if communicating through telepathy, the women simultaneously hurried Cody over to the sink and began to scrub his fingers and arms.

To Steve's surprise, the young man had started to look almost human. He had ears and a mouth, a long neck, and thin, ropy arms. He was skinny. Much too skinny. But he stopped weeping when Brenda ordered him to blow his nose into a tissue and then washed his face with a thick white cloth.

When Cody straightened from the sink, he focused his blue eyes on Brenda. "Okay. I'm better now."

"Lots better," Brenda echoed.

"Amen to that." Patsy shook her head as she threw her tools into a plastic bag. "I'm going to have to sterilize all this stuff and then soak it in antiseptic liquid. Now listen here, people," she said, turning to address everyone, including the two women huddled in the corner. "If word of this gets out, my customers are going to be wary about coming to Just As I Am. So we'll consider today's activity a TLC matter, and none of us will breathe a word of it. And I'm talking to you, Esther Moore. No matter what, don't you dare tell Charlie."

"I never keep secrets from my husband," Esther said firmly. Then her shoulders sagged. "But . . . okay. On this, my lips are sealed. Charlie doesn't care about the TLC anyway. Says we're nothing but a gaggle of silly geese."

"How about you, Steve?" Patsy asked.

"I'm mum." He held up a hand in the Boy Scout pledge of honor.

"Cody?" She turned to the young man. "Don't you say a thing about lice or fleas; you hear me? You just tell people that Patsy Pringle cut your hair, and she did a mighty fine job of it too."

"Patsy Pringle cut my lice," Cody began. "Wait . . . oh no . . ."

"I'm done for," Patsy moaned. "Well, I guess I've weathered worse. No one ever lets me forget the time our new nail girl gave everybody a fungus. That was ten years ago. Lord, help us all."

Still muttering what sounded like a prayer, Patsy grabbed her tools and the bags of hair and opened the sliding glass door. Steve watched as she climbed the hill to the street like a Sherpa headed for the summit of Everest. Esther and Ashley, still clinging to each other, made a wide circle around the area where Cody's hair had fallen, and they, too, hurried outside.

Steve took a step backward as Brenda began dumping a variety of liquids and powders on the new vinyl floor. What could he do but help? He fetched a mop and several old rags, and together they bent over the task of disinfecting their basement.

"Smells like the hospital," Cody said. He was standing near the sliding door. "Like when my daddy and me went there, and they said, 'Mr. Goss, we can't help you no more, so you'll just have to make your way.' That's what they said. And then my daddy said to me, 'Cody, you're twenty-one, so you'll just have to make your way.' And that's what we did."

Brenda stopped mopping and looked up. "Cody, what happened to your daddy?"

He sucked on his lower lip for a moment. Steve could see those blue eyes filling with tears, and he braced for another scene. Though he needed to call his office, needed to hurry off to an appointment for a house showing, needed to do a hundred other things, Steve realized that for the first time in weeks, something was happening in his house.

Cody had become a human being . . . and Brenda had too. Maybe there was hope for them after all.

CHAPTER FIFTEEN

"My daddy put me out on the side of the road." Cody spoke as he stared at Brenda, teardrops hanging from the ends of his long dark eyelashes. He reminded her of a newly pared potato, his bald head gleaming white and slightly misshapen. He sniffled loudly and shook his head. "Then he drove off, and that's what happened to my daddy."

Brenda reached out and laid her hand on his arm. So gaunt that he almost frightened her, Cody placed his free hand on top of hers. She knew the whole story was buried somewhere inside this troubled young man, but she had no idea how to release it.

Cody kept gulping down deep bellyfuls of air. He glanced at Steve. "Who's he?" Cody asked Brenda. He looked at Steve again. "Who do you think you are, fella?"

"This is Steve Hansen," she answered quickly. "You know him, Cody. He's my husband."

"He doesn't look like Nick."

A chill washed down Brenda's spine. "Of course not. Nick was a handyman, remember? He painted the basement. Now, let's get you upstairs and see if we can find some chocolate cake."

"Nick didn't share his hot dogs with me," Cody complained to Steve. "He's not like Jesus."

Brenda knew she didn't have any cake. She hadn't felt like baking — or doing much else — for the past few days. But she had to divert Cody from the subject of Nick. If he said anything . . .

"Do you share your hot dogs, Steve?" Cody blurted out the question as Brenda urged him toward the staircase. "Because I like hot dogs."

"I always share my hot dogs," Steve replied. "Did your daddy give you hot dogs? I bet he did."

Cody stopped walking and blinked his big blue eyes at Steve. "Yessir, he did. Whenever he could find work, they would pay him money, and then he bought hot dogs for us. We built a fire near our car, and my daddy read the Bible to me while we waited for the hot dogs to cook. We always said our Bible verses a few times, so we wouldn't forget them. Sometimes the hot dogs got sort of black while we were doing Psalm 139, but we ate them anyway. Do you like hot dogs?"

"I sure do." Steve stood from the chair where he'd been resting after mopping the floor. "If I had some, I'd share them with you. We could cook them over a fire, just like you and your daddy."

"Hey, I like you!" Cody's face broke into a smile, the sight of his joy marred only by his brown teeth. He turned to Brenda. "I like Steve better than Nick. You should like him, too, and not Nick."

"Cody, I'm married to Steve." Brenda continued to try to push the young man toward the stairs. "Of course I like him. He's my husband. Now let's go see what we can find in the kitchen."

"Do you, Brenda?" Steve asked.

She paused. "Do I what?"

"You told Cody you like me. Do you?"

Brenda clenched her teeth for a moment. "That's a ridiculous question. We're married."

"I know, but I've lost track of you. You've been gone a long time, and I'm not sure how you feel anymore. Do you like me?"

"I like you." She shrugged. "I used to like you, anyway."

"You called me a bum."

343

"Well, you called Cody a bum."

"What's a bum?" Cody asked.

"Never mind," Brenda said, "just go on upstairs. This has been an exhausting afternoon. Esther and her gaggle of women came barging into the house, and the next thing I knew, they were shaving you and everyone was screaming."

"We all screamed because of the mice in my hair."

"Lice . . . oh, never mind. Just go." She gave him a gentle shove, and he stumbled onto the staircase.

"Don't hug Nick anymore, okay?" Cody told her over his shoulder. "He's not as nice as Steve. He doesn't share, and you shouldn't let him kiss you. Steve is like my daddy, because he wants to cook hot dogs on a fire with me, and we can eat them even if they're black. That's like Jesus. 'And he commanded the multitude to sit down on the grass, and took the five loaves and the two fishes —' "

"Cody, stop!" Brenda ordered as they reached the foyer. She could hear her heartbeat hammering in her ears. Her cheeks felt blazing hot. "Stop talking and just get out that door. Sit on your swing, and be quiet. Stop blabbering all that nonsense, Cody. I mean it. Don't say another word, because if I hear you, I'm going to stop bringing you soup and sandwiches. I told you before — just leave me alone!"

She shouldered him through the front door and shut it behind him. Sinking to the floor, she hugged herself around the stomach. Cody had said the words! He had told Steve about Nick. Her worst fear.

How could she convince Steve that Cody had been confused . . . or that he had lied . . . or misinterpreted what he had seen? She had to think of a way to cover it. Hide it.

This was what she had been dreading most. And yet, she had wanted it too. Let Steve know that another man desired her. Let him hear how deeply he had hurt her by abandoning her day after day. Let him understand how his apathy had choked off her hope bit by bit.

If Steve knew the truth, he might leave her. Or turn her out of the house. She deserved it. Maybe she even wanted it, didn't she? A reason to turn to Nick. Or to flee to her parents in St. Louis. Or just to leave this house — desert Steve the way he had discarded her.

"Brenda?" Her husband's voice drifted up from the stairwell. "Will you please come down here a minute?"

She wouldn't go to him. She would leave now, and then she would never have to discuss anything. Covering her eyes with her hands, Brenda searched her mind for direction. Where was God at a time like this? Where had He been all along? How could He have allowed her such pain — a woman who had served Him faithfully all her life, whose home had glorified Him, whose oldest daughter had given herself to mission work on His behalf?

God didn't care! He couldn't possibly love her. He had known this was going to happen, and He had permitted it.

"Hey, Brenda? Are you up there?" Steve's head and shoulders appeared, and his eyes fastened on her. "I need to talk to you. Right now."

"I don't want to talk," she ground out. "Leave me alone."

"I'm not leaving you alone anymore. I'm staying here in this house until you talk to me. And you'd better get down here and start talking, or I'll come up there and we can let Cody and Charlie Moore and half the neighborhood hear us."

Brenda leaned her head back against the door. This was it. The moment. She could lie, and lie again, and then do her best to cover those lies with more of the same. Or she could tell the truth. Confess. Admit her guilt.

Before everything crumbled, her life had been open and free and honest. But now . . . now she hated herself, her world, and everything in it.

Rising to her feet, she faced her husband. She realized they could never turn back time. There was no hope that things would be the way they once were. The kids had gone away. Steve's focus had changed. Brenda had allowed Nick into her heart.

"Don't you have a meeting?" she asked Steve as she started down the stairs. She tried to keep the sarcasm from her voice, but she couldn't. "Or a house to show? Or a dinner guest waiting for you at the club?"

"No," he said. "Not today. Not now."

She stepped into the basement and perched on the stool where Cody had been shorn of his matted hair and raggedy beard. That's how this would end too, she realized. She and Steve would shave their marriage. They would shear off all the layers, all the vermin, all the hurt and spitefulness that had built up between them. It would be painful . . . and ugly . . . and it had to be done.

Steve sat down on a chair and stared at her. He looked worn and pale. Older. Tired.

Brenda drew down a deep breath. "Well, while you were out selling houses from dawn till midnight, I started to care for Nick LeClair. And he cared about me too. We had very strong feelings for each other." With great effort, she held her head high. "There. Isn't that what you wanted to know? Nick came to the house every day; he talked to me; he liked me. After a while, I realized how much I enjoyed being with him. He was funny and sweet. He admired my sewing and painting, and I admired his carpentry. We became friends, but we both wanted something more. On his last day here in the basement, he held me. Then Cody came in. After that, Nick left, and I haven't seen him since."

Not moving a muscle, Steve sat in silence. He blinked once. Then he swallowed. "So that's what I saw the other day," he said. "When I came home to change clothes and caught the two of you in the foyer."

"You didn't *catch* us." She bristled. "We didn't do anything."

"Except fall in love."

"Why not? What did you expect me to do with my heart, Steve? It was empty, and you didn't care. Nick filled it."

"He wasn't interested in your heart, Brenda. He was touching you. I saw him, the way he was grabbing after you. He had his hands on you!"

"And that night at the country club, Jacqueline Patterson was touching you. What's the difference?"

"You know the difference!" He jumped up from the chair and began pacing. "Jackie is a client, that's all. She's . . . she's part of my business. But you're my wife, and that loser had no right to —"

"I'm not your wife. You're married to your business, Steve. That's your one and only true love. When you started selling real estate, I supported you. I was proud of you and everything you were accomplishing. But then you betrayed me. You fell in love with your work, you married it, and you gave your whole life to it. Jackie touching you was no different from Nick touching me."

"That's a lie, and you know it!" Clenching his fist, he slammed it down on the stairway handrail. "I can't believe this! I *don't* believe it! You and that handyman. That low-life weasel covered in paint. You let him put his arms around you."

"I let Nick hold me."

"Brenda, how could you do that? You're my wife, and you let another man hold you in his arms. The way I used to hold you. He put his hands on you and ruined you."

Steve's face was red now, the vein in his neck pulsing. "Did he . . . did he kiss you?"

"No."

"Why not?"

"Because —"

"Because Cody came in, right? Would you have let him? Did you want that man to kiss you?"

"At the time, I did. Now . . ." She shrugged. "I haven't answered his calls."

"He's been *calling* here? Calling you on *my* phone?"

"*Your* phone? Is all this yours, Steve?" she asked, holding out her arms. "Are these your possessions — the house, the furniture . . . me?"

"You are my wife. *Mine!* You made a vow before God to be faithful to me! You gave birth to my children. You belong to me."

"What? Like a chair? Or a lawn mower? Or your car? I mean less to you than that stupid hybrid, don't I? You take it everywhere. You keep it clean and polished, you buy it things, and you brag about it. What about me, Steve? What am I to you?"

"You are my wife!"

"What's a wife? Can you tell me that?"

"I can tell you what it's not. It's not someone who sits around all day long and never even bothers to get dressed. It's not someone who shudders every time her husband tries to touch her. And it's not someone who falls in love with an ignorant, worthless, slob handyman."

"Nick has exactly the same amount of education as you, Steve Hansen. But I'm not going to try to defend him. Nothing happened between us except a hug, and nothing will. What started is over. It's finished."

"How can you say nothing happened except a hug? You intended for more to happen. You just told me how you felt about him! You wanted more. If Cody hadn't come in, what would you have done? Would you have gone to bed with the man?"

"I don't know."

"Unbelievable!" He clenched a clump of his hair. "All this time I've trusted you and provided for you. I've been faithful to you while you pushed me away and refused to let me near. I stayed loyal even though you hid from me under your blankets and bit my head off every time I tried to talk to you."

"Don't elevate yourself, Steve. We both betrayed our marriage vows."

"I stayed with you through sickness and health, through richer or poorer —"

"You started creeping away from me the

minute you sold your first house. You fell totally and completely in love with your job. You gave yourself to it, body and soul."

"It's a job, Brenda. You can't compare it to what you did."

"No? Why do you suppose I was vulnerable to Nick?"

"Because he's a sleazy con artist who —"

"Because you had left me — and don't give me your usual rigmarole about coming home every night and waking up here every morning. You have been gone. Gone, gone, gone! If you had been here, spent time with me, cared enough to honor me with your attention and maybe even a little appreciation, I wouldn't have left my heart wide-open. Our ruined shell of a marriage is as much your fault as it is mine."

"That is bunk."

"It's the truth, and you know it. I've admitted my failure. I confessed everything. It was wrong, and I knew it, and I put a stop to it." She paused and lowered her eyes before continuing in a barely audible voice. "So . . . can you forgive me?"

"Forgive?" he echoed. "Are you kidding? I'm not going to forgive you!" He stormed to the far corner of the basement and back again. "You're trying to make your affair sound as innocent as my dedication to my work. Well, do you know why I work? It's to provide for you and the kids. Don't tell me that's why you fell into another man's arms. What you did was just good old-fashioned lust, Brenda. A mixed-up kid walking in is the only thing that kept you from having a full-blown affair with your grubby little handyman. And that same kid is the only reason you confessed to me today. If Cody wants hot dogs, you better believe I'll get him some. But if you want my forgiveness, you can forget it. You betrayed me. Then you tried to blame me for your sins. And now you expect me to just let it go?"

"I don't expect anything of you anymore, Steve. I've learned you're never around when I need you. I have no expectations. . . . I know I made a mistake and I'm just asking for your forgiveness, that's all."

"No way. What you've asked for is a divorce — and that's exactly what you're going to get."

"Strawberries!" Esther sang out, lifting high a pint of the red fruit inside a disposable container. "Right out of Charlie's garden this very morning. So fresh you'll just melt when you taste them!"

Brenda attempted to muster a smile. "Thank you, Esther," she said. "You can put them in the fridge."

"I haven't seen you since we were here the other day, honey. What have you been — why, you look lower than a dog's belly! We got you up and out of that chair, and there you are again! At least you're dressed." Esther set the strawberries in the refrigerator. "My stars, child, these shelves are almost bare. What's going on? Is Cody giving you trouble?"

"No, he's fine."

"Where's Steve? If you're feeling this poorly, he ought to be home looking after you. I'm telling you, these men might as well be wearing blinders for all they notice around them. Yesterday I cut a beautiful bouquet of purple irises from the front yard, and then I put them in a vase smack-dab in the middle of the dining-room table. Do you think Charlie mentioned them? Not a word! There they sat, right in front of his chicken-fried steak, and he ate as if nothing was on the table but the salt and pepper."

Esther seated herself on the sofa across from Brenda. "I don't know what I'd do without my Charlie, but sometimes that man makes me mad enough to chew splinters. Do you ever feel that way about Steve? The two of you look picture-perfect all the time, but I'd have to guess you have your moments."

Focusing over Esther's head at the portrait of the Hansen family, Brenda had to suppress a surge of sadness. Had they *ever* been picture-perfect? No. But there was a time when the world had felt like summer all year round. They'd all been so comfortable with each other. So committed and supportive. Once upon a time, they had all been together. And now . . . now Steve had vanished. Brenda didn't know where he had gone the day he vowed to divorce her and went storming out of their home after she told him about Nick LeClair. She had left messages on his cell phone, but he didn't return her calls. Had he disappeared forever? Gone like a tuft of dandelion seed, leaving behind this bare, lonely stem of a wife?

"Well, anyway," Esther said, filling in the emptiness in the room when Brenda didn't respond to her question.

They sat for a moment, awkwardly silent. Brenda wished the woman would leave her alone. She didn't need Esther's chatter and prying questions. Steve was probably never coming home again, and soon she would have to tell the children about the divorce, and then the black box around her would fold in on itself like an accordion.

"You know, I've been thinking about the flower beds at Patsy Pringle's house," Esther spoke up again brightly. "The other day I was having my usual set and style at Just As I Am, and Patsy told me that last fall she had planted two hundred tulip bulbs. And do you know what happened?"

Brenda managed to focus on Esther and shake her head.

"The deer ate every single bulb! Can you imagine that? Well, of course, now her flower beds are nearly empty except for a few perennials. She's got weeds, poor thing. Brenda, I propose that the TLC ought to help Patsy by cleaning up her garden and planting a few nice annuals. Maybe some marigolds. I hear the deer won't touch those."

Again Brenda made an attempt to focus on her neighbor and to speak. But nothing she could think of was worth saying.

"As a matter of fact," Esther went on, "I'd like for you to come with me to have a look at Patsy's yard and figure out what we can do. I've got the golf cart parked in your driveway, and I'm sure it won't take but a minute. You've always had the prettiest gardens in Deepwater Cove. Oh, come on, honey. Please say yes!"

Before Brenda could beg off, the older

woman was practically pulling her out of the rocker toward the front door. Moving awkwardly, Brenda felt dazed, almost shocked, that her legs still worked and her feet could find their way across the porch. As the women walked toward the golf cart, they passed Cody dozing on the porch swing. He waved at them and put his head down again. As if from some strange distance, Brenda watched herself slide onto the cart's red vinyl seat.

"Whee!" Esther said as she put the two-passenger vehicle in gear. "I have to tell you that when I can get this golf cart away from Charlie, I really let 'er go! You know how he always piddles along, checking out everyone's yards and studying the houses to see who's home. And, of course, he takes Boofer along with him most of the time, so that means he barely goes two miles an hour. He's deathly afraid the old dog is going to tumble out of the cart and get hurt, so I say, 'Leave Boofer here at home, why don't you?' But Charlie loves that mutt, and you know how hard it can be to make a man listen."

Brenda closed her eyes and leaned back on the seat, realizing how much she had missed the kiss of fresh air and sunshine on her skin. She couldn't imagine life without

Steve, and yet — despite the collapsing black box around her — it had to go on. Beside her, Esther smelled of soft lavender lotion and clean laundry. The golf cart bumped along the road, and the movement sent a tremble of life up Brenda's spine. She was alive, she realized numbly. Able to feel and smell. Able to walk and talk and do things. As bad as everything seemed, she still had the earth and the sky. Her heart still pumped and her lungs took in air.

"Men don't listen, and they never look at what's right in front of their noses," Esther was saying. "It's a wonder to me how they make it through the day. I am forever searching for things Charlie has lost. And complain! I'm telling you that man gripes about every ache and pain in his skinny old body. After he retired, I thought he would drive me crazy as a June bug."

Looking around now, Brenda saw that even though her life felt radically different, nothing had changed in Deepwater Cove. Children and dogs played down by the lakeshore. Men mowed lawns. Women washed windows. Cars and golf carts passed each other on the narrow roads. Robins bounced along the ground in search of worms. Squirrels scampered up and down tree trunks.

"Of course, it didn't take me long to figure

out how to make Charlie happy and easier to get along with." Esther drove the golf cart into Patsy Pringle's driveway and switched off the engine. "All he needs is a little cuddle now and then. A pat on the arm. A good-morning hug. A kiss on the cheek. Men just melt in your hands for that kind of thing."

As Esther stepped out of the cart, Brenda sat still for a moment, absorbing the simple remedy for marital happiness that her friend had proposed.

Hugs and cuddles.

Was that what Steve had been wanting? She could recall his accusations: *you never touch me anymore; we never sleep together; you always pull away from me.* Her anger and hurt had caused her to shut herself off from him. Of course she hadn't been kissing or hugging him. He had abandoned her, and it was so painful that she couldn't bear his proximity in their bed. But maybe she had taken away the very thing he most needed and wanted from her. The thing that would draw him close and make his heart grow softer toward her.

Brenda left the cart and walked along beside Esther toward the weedy garden patch in Patsy's front yard. Would Steve even come back? she wondered. Would they divorce? Would he vanish from her life forever?

"Impatiens!" Esther announced. "Would you look at that? They've self-seeded from last year's batch. A whole crop of little ones. All they need is some tender loving care from the TLC, and Patsy will have herself a pretty bed of flowers."

"A cuddle now and then?" Brenda asked as Esther yanked out a dandelion about to go to seed. "Is that really all it takes to make Charlie happy?"

"Not much more, honey. Oh, you've got to feed and water them — husbands, I mean. But really they're not too different from a flower bed. Most of them aren't pondering deep matters. It's football or golf or fishing. A building project or a house to sell. That's what occupies the biggest part of a man's brain, honey. That and . . . well . . . you know. *Women.*"

Brenda had to smile. The thought that knobby-kneed Charlie Moore kept a keen eye out for a pretty woman amused her. But she knew Esther was right.

"If you want a full, beautiful flower bed in the summertime," Esther said, "you need to treat it right. That means you've got to get your hands in there and make it feel good. Husbands are no different. If you want a summertime marriage — even when you're as crotchety as Charlie and me — you need to do what it takes. And a man needs his hugs, kisses, pats, and, of course, the rest of it."

A summertime marriage, Brenda thought as she knelt next to Esther and cupped her fingers around the fragile green leaves of a baby impatiens. She and Steve had enjoyed that once. Could they ever get it back?

Steve sat on the end of Deepwater Cove's community dock and worked a minnow onto Cody's fishhook. For the past week, he had stayed away from home, unwilling and unable even to look at his wife. After calling his office to let them know he would be away for a few days, Steve had driven to Arkansas and checked into a cheap motel. He'd spent his days fishing and his nights trying, unsuccessfully, to sleep.

He hated Brenda. That much he knew. She disgusted and revolted him. Every time he thought of her in Nick LeClair's arms, he wanted to vomit. Sometimes he did. Never in his whole realm of thought had the idea crossed his mind that Brenda could be unfaithful. It was impossible. They had loved each other so long and so well. They shared their three children. Their home.

Years and years of memories. Even a cat.

He could never forgive her for smashing that perfect picture he had cherished in his mind all these years. She had ruined their marriage. Destroyed everything they had worked so hard to build.

He wanted to kill the handyman. If he could, he would wring the jerk's scrawny neck. Nick LeClair had come into Steve's home and seduced Brenda! He ought to buy a gun and blow the guy's brains out. Holding her and touching her arm — when she wouldn't even let her own husband near! He'd like to tie them together with a couple of cement blocks and drown them both.

"I think we could eat these fish," Cody observed, breaking into Steve's reliving of the past few days. He pointed to the bucket of minnows. "They're small, but my daddy and me learned how to eat bugs and craw-dads and mice and all kinds of little things. If you're hungry, you don't mind."

Steve let out his breath. Just thinking about how angry he had been made him furious all over again. His trip had cost him several potentially lucrative house showings, and no doubt his whole office was curious about why he had suddenly vanished. On returning to the area this afternoon, he had decided not to stop by the agency. He hadn't shaved or slept well, and he didn't feel up to seeing anyone.

"People don't eat minnows," he explained to Cody. "Big fish eat these little fish. Then people eat the big fish."

"Okay."

"That's just the way it is."

"Okay."

"I mean, you could eat minnows if you wanted to, but you wouldn't get full. See?"

"Uh-huh. But if you're hungry, you could eat 'em, and your tummy might feel better."

Steve gazed out across the lake, remembering again. After those days of fishing, watching TV, and eating Snickers bars and peanut-butter crackers, he had finally decided it was time to deal with reality. He would drive back to Deepwater Cove, walk in the front door of their house, and tell Brenda their marriage was over.

Then he would ask her if she wanted to file for the divorce, or if he should do it. He would give her the house and her car, and they would divide things evenly. Plenty of small homes had come on the market recently, and he could buy one and move in. The kids could visit him and their mother when they had time. Steve would continue working at the agency, and maybe one day he might find another woman to love. At this point, he didn't even want to think about that. If he couldn't trust Brenda Hansen, whom could he trust?

When Steve got home, he had found Cody sitting on the front-porch swing. Brenda was at Just As I Am getting her hair cut, Cody said. So Steve took the boy to a nearby gas station and bought a couple dozen minnows. Then they drove back to Deepwater Cove, grabbed two poles, and walked down to the dock. So far, they hadn't had a nibble.

"Did you buy any hot dogs while you were gone?" Cody asked. "I told Brenda I thought that's where you were, but she didn't believe me."

"I went to a motel and rested for a few days." He watched his bobber for a moment. "How is Brenda?"

"She cries and yells a lot, but she still makes me sandwiches. Yesterday she baked a chocolate cake. It was good. I told her she was a Christian for baking me that cake, but she just yelled and cried some more and made me sit on the swing. I like fishing with you, Steve. I'm glad you came back."

"Has anyone else been to the house?" he asked warily.

"Lots of people. The lady and man on the golf cart drive by a bunch of times every day. They wave at me and say, 'Hi, Cody!'

so I wave back at them. The hair-shaving lady came over to check on my head. She said all the mice are gone, and so is everything else that was hiding in my hair and beard. She and Brenda drank tea on the back porch, but they didn't invite me. They have a club — the Tea Ladies' Club — and you can't be in it if you're not a lady. I don't think that's sharing. All the ladies of the club visited. I swept and mopped the floors in your house, because I'm good at that. When I lived with my daddy, I always kept everything span. Brenda said I could wash the windows again if I wanted to, so I've washed them lots of times."

Steve tried to picture all this activity going on at the house in Deepwater Cove. He wondered what Brenda had told her friends about him. Had she confessed? Had she blamed him for abandoning her and made it look like their problems were all his fault? He frowned.

"Anyone else drop by?" he asked Cody, getting around to his real concern. "How about that handyman, Nick LeClair?"

"He doesn't share his hot dogs —"

"I know, but have you seen him? Has he been to the house?"

Cody gulped. "No. I don't like him."

"I don't like him either."

"He said, 'Who do you think you are, fella?' in a mean way, like he wanted to fight me. I don't like to fight, because I always get hurt."

Steve's breath hung shallow in his chest. "What was he doing? That day when you came to the house . . . what did you see?"

"He was hugging Brenda, but she pushed him away and said, 'No!' Just like that. I don't think she wanted him to hug her."

"Yes, she did," Steve blurted out before he could stop himself. "Never mind. Forget I said that."

"I forget lots of things, all except my Bible verses. My daddy and me used to say them over and over so we wouldn't forget. Shall I say a verse since the big fish aren't eating the little fish?"

"I guess so."

"Psalm 139," Cody began. " 'O Lord, thou hast searched me, and known me. Thou knowest my downsitting and mine uprising, thou understandest my thought afar off —' "

"Steve?"

Brenda's voice carried across the green lawn toward the lakeshore. He turned and saw her, dressed in a pink top, blue jean shorts, and sandals. Her hair was too short — almost boyish — and she looked thinner than she should. She lifted a hand in greeting.

"Cody?" she called. "Is that you?"

"It's me and Steve." Cody dropped the rod and clapped his hands. "Look, he came back! I told you he would. I told you!"

Brenda approached, stepping onto the gangway that led from the shore onto the dock. As she made her way down the aisle between two rows of boat slips, Steve pictured her melting into Nick LeClair's arms. Slender, beautiful, looking younger than her age, she had wanted that man to hold her and kiss her. She had longed for his touch — and more. Rage boiled up inside Steve's chest, and he fought the urge to bark out his fury in front of Cody.

"See all the little fish, Brenda?" the young man said, motioning toward the minnow bucket. "We don't eat these. We eat big ones."

Brenda laid her hand on his arm. "Have you caught any big ones?"

"Nope," Cody said. "Steve came back after you went to the beauty shop. We bought these little fish and then we came down to the dock."

Her green eyes focused on Steve, softening as she gazed at him. "I'm glad you're back," she said. "Are you all right?"

"Yeah," he growled. "Doing great."

Her face froze. "I see. Where have you been for the past week?"

"I'm going back to the house," he said.

"Good!" Cody exclaimed. "That means it's time for my shower, Steve! Brenda told me that when you came back, we would take a shower — you and me — and get all clean and put on my new clothes."

"I thought you might be willing to help Cody," Brenda clarified.

Steve eyed his wife as he gathered up the fishing rods and the minnow bucket. Was she frightened now — scared that he would divorce her, force her out of the house, compel her to get a job? He hoped so. The taste of bitterness soured his mouth as he placed the tackle in the storage cupboard near their slip. Let her worry. Let her feel some of the hopelessness and hurt he had suffered.

He started for the house with Cody and Brenda trailing behind him. The thought of dragging out his anger for weeks and months somehow satisfied Steve. He would punish Brenda, keep her in a state of dismay and fear, and then he would leave her.

She had admitted her failing, apologized, asked him to forgive her. He held all the power now, and it felt good to watch her grovel.

A touch on his hand caused him to stiffen. She wouldn't dare —

"A shower, a shower!" Cody sang out, wrapping his skinny fingers around Steve's hand. "This is going to be lots and lots of fun. Just me and you and Brenda, back together again. It's a happy day!"

CHAPTER SIXTEEN

"Steve Hansen came home." Charlie Moore made the announcement after parking his golf cart in the driveway and stepping onto the front porch of his tidy little home in Deepwater Cove. "He took Cody fishing. I saw them down on the dock. They had a bucket of minnows."

Esther glanced at Kim Finley, who had dropped by to pick up a quart of strawberries. The Moores planted a big garden every year, and their strawberry patch was famous around the lake. Esther had invited Kim to drop by and take home some of the fruit in the hope that it would help little Luke feel better. The boy had missed so much school that Kim was afraid he might not be able to advance to the next grade level. That would put him a full year behind his twin sister, Lydia, and Kim feared it would damage his self-esteem.

Esther watched Charlie grimace as he

settled into a white wicker chair. His knees were getting worse, though he did his best to deny it. She hated to see him in pain, but what could she do if he refused to go to the doctor?

As Boofer, their little dog, settled into her husband's lap, Esther stroked Charlie's arm. "Did you talk to Steve, honey? Surely Cody must have seen you drive by." She smiled at Kim. "The boy may be slow, but he never misses a chance to wave at us on our golf cart. I think he's just a sweet, simple young man who wouldn't hurt a fly. Don't you, Kim?"

"I haven't talked to him much, but he's always friendly."

"It was good of Brenda Hansen to try to help him. Did you see her on the dock too, Charlie?"

"Not when I drove by. But I can tell you one thing — I'm awful glad Steve's back."

"So am I," Esther agreed. "I don't believe for a minute what people were saying about the two of them. He and Brenda have always been the happiest couple — raising those beautiful children, working hard, going to church every Sunday. What could possibly have come between them? No, I'm sure he was on a business trip."

Charlie shook his head. "Now, Esther, you

can't go making things all apple pie and ice cream. There's not a married couple in the world that doesn't have a little trouble now and then."

"Not us. We've been happy since the day we said, 'I do,' and don't tell me otherwise."

"Oh, Esther, you know we've had our rocky times. If Steve needed a little breathing room, then so be it. And Brenda — well, she's had her hands full with Cody and that basement project."

"She was very quiet when the TLC visited her," Kim put in. "It was the middle of the afternoon, and she hadn't even changed out of her nightgown. I think she's been suffering a deep depression."

"I wouldn't know a thing about depression," Esther said, waving a hand to brush off the unpleasant thought. "It doesn't make a bit of sense to me."

"When my husband left the twins and me, I sank into a depression," Kim told Esther and Charlie. "At first I couldn't believe he was really gone. Then I got so angry that I could hardly keep it inside. I yelled at the kids a lot, and I even snapped at my clients. Everything irritated me. Finally, I went numb. Even though I had my precious children, a stable job with benefits, and a nice home, the whole world looked black to me. I felt like I was inside a box with no way out."

"Now that sounds pretty awful to me," Charlie said. "My mother went through a time like that when her last baby died. My father put her in the hospital for what seemed like forever to me. One day she came home, but she was never the same after that. She had lost her joy."

Kim nodded. "A friend talked me into seeing a counselor, and I took some medicine for a while. Finally the darkness started to lift, and I got back on my feet. But when I saw Brenda the other day, I recognized all the signs of depression."

"Depression is nothing more than a state of mind," Esther argued. "People have to be tough. When hard times come, they ought to buckle down and face things head-on. I'm sorry to be plainspoken, but all this psychology stuff sounds like a bunch of hooey to me. I realize you feel better now, Kim, but why didn't you grab yourself by the bootstraps and pull yourself up? *Snap out of it* is what I tell myself."

"For some of us," Kim said softly, "it's not that easy."

"Well, I just hope things get back to normal around here now that Steve's home." Charlie took a large white handkerchief from his back pocket and wiped his forehead. "Sure is hot today. I think we're about to have to call an official end to spring. How are the strawberries holding out, Esther?"

"They're still coming on," she told him. "I baked a strawberry cobbler for dessert. We ought to have fruit for a good while yet. But I found a hole in the garden fence this morning. The rabbits got into the lettuce already."

"Aw, shucks," Charlie grumbled. "If it isn't one thing, it's another."

As Ozzie rubbed against the side of her leg, Brenda stood outside the open door of the master bathroom and cradled a stack of clean, new clothing. In anticipation of this moment, she had purchased three pairs of blue jeans and five T-shirts for Cody, plus socks and underwear and some shiny white sneakers. As the water hissed, steam crept out above the curtain. She could hear Cody laughing as Steve, standing just outside the shower, gave instructions.

"Wash right there," Steve was saying as he peeked behind the curtain. "Get that soap on good, Cody, or I'll have to make you do it again."

"It's slippery!" The younger man giggled

from inside the tiled shower stall. "Like a fish! Like one of those big fish we didn't catch!"

"Hang on to it." Steve mumbled something Brenda couldn't make out. "When was the last time you had a bath, kid?"

"Me and my daddy washed off in gas-station bathrooms. If you buy a piece of bubble gum, you can get the key and use the bathroom. That's how we did it."

"I believe it. The dirt is ground into your pores. Get your neck, Cody, and use that washcloth. You have to scrub every bit of yourself, even in the back."

Brenda closed her eyes and settled her chin on the clothing. Steve had come home. For days she had lived with the fear that she would never see him again. He never called home, though Brenda left several messages on his voice mail. It was as if her confession and their argument had propelled him out of her life forever.

Though Brenda had longed to slide back into her cocoon after Steve left, the members of the Tea Ladies' Club prevented it. After the day Esther Moore showed up with fresh strawberries, she began to stop by regularly, bringing fresh spring lettuce, a bouquet of irises, or a card signed by all the women. She always had some activity in mind for herself and Brenda — baking pies or cookies together, drinking tea on the porch, weeding a neighbor's flower beds, or figuring out how to use the new computer Charlie had purchased. Brenda resented the intrusion at first. But she gradually acknowledged that she looked forward to Esther's visits as an uplifting way to start each day.

By noon, Esther would zip off in her golf cart to fix lunch for Charlie. Within minutes, Ashley Hanes usually showed up at the Hansen house. She longed to do beadwork in the new basement crafts area, she told Brenda. And she needed help. Together they strung necklaces, bracelets, and anklets. Ashley taught Brenda how to form clay into colorful beads that could be baked rock-hard in the oven. She begged for sewing lessons, too, and Brenda felt obligated to drag out her machine and help the young woman stitch new kitchen curtains.

About the time Ashley left for work each afternoon, along would come Kim Finley and her twins. The kids wanted to play on the swing set in the backyard, paint pictures in the basement, or chase the cat around the house. Kim helped Brenda prepare Cody's meals and assemble goody packages to be mailed off to Justin and Jessica at college.

At the end of each day, Brenda was exhausted. But she had her new friends to thank for keeping her so busy. None of them had questioned her about her relationship with Steve, and she was grateful. She didn't have time to dwell on her absentee husband. In fact, Steve had been away from home so much anyway that things almost felt normal.

By the time Brenda had spotted Cody and Steve down on the dock, she had been up and about enough to find the energy for a trip to Just As I Am. Patsy Pringle had been her usual cheerful self that afternoon, asking about everyone in the family and clucking in sympathy each time Brenda hinted that she and Steve were going through a hard time.

The sight of her husband fishing on the dock had lifted Brenda's heart. But his anger and surliness quickly squelched any hope she may have held for a reconciliation. Clearly Steve's time away from her had done nothing to heal his hurt. He had returned home — but she had no doubt he intended to end their marriage.

"Ha!" Cody cried. Stark naked, he tore open the shower curtain. "I'm clean, even in my ears! Even behind my neck! Even —"

"That's enough, Cody," Brenda said as Steve attempted to push him back into the shower. "It's bad manners to let people see you without any clothes. Now, get back in there until we shut the door. Then put these things on, and you can come out again." She handed over the new outfit.

Yanking the curtain closed to block Cody, Steve stepped into the bedroom and shut the bathroom door behind him. He blew out a breath as he held out Cody's rags. "You probably ought to burn these. They smell."

Brenda took the clothing into the kitchen and dug in the pantry for a plastic grocery bag. She could hear Steve behind her, his footsteps on the tile floor. He sounded so normal, so much at home. For the hundredth time since her confession, she shuddered at the enormity of what she had been ready to risk — the loss of Steve's stability, his stalwart practicality, his comforting presence.

During his absence, remorse had driven Brenda back to her knees. She had finally admitted — to herself and to the Lord — that she'd chosen to distance herself from Him and from the support and teaching of her local church. What a mistake that had been. She prayed that God would forgive her for wandering from the path she had chosen to follow so long ago. She begged the Lord to change Steve's mind and bring him home to her. The past Sunday, she had returned to LAMB Chapel and asked God to help her understand how to rebuild what she and Steve had almost destroyed.

But then her husband had come back with all his rage and hostility tied up in a weapon that he had already flung at her more than once. What would he say to her now? How would he begin their ending?

Praying for strength, she stuffed Cody's old T-shirt into the bag. As she gathered up the jeans, she instinctively checked the pockets. Years of doing laundry had taught her to expect coins, stones, keys, wallets, even fishing worms. This time her hand closed on a piece of paper.

"There's a note in Cody's pocket," she told Steve. He stepped to the counter beside her. Grimy and worn, the page nearly tore as she unfolded it.

" 'Dear Friend,' " she read aloud. " 'I know you have found my son, Cody Goss, or you would not be reading this letter. Cody is backward, but he never means any mischief. His mama died when he was born, and I have had the sole care of the boy ever since. I did not send him to school lest the other children tease him. Cody knows his numbers pretty good, and he can say some of the alphabet. He can't read, but he has learned lots of Scriptures. He can also clean things up spic and span. Cody is a Christian, and you can trust him. He don't steal nor tell lies. I have got cancer that is going to kill me pretty quick, and I don't want Cody to watch me die. He cries real easy. I checked all over for a place he could live. But they all said he's twenty-one, and he's going to have to make his way. So I am putting him out on the road for Jesus to watch over, and then I will head for the nearest hospital wherein I shall cross the Jordan River and pass on to glory. I don't have nothing to leave Cody, not even my car. It is plumb shot after all these years. Please be kind to my son and don't harm him. Sincerely, William Goss.' "

Brenda laid the wrinkled note on the kitchen counter and turned to Steve. "Look at the date," she said. "This letter is almost two years old. Cody's father must have died by now. I guess . . . well, I imagined that somehow we could find him . . . we could fix it all. I thought if we took care of Cody and helped him, eventually things would . . . things would be okay again."

Tears welled in her eyes. She had cherished the same hope for herself and Steve, Brenda realized. Somehow, someway, the problems would fix themselves. Cody's father would reappear. All memories of Nick LeClair would vanish. Steve and Brenda would be just like they had always been. Together. Happy. United.

"Why are you crying?" Steve asked. His voice had softened a little. "You didn't expect Cody's life to be easy, did you? The kid was a mess when he showed up here. His father is gone, buried who knows where. Cody's too old to become a ward of the state, and he's way beyond anything a foster family could do. I tried to tell you . . . everyone tried to tell you that Cody was a homeless man, not a little boy who could be rescued. He's just like the other destitute, down-and-out people who sleep on the streets of cities and towns all over the world. He needs a place to live. A job. Transportation. If you want to make Cody's life better, it's going to take a lot of work."

Brenda nodded. "Good things take work. I'm willing to put out the effort to help Cody. I raised the kids through all their ups and downs. I took care of our family — fed and clothed everyone, drove endless miles to ball games and dance lessons, kept up with homework. And us . . ."

She looked up at her husband, recalling Esther's words of advice and encouragement. "I did my part to make a good marriage, Steve. I worked very hard at it. I want you to know that I've had a lot of time to think and pray and cry . . . and I'm willing to do whatever it takes to put us back together. Maybe not the way we were. But maybe better."

Steve focused on the lake, gleaming orange and blue in a sunset that gilded the living-room windows. For a moment he said nothing, his jaw twitching and the vein in his neck pulsing. Brenda could feel his anger. So many years together had taught her to read his silences as well as his words. He was furious. He hadn't forgiven her. He wouldn't be willing to try. She could see the message in the stiff set of his shoulders and the fists clenched at his sides.

Finally, he turned to her. "You betrayed me, Brenda. Don't try to tell me it was nothing just because you didn't sleep with that man. You wanted to. You would have. You gave your heart to him. You broke our marriage into pieces."

"I know," she said softly.

"And don't try to rationalize it by blaming me for working too much. You know what I do. You've been to my office, and you've seen the load I carry. When I left the auto-parts business, you supported me.

Everything I did got your blessing. And then you turned on me. You started resenting me and treating me like dirt. You wouldn't talk to me or touch me."

He gritted his teeth. "You let him touch you," he ground out. "You let that man hold you in his arms when you wouldn't even look at me. I needed you, Brenda. I needed you in our bed at night, and you turned me away. I needed you to be there for me when I came home from work — to sit on my lap and hug me the way you used to. But you wouldn't come near me."

She sniffled, struggling to hold back the words of recrimination that rose inside her. *I needed you too, but you were gone!* she wanted to shout at Steve. *You weren't there for me, so why should I be there for you? You abandoned me! You ignored me! You deserted your own wife!*

But she had said those things already — too many times. If Steve had heard them, he knew how she felt. And if he hadn't heard her before, he wasn't likely to listen now. Now was not the time to cast her own hurts on him. She owed him this chance to vent his rage at her. She deserved everything he said.

"You know what kind of man I am," Steve said, fastening his eyes on her. "You've known me since high school. I needed a wife who would be there for me, always by my side, holding me up. I married you because you were the woman whose touch I needed. I promised to take care of you and provide for you and our children, and I have. I kept up my part of the deal. But you just blew it off. You treated my love and faithfulness like trash!"

"I'm so sorry," she whispered, brushing her damp cheeks. She recalled her hope of rebuilding a summertime marriage and Patsy's tiny impatiens that had begun to sprout from the seeds of past years. "I know what I did was wrong. I know I hurt you and deceived you. I realize I was disloyal to our wedding vows. I can't defend myself, and I won't try, Steve. I deserve your anger. But I wish . . . I really wish you could find a way to forgive me."

"Why should I? Give me one good reason."

"I'll give you three good reasons," she said immediately. "Our children. It would kill them if we divorced."

"The kids don't live here anymore, Brenda. They have their own lives, even though you haven't figured that out. They don't need us or our happy little home. Most of their friends have parents who've been divorced. If we went our separate ways, it might rock their boat a little, but it wouldn't kill them."

"What about your parents? And my dad?"

"Same thing. They'd be disappointed, but that's no reason to maintain this sham of a marriage."

"It wasn't always a sham. We loved each other. We could learn to do that again. But not if you won't forgive me. If you can't do it for our family or for me, then do it for yourself. Don't let my failure make you bitter and angry, Steve. And please . . . please don't give up on us."

"Hey! There's my daddy's letter!" Cody padded in his stocking feet into the kitchen. "You found it in the pocket of my pants. I almost forgot about it. Daddy wrote it before he put me out of the car. He said I was twenty-one, and it was time to make my way."

Brenda turned toward the voice and was stunned at the sight of the young man. Cody positively gleamed. His hair had begun to grow back. His blue eyes sparkled, his cheeks glowed pink, and his freshly shaved jaw looked as smooth as silk. In the new T-shirt and jeans, he looked almost like one of Justin's friends — maybe even a little better, to tell the truth. Cody had an appointment with the dentist next week, and he'd started using the toothbrush Brenda bought him.

"My daddy wrote that I'm a good boy," Cody announced, pointing to the letter. "He read it to me. He said I'm a Christian, and I don't lie or steal, and I know how to keep things span. I can do my numbers and say my Bible verses too. And my daddy crossed the river and went to glory, so we won't see each other again until the great by-and-by. Do you know when that is? I really miss him. We used to eat hot dogs together."

"I think it will be a while," Brenda said. "The main thing to remember is that your daddy loved you very much, and he was proud of you."

Cody nodded. "After he drove away and left me behind, I didn't know what to do. I cried. I walked on the road, and I walked into towns. People shouted at me. One time some boys threw rocks at me. Another time, some men got me into a fight, and they pushed me onto the ground and hit me hard. It hurt a lot. I didn't like being alone without my daddy. But then the storm came, and I found you and the pink cat. You're a Christian."

Brenda rubbed her hand up and down Cody's thin arm. "It's all right now. We'll figure something out."

"Okay," Cody said.

"Why are you carrying your shoes? You should put them on."

"They have strings, see? I don't know how to tie things. I never got the hang of it."

Taking the shoes, Brenda pointed out a spot on the kitchen floor. They sat down together, and she pulled a sneaker onto his foot. "I'll do this one," she told him, "while you copy me on the other one."

"Okay," Cody grunted as he tugged his foot into the second shoe.

"Take the two ends like this," Brenda said, demonstrating. "They're called shoelaces. Now cross them over and then under. Now, pull."

Cody fumbled with the laces, his fingers tangling together and getting caught in his jeans, until finally Brenda helped him make the first tie. Recalling hours spent teaching her children this very skill, Brenda worked with him on making loops and finishing the bow. When they looked up at each other at last, Cody had created something of a loose knot that no doubt would come undone within three or four steps. But he was beside himself with joy.

"I did it!" he exclaimed. "Hey, I did it!" He threw his arms around Brenda, nearly knocking her over on the kitchen floor.

She laughed and ran her hand over his stubby hair. "How about some of our favorite chocolate cake?"

"I love chocolate cake! In triangles or squares?"

"Squares, of course. That's the way we like it best."

Smiling, she stood and helped Cody to his feet. As she turned toward the cupboard, she saw Steve standing in the doorway where the kitchen met the foyer. He had turned away from her. Head bowed and shoulders bent, he was rubbing his eyes.

"Steve?" Brenda stepped to his side and laid her hand on his arm. He felt cold, trembling. "Are you all right?"

He lifted his head, and she could see that his eyes were red. "You always used to do that," he managed, his voice husky. "With the kids . . . you helped them learn to tie their shoes."

"I miss them," she admitted. "It's been hard for me since Jessica left. They're all gone now, and . . . and I'm lonely."

Nodding, he covered her hand with his own. "I don't know how to forgive you, Brenda. I can't figure out how to stop thinking about what happened. How to let it go. How to get rid of the anger."

"I've been angry too, and it's not a good thing. It's been eating me up inside. I felt so empty."

"Is that why you gave someone else your heart?"

"Maybe." She closed her eyes, wishing she could erase everything she had done. "Probably."

"You were angry with me for being so busy?"

"For being gone." She laid her head on his shoulder. "I realize it doesn't make sense, Steve, but I rejected you because I felt abandoned by you. A few minutes ago, you said you married me because you needed my touch. Well, I married you because I needed your presence. I've missed you. This fall, with the house so empty, it began to feel like we never talked or went on walks together or sat on the sofa in each other's arms."

"But that's what I've been wanting."

"Me too."

He swallowed hard. "I don't know if I can forgive, Brenda. It's like you stuck a knife in my heart and turned the blade until you made sure I was dead. The idea of us ever being that way again . . . the way we were . . . seems impossible."

"Could we try?"

"I'm not sure," he said.

"I'm willing." She turned to face him. "I know it will take a lot of hard work. Maybe it'll be years before we get things to feel really right again. But I'm ready to make the effort. I want to try to support you in your work like I used to. I want you to succeed, and I really am proud of everything you've accomplished. I respect you, Steve. You're a good man."

Pressing his lips together, he lifted his focus to the ceiling. "You don't know how long I've waited to hear those words. To feel your hand on my arm and your head on my shoulder. To believe that you don't despise me."

"I love you, Steve. And I never stopped." Fearing the worst possible reaction from him, Brenda summoned her courage and slipped her arms around her husband. Drawing him close, she held him tightly and brushed her fingertips up and down his back.

At last, he lifted his own arms and encircled her. Laying his cheek against her head, he rocked her lightly, the way he always had.

"All right, honey." He breathed the words against her ear. "I'll try. . . . I'll try."

Through her tears, Brenda spotted Cody

heading toward them. Three plates — each holding a mangled square of chocolate cake — balanced precariously in his hands. He grinned through chocolate icing smeared around the corners of his mouth.

"I'll try too!" Cody said happily. "I'll try this chocolate cake, because I know it's gonna be good. Brenda always does the best chocolate cakes, and that's because she's a Christian. I think you are too, Steve. You helped me try to catch fish, and that's like the five loaves and two fishes and everyone eating till they were full. My daddy learned me about it in Matthew 14:16: 'But Jesus said unto them, They need not depart; give ye them to eat.' And here we are, all three of us together, sharing our chocolate cake just like Jesus!"

Brenda grabbed a plate before the cake could topple onto the floor. She handed it to Steve and took another. "Thank you, Cody."

Cody stuck a fork into his cake. " 'Give ye them to eat,' and that's how you be a Christian. That, and forgive. When those men were hitting me, I said Luke 6:36 and 37 over and over. 'Be ye therefore merciful, as your Father also is merciful. Judge not, and ye shall not be judged: condemn not, and ye shall not be condemned: forgive, and ye shall be forgiven.' That's a really good one if you want to be a Christian and pass on to glory in the great by-and-by."

As Cody ate, Brenda shifted her focus to Steve and recognized in his eyes a tenderness she had not seen for a very long time.

Walking away from his office and driving home while the sun was still shining turned out to be one of the hardest things Steve had ever done. For three days, he had jerked his attention from the active, bustling world of real estate and gone home to eat dinner with a woman he wasn't sure he could ever truly love again. He had told Brenda he would try, and he was trying. He had decided to give it a week, and if things hadn't improved — at least slightly — he would have to reevaluate.

The first night he had come home early, Brenda was so surprised to see him that she dropped a pan of lasagna on the floor, and they had to go out to eat. The second night, she grilled steaks and served them with baked potatoes and fresh green salad.

Now, on the third night — right in the midst of negotiations between the potential buyer and the seller of a million-dollar lake home — he had forced himself to call a halt to the proceedings. He had turned off his cell phone, instructed his secretary to hold all his calls until the following morning, and pressed the button that would lock his office door. After driving to Deepwater Cove, greeting Brenda at the door, and eating a big helping of stir-fried chicken, he pushed his pink plaid chair back from their table.

"Let's walk again like we did yesterday!" Cody spoke up. "Let's go down to the lake and see if Charlie Moore has caught any fish."

As Steve had learned, the young man typically showed up at the front door the moment Brenda took dinner out of the oven. Brenda explained that ever since Cody's return to the neighborhood, he had been eating most meals with her. She seemed to have substituted Cody for her husband at the table, and Steve had felt almost awkward resuming his traditional place at its head.

"I'd like to go for a walk too." Brenda glanced at Steve, her expression wary. "Do you want to join us?"

If he were to tell the truth, Steve would have to say no. He didn't want to walk around the neighborhood or watch Charlie Moore fish. He wanted to be back in his office negotiating a lucrative sale. Or taking a valued client to the country club for dinner. In fact, the last two people on earth he wanted to spend time with were Brenda and Cody.

"Sure." He forced the word out of his mouth. "I'll get our jackets. It was a little cool outside when I drove home."

Struggling to be more pleasant to his wife than he felt, Steve brought jackets from the coat closet. He helped Cody get his arms into the long sleeves — a major endeavor, as it turned out. Then they set off into the gathering dusk, Cody hurrying ahead and Steve walking dutifully beside his wife.

Every time he thought about what she had done with that scrawny handyman, Steve faced an array of arrows aimed straight at his heart. Part of him wanted to shake his wife, yell at her, make her cower in the dirt in repentance. Part of him wanted to hunt down Nick LeClair and challenge him to a fistfight. Instead of giving in to those emotions, Steve had decided to take pride in the fact that he was maintaining his cool, doing his best to meet Brenda's requests, and remaining steadfastly at her side.

It was a stretch, he knew. But didn't he deserve some credit? After all, how many men would have even gone this far in trying to salvage a broken marriage?

But he knew congratulating himself wouldn't make him feel good for very long.

The fact was, the challenge of making his marriage work held little allure. Steve inevitably found his thoughts traveling in circles — always back to Brenda's betrayal and his own pain.

"Thank you for coming home for dinner again tonight," Brenda said as they strolled down the narrow paved road toward the lake. "It almost feels like before — when I could count on you and prepare a meal I knew you would enjoy. I realize it must be difficult for you to leave your office so early and —"

"No," he snapped at her without thinking. "No, I don't think you do. Tonight I was in the middle of a sale on a three-tiered, seven-bedroom, ten-bath home with a swimming pool near Sunrise Beach. Right on the dot at six o'clock, I got a counteroffer from the prospective buyer, but I decided not to call the seller about it until tomorrow."

"Oh," she said meekly, "I see."

Steve sighed. "It's not easy — that's all I'm saying, Brenda. I told you I'd try, so I am. See, I came home, and now I'm walking to the lake. I hope you're happy."

She moved beside him in silence.

"Look, I didn't intend to sound harsh," he continued. "But I mean, look at it from my point of view. I'm the one who got burned, and now I'm the one who has to make sacrifices."

"When a marriage goes down in flames," Brenda said, "both people get burned. I've been hurting for a long time. You've been gone so much I began to think I might actually get used to it. But I never did."

"I haven't been *gone.* Not like guys who fish or golf all the time. I've been *working,* Brenda."

"Is it any different?"

"Of course it is! I'm not goofing off. I'm earning money for my family."

"You've been gone. That's the only thing that matters."

"Well, now I'm here. What else do you want?"

Instead of answering, Brenda pasted on a smile and waved at Esther Moore, who was sitting on her porch brushing her dog. Boofer spotted Cody and tried to run to him, but Esther held on tight.

"Animals love Cody," Brenda observed. "I guess he must be very gentle with them."

Way to change the subject, Steve thought. Well, good. He didn't want to talk about their marriage anyway. There was nothing more he could do except endure it. That, and alter his entire pattern of existence.

"You know, it might help if I wasn't the

only one working on this relationship, Brenda," he said. "I've been coming home early, eating dinner with you, taking these walks. I'm trying to be civil to you —"

"And you have no idea how much all that means to me. We used to enjoy spending time together, remember? You would tell me about your work and all the people who came into the auto-parts store. I'd like to hear what's going on in your agency now. I want to be supportive, because I know how much your work means to you. Everyone in the community talks about what a great salesman you are, and it makes me really proud to be your wife. I love it that you're smart and successful. But mostly, I'm just glad you come home to me. I feel . . . it's hard to explain, Steve . . . but I feel *better*."

Before he could respond, she reached over and slipped her hand into his. Instinctively, he wrapped his fingers around hers. Like kids on an awkward date, they walked along the gravel path toward the lake in stilted silence.

Steve could feel every part of Brenda's hand as though it were pulsing with electricity. Her slender fingers slipped between his own, much larger ones. The heel of her hand pressed against his palm. Her elbow brushed his arm. As she stepped closer to him, her shoulder leaned into his, and she let out a long breath.

"There's Charlie at the end of the dock," she said in a low voice. "He's already showing Cody his stringer of crappie. Every night I figure Charlie must have pulled the very last fish out of the water around the dock, but the next night, he's caught at least one or two more keepers."

Steve tightened his hold on Brenda's hand. Holding hands with her again felt so good. If only he could be certain the gesture wasn't just an act. Part of her campaign to salve her conscience. His heart was thudding in his chest, and he searched for something to say as if the word repository in his mind had suddenly been deleted.

"Esther told me that she and Charlie eat so much fish she's surprised she hasn't started to grow fins." Brenda chuckled. "Lately she and I have become good friends."

Steve nodded and managed to say, "I'm glad."

"Oh, look! Charlie has one hooked, and he's giving Cody the rod!"

Brenda's hand jerked suddenly out of Steve's grip as she cupped her mouth. "You can do it, Cody!" she cried, jumping up and down on her tiptoes. "Reel him in slowly!

Charlie, show him which way to crank it!"

Beaming, she grabbed Steve's hand again and squeezed it. At the sheer joy on her face — and the certainty that this time her grasp was genuine — he couldn't hold back a grin.

"Come on!" she said, drawing him forward. "Let's go watch Cody pull in his first fish. Isn't this fun?"

As they picked up their pace, hurrying hand in hand toward the dock, Steve had to agree. This *was* kind of fun.

CHAPTER SEVENTEEN

Steve pulled up to the gas pumps outside Rods-n-Ends two weeks after his return to Deepwater Cove. As he stepped out of his car, he saw Pete Roberts leave his place behind the counter and saunter toward the door. For once, the thought of shooting the breeze with the hefty store owner didn't make Steve cringe.

His trial week had turned into two. Things with Brenda were still far from perfect, but coming home early had made a difference. So that morning at his office, he had gathered the other real-estate agents and his staff in the conference room to make an announcement. He would be heading home no later than six each evening. The agency would be open on Saturdays, but Sundays would be reserved for church and family. The news had come as a surprise, and one employee objected to the changes, but Steve had refused to hear any arguments. His declaration stood.

"Heard you took a trip to Arkansas," Pete drawled as he ambled to the pumps. "Pretty down there this time of year. Thick forests and lots of streams. Do any fishing?"

"Some," Steve said. "I needed a little break, time to think things over. So I mostly just put up my feet and rested."

"I don't blame you a bit. That agency of yours is going great guns day and night. I see your signs and billboards everywhere."

"We're busy, but I decided to make a few adjustments. Get home a little earlier, take Sundays off, visit the kids now and then — that kind of thing."

"Sundays off? Now that does surprise me." Pete spat a thin stream of chewing tobacco from the side of his mouth. "I thought that's when most people came to the lake to look at properties."

Steve shrugged. "My agents have keys to the office. But you won't see me there."

Pete smiled. "I like a fella who knows his own mind. If I could afford it, I'd do the same thing. You may not rake in as much money as you used to, but some things are more important."

"Brenda and I talked it over. I realized we could make do with less. When I sold auto parts, we barely got through the month.

Now college is paid up for the kids, and we don't have but two mouths at home to feed."

"What about that young fellow? You know the one that's a little bit . . ." Pete pointed his index finger at his ear and drew a few circles. "You don't like to say someone's dumb or retarded these days, but what else could you call him?"

"Cody? He's slow, but I don't think he's had much of a chance to show what he can do. Brenda's been working with him, teaching him a few things. Turns out he's smarter than we all thought."

"No kidding? Well, don't that beat all? You think you've got a fella pegged, and then he up and surprises the socks off you. Like you shutting down your agency on Sundays." Pete leaned on the gas pump and gestured toward the strip mall. "Anything come of your idea about buying this place? The video-store guy has been getting boxes delivered every day. I think he's about to open up. And the chiropractor is threatening to shut down. He gave notice that he's looking for new digs. It's a mess."

Steve finished pumping gas into his tank and settled the nozzle back in its holder. "I seriously considered purchasing the mall," he told Pete. "I even had a financial backer. Someone from St. Louis came down to the lake to work out the details with me, and I thought I could make a go of it. We had a few meetings, but I finally called off the deal."

"Didn't like the terms, huh?"

"It wasn't that so much as the time. If I go into commercial real estate, I'll have to work even more hours than I do right now. I hate the idea of an adult-video store moving into Tranquility as much as the rest of us around here, but I just couldn't see adding that to my load."

Pete nodded. "Well, if I had the wherewithal, I'd buy it, but there you go. Spent my best earning years drinking up my wages. Sacrificed two marriages and my good health, all for booze. My second wife, when she left me, she told me I was married to beer. That really got me, you know? *Married to beer.* But she was right . . . I loved getting drunk better than I loved her, better than I loved myself. Now here I am trying to make a living selling minnows, gas, and hot dogs."

Though Pete's story was different from his own, Steve could relate. Brenda had accused him of being married to his work, and he couldn't deny how much he loved selling real estate. It was almost an addiction — writing advertising copy, ordering billboards, convincing sellers, reeling in buyers, finalizing sales.

As he thought about the vocation to which he had given his time, energy, and passion, his gaze wandered over to the beauty shop next door to Rods-n-Ends. Before his last haircut, a group of Patsy's regular customers had dragged him into the tearoom to tell him their feelings about the video store. At the time, Steve had paid scant attention. But now he recalled what Kim Finley had said: *"If a man wants a real woman to meet his needs, he has to do his part."* Steve had always considered "his part" to be earning money and providing for the family. But that wasn't what the ladies were after.

"Real women want to be loved and cherished, not treated like some kind of object," Patsy Pringle had told him. Esther Moore had chimed in with her view on men: *"My husband has learned that he had better listen — and listen good — if he wants me to feel any affection for him."* Even the usually quiet Kim Finley had an opinion on what a woman truly wanted. She described how Derek was supportive and did all he could to help make her life easier, despite his heavy workload with the Water Patrol. *"Derek is always trying to figure out how to be a better husband,"* she claimed.

Pretty rigorous standards, Steve thought. But if other men had learned to please their wives, couldn't he? With a lot of effort, Pete Roberts had managed to overcome the things that were destroying his health and ruining his relationships. Steve had begun to look at repairing his marriage as a similar kind of challenge. His first step had been to start coming home early and spending time with Brenda. While it had seemed impossible at first, he was actually learning to enjoy their evening walks. He figured all the steps ahead would also be difficult and require hard work, but he had never backed down from obstacles before.

Recalling Pete's regret at the way he had wasted so many years of his life, Steve clapped the burly man on the shoulder. "Don't be too hard on yourself, Pete," he said. "You've turned your life around, and that's more than a lot of people can say. You don't drink, you work hard, and I've seen you in church every Sunday. I think you've even won Patsy Pringle's heart."

Laughing, Pete shook his head. "Not even close! That woman is more stubborn and hardheaded than I am, and that's saying a lot. Aw, we're on speaking terms since I built that soundproof wall between our businesses. But she won't hardly give me the time of day."

"Don't give up," Steve urged Pete as he climbed back into his car. "One of these days, if you and I listen to our women and spend enough time with them, we'll know exactly what they're looking for in a man."

"Good advice," Pete said, waving as Steve pulled out of the parking lot. "I'll try to remember it."

"Mercy sakes, look what just walked in the door!" Patsy Pringle exclaimed from her station inside Just As I Am. "If that isn't the handsomest young man in the world, I'll eat my hat."

Cody paused, confusion written on his face. "You don't have on a hat, Patsy."

"It's just an expression," Brenda told him. "She thinks you look wonderful."

"That's because I take a shower every day," he announced, loud enough for everyone in the salon to hear him. "I don't have any more mice in my hair, and I wear clean clothes, and I can almost tie my shoelaces."

"Well, I'll be," Patsy said. "A shower every day? Why, that's just about the best news I've heard this century. And learning to tie your shoes too? Are you sure your name is Cody Goss?"

He chuckled. "You know who I am, Patsy

Pringle."

"And I couldn't be happier about it." She smiled at the sight of Brenda Hansen, who was starting to look a little more like her old self. "What are you two doing here today? Did I goof up my schedule book again?"

"It's Wednesday," Brenda reminded her. "We have a meeting of the TLC."

"The Tea Ladies' Club," Cody said. "It's for ladies, but Brenda said I could come today. I want to see if you have any chocolate cake, because my daddy said —"

"Are the others here yet?" Brenda asked, cutting off Cody's recital of the holy benefits of that particular dessert. "Esther dropped by on her golf cart this morning to remind me."

"Any time now," Patsy sang out. "In fact, Kim may be back there already. I forgot about the meeting, but I'll see if one of the other stylists will take my three o'clock manicure and pedicure. We're always filling in for each other."

Brenda ushered Cody back to the tea-room, where Kim sat browsing through a magazine. They greeted her and settled their belongings before heading over to the pastry case and the urn. Brenda selected a peanut-butter cookie and some Earl Grey tea while

Cody agonized between a slice of pecan pie and a helping of apple cobbler.

"I guess it won't be long before school's out for the summer," Brenda remarked to Kim as she returned to the table. "I remember my kids could hardly wait for vacation to start. They would get so antsy and excited, but by mid-August, they were always ready to go back to class and see their friends."

Dark-haired Kim closed the magazine and stirred her tea. "Are yours coming home from college soon?"

Brenda glanced away for a moment, swallowing down the ache. It wasn't quite as sharp now, but it still hung on. "Jennifer doesn't complete her mission in Africa until the end of August. The other day, she sent us a message that she had finally made the decision to commit to full-time service."

"You mean she'll be a missionary? And live in a foreign country for the rest of her life?"

"That's what she says." Brenda reflected for a moment on her lovely, golden-haired older daughter. So dedicated and selfless. What would Jennifer think if she knew what her mother had done? Even the fact that Brenda had stopped going to church until just recently would shock Jennifer. The idea that her parents might still separate — even divorce — would dangerously tilt her view of life. Of the three children, it was Jennifer whose face Brenda most often saw when she thought about the incident with Nick LeClair. Struggling to hold her emotions at bay, she took a sip of tea.

"Jennifer believes God has called her to teach at a boarding school for missionary kids," Brenda informed Kim. "She's already getting her paperwork ready to enter a seminary in Texas. When she graduated with a teaching degree, I pictured her in a classroom full of kindergarteners here in Missouri. But evidently that's not what the Lord had in mind."

"I guess I never thought about young single women becoming missionaries," Kim said. "You must be very proud of her."

"We are, but we miss her a lot. And as it turns out, both Justin and Jessica will be spending the summer in Springfield. Jessica wants to take classes toward an early graduation."

"Jessica? I can still see her running down to the lake with her friends. Skinny young girls in bathing suits, giggling and acting so silly. It's hard to imagine that she's old enough to be thinking about college graduation already."

Brenda nodded.

"And Justin?"

"Believe it or not, he got a job at a car dealership in Springfield. He's still so goofy that I can't imagine why anyone would hire him, but I guess he convinced them. At first, he'll just be moving cars around on the lot and that sort of thing. But he's hoping to get into sales by the end of summer."

"Takes after his father," Kim said. "Everyone's predicting Steve will win Realtor of the Year, and his agency is sure to be honored at the chamber of commerce banquet this Christmas. How is Steve, by the way? I heard he went to Arkansas on a business trip."

Brenda had been fielding this question often enough to have the answer down pat. "He took a little retreat to do some thinking about his work and how it's impacting his life. He's decided to cut back on his hours and close the agency on Sundays."

"Wow, that's a radical change." Kim's dark eyes softened. "How are *you*, Brenda? When the TLC visited your house the day we cut Cody's hair, your condition really concerned me."

"I'm better, I think. At least . . . I'm not spending most of the day in my rocking chair. All of you really helped by getting me up and forcing me to stay busy. I've had a hard time lately. The kids left home, and things just became awkward, confusing . . . overwhelming."

"I understand, at least a little. During my divorce, I got very depressed. It took a lot of work to recover. Now we're facing something that might knock the wind out of me again. I could use your prayers."

"What's going on, Kim?" Brenda reached across the table and closed her fingers over Kim's hand. "Is there anything I can do?"

"It's Luke," she said. "We took him up to St. Louis. The doctors ran all kinds of tests. It seems like things aren't working right . . . his pancreas and his endocrine levels. Things I never even heard of before. Brenda, they think Luke has diabetes."

"Oh, Kim, I'm so sorry."

Kim began to speak again, but Esther Moore and Ashley Hanes arrived together at the table. Cody had finally made his selection, so he took a chair and settled in.

"Well, you ladies look as sad as a fallen cake," Patsy said, setting down her teacup and joining the group.

"Chocolate cake?" Cody asked. "Because my daddy says that —"

All the women chimed in at once to drown out Cody's chant.

Ashley's voice carried over the rest. "It's Luke," she told Patsy. "The doctors in St. Louis say he's got diabetes."

"Well, mercy sakes alive," Patsy said, reaching around Kim's shoulders and giving her a squeeze. "No wonder you hardly looked up when you came into the salon, sweetie. What can we do for you?"

"Derek and I aren't sure what to do," Kim said. "We both work long hours —"

"You work at the dentist's office," Cody interrupted. "I saw you there. I went to the dentist and got my teeth cleaned by a lady. Look." He rolled his lips back and displayed his newly scrubbed and polished teeth for everyone to admire.

"That's nice, Cody," Patsy said, "but I think it's high time we addressed the Lord about this. If nobody minds, I'll do the out-loud praying, and the rest of you can follow along with me or talk to God in silence. We'll cover Luke and his diabetes, Brenda's recent spell of discouragement, and my attitude toward my neighbors in the mall — particularly that new place going in down the way."

"And me," Ashley said in an uncharacteristically timid voice. "Me and Brad."

Everyone turned to her, but she lowered her eyes. Patsy bowed her head and began

412

to pray. As she lifted up Luke and all the Finleys, Brenda felt movement from Cody's chair beside her. She didn't want to look up, but the idea that Cody might run off again troubled her. Still, she really did need to focus on this shared conversation with God. Patsy had a way of speaking to the Lord that made Brenda feel as though He were sitting right there with the Tea Ladies' Club.

And come to think of it, He was. *"For where two or three are gathered together in my name, there am I in the midst of them."* The Bible verse Brenda had learned so long ago was true, she realized. She had never doubted it, no matter how far she had wandered from the straight and narrow path. At first, she wanted nothing more than to hide under the table at the very idea that Christ's Spirit was there in the salon, looking at her, knowing all about her, aware of everything she had thought and done this past spring. And then . . . as once again she silently poured out all her shame and begged His forgiveness, she knew a wash of relief.

As sick, lonely, depressed, angry, and hopeless as she had felt — and still did at times — Brenda knew God was with her, forgiving her, holding her up, and surrounding her with wonderful people like these women in Patsy's salon. Brenda realized that, in fact, she no longer needed to keep reminding the Lord of her errors and asking His pardon. Once was all it took, and God erased everything. She only wished it was that easy with Steve.

When Patsy had finished praying for everyone and the amens were finally echoed, Brenda lifted her head to find that all of the women were crying. Patsy got to her feet to grab a tissue box from her station, but her squeal of surprise startled everyone out of their tears.

"Glory be!" she exclaimed. "Cody, honey child, what are you doing over here? I'll get that swept clean in a minute. You come on back and have tea with us."

Brenda stood, concern knotting her stomach as she watched the young man rise from the floor, a broom and dustpan in his hands. His blue eyes focused on her, then on Patsy, and then on the broom.

"I like to keep things span," he told Patsy. "My daddy said I was really good at it. I can sweep better than anybody, and I like to wash windows and mirrors."

"But you don't have to do that *here*," Patsy insisted. "You're our guest. I had no idea you had gone over to my station while

I was praying. 'Course, my mother always said if I was talking to the Lord, I wouldn't feel a tornado suck the house out from under me. Anyhow, you just leave that mess to me, Cody. I'm used to cleaning up."

"But I'm good at keeping things span," Cody reiterated.

Brenda had joined them, hoping she could help sort out the confusion. "Cody has washed my windows about fifteen times since he came back to Deepwater Cove," she told Patsy. "He did a nice job. Last week, he found an old broom on the burn pile down by the lake, and now he sweeps my porch three or four times a day."

"Mine too!" Esther called out, waving her napkin. "He would have washed our golf cart, but Charlie ran him off. Charlie likes to wash and polish the cart himself. Listen, Patsy, you just let Cody sweep. We need to talk about this video-store problem. I'm thinking of organizing a protest with placards and flags and megaphones and everything. I've already looked into printing up pamphlets, and I think we can do them on Charlie's computer. While we have our meeting, give that boy a chance to do something he likes."

Patsy glanced at Brenda for her reaction. "He won't do any harm," Brenda assured her. "Cody's very careful."

The young man's newly whitened teeth gleamed as he grinned. "I'm always careful. I never touch buttons, neither. My daddy told me not to touch any buttons or switches, because you could fry yourself like a Thanksgiving turkey."

"Are you sure you don't want to come back to the table, Cody?" Patsy asked. "I'll get you another dessert, and you can listen to us talk."

Cody leaned over. "It's the Tea *Ladies'* Club," he murmured into her ear. "*Ladies.* I know what that means. It means women. And I am not a lady. I'm a man, twenty-one, time to make my way."

"You certainly are," she said. "You're a very fine young man, if I do say so myself. Well, if it'll make you happy, go ahead and sweep all you want. There's a bucket of cleaners and sponges under the sink in the back room. Just don't bother the other stylists while they're working, and let the customers read their magazines if they don't feel like talking."

"Yes, sir," Cody said, beaming. "I can do that. I can do it all really good."

Brenda thought of about ten warnings to give Cody; then she recalled having to turn loose of her own children long before she felt they were ready to be independent. As she rejoined Patsy at the table, she thanked her for allowing Cody the opportunity to do something helpful.

"Helpful?" Patsy said, lifting a carefully outlined brown eyebrow. "The boy is a godsend."

"You couldn't ask for a finer addition to the community," Esther declared. "I always knew there was a good person hidden under all that hair. Now, ladies, about my protest march . . ."

"Hold on a minute." Patsy crossed her arms the way she always did when she meant business. "I have a proposal to put before the club."

"What is it?" Ashley asked.

"Hey now, girls, this is not how you hold a club meeting," Esther protested. "You've got to follow parliamentary proceedings and such. We need to get us a copy of *Robert's Rules of Order.*"

Patsy gave a snort. "Order schmorder. I don't cotton to all that folderol anyhow. I have something to say, and my next client will be here in fifteen minutes. Now, do you want to hear my proposal or not?"

"All right," Esther said. "If that's the way you prefer it, though I think a few club rules would be appropriate."

After glancing back over her shoulder, Patsy leaned forward. "I propose we change the name of our club. Cody's helped me see the light. Calling ourselves the Tea Ladies' Club comes across as downright narrow-minded. I don't care if a person is male, female, red, white, black, or blue, smart or dumb, tall or short, fat or skinny — if they want to be a club member, we should let 'em join."

"But TLC has such a nice ring to it," Kim said. "Every time I think about all of you, I see tender loving care written all over your faces."

"Me too," Ashley said. "I like TLC."

"Then how about something similar. . . ." Patsy thought for a moment. "We meet in the tearoom, so that's important. And we're a club, too. So . . ."

"The Tea Lovers' Club!" Brenda burst out.

"There you go!" Patsy cried. "It's perfect. The only rule or requirement of our club is that you have to love tea. And we might even bend that one if someone's partial to coffee."

Ashley lifted her teacup, and everyone joined in the toast. "To the Tea Lovers' Club," she said. "May we give each other nothing but tender loving care."

As the china cups clinked together, the women chuckled. "In that case," Esther said, "I recommend we add one new member right away."

The group turned as one to study the tall, handsome young man who was polishing the mirror in Patsy's station while admiring his shiny white teeth.

"To our newest member," Kim said, raising her teacup a second time. "Here's to Cody Goss."

After taking a sip of tea, Esther leaned forward on the table and said, "And now, ladies — and gentleman — I have a plan for how to get rid of that adult-video store."

CHAPTER EIGHTEEN

As he eased onto the highway, Steve looked in the rearview mirror. A glimpse of his own face startled him and caused him to glance back at the mirror for a moment. He hadn't slept well since his return to Deepwater Cove, but he didn't realize he looked so haggard. Turning his attention to the road again, he prayed that he could keep his mind centered on holding up his end of the agreement he'd made with his wife.

Steve had told Brenda he would *try*. He would work with her to restore their relationship and rebuild their marriage. Since then, he had come home early every evening, eaten dinner with her and Cody, walked with her around the neighborhood in the evenings, and done his best to be pleasant.

But each hour of the day brought a new assault in the exhausting two-front battle Steve was waging. Not only did he fight to block out the name of Nick LeClair, to erase the mental image of Brenda in another man's arms. He also labored to love his wife for who she had always been, even though part of him wanted to despise her for the one thing she had done to hurt him so deeply.

He'd heard Pastor Andrew say that forgiveness was a decision, not a feeling. Steve thought it was a great concept. But he'd never had a life-shattering offense to forgive before.

It was hard. Sometimes he thought it was too hard. There was a barrier standing in his way, and he didn't even know what to call it. Yet he ran up against it every time he tried to move on.

When he wasn't distracted by work, the newspaper, a book, or television, he struggled against the gag reflex that always hung at the top of his throat. Anger and hurt had formed into a ball lodged inside him, and he didn't know how to get rid of it. He needed to say something, but he wasn't sure what. It was about Brenda . . . but it was also about himself. He wondered if he had been part of the problem. Could there be any truth to Brenda's accusations that he had abandoned her for his job?

No matter how he tried to sort through it

all, he kept coming back to Brenda's betrayal. Finally he realized that all he actually could do about it was to pray. So that's what he'd been doing.

But it wasn't working, Steve realized as he drove into the garage, let the door drop, and got out of the car. Everything he trusted had been shattered in a single instant. His wife, God, even his own confidence in himself as a good husband and faithful family man.

Leaning one arm on the roof of his car, Steve once again tried to find the words to pray. All that came out of him was a deeply uttered "Why?"

Hearing no answer, Steve put his head down on his arm and shut his eyes. At that moment, a verse from St. Paul's letter to the Romans drifted through the fog in his brain. Though the passage hadn't made much sense to him in the past, now he understood exactly what the apostle had meant when he wrote about people not knowing how to pray or what to pray for. Paul had promised that at such times, the Holy Spirit would pray for believers with groanings that could not be expressed in words.

Steve took comfort in the knowledge that the Spirit understood exactly what he needed and was pleading with God on his behalf. But it didn't resolve the problem he encountered every evening after work. Steve still had to step inside his house in Deepwater Cove and face the woman he could barely think of as his wife. Since his return from Arkansas, Brenda had done her best to be cheerful, kind, and supportive, but Steve's heart felt like a chunk of rock-hard ice.

Pushing open the door from the garage to the kitchen, he immediately smelled the dish that had graced the Hansen family table every spring. At the first appearance of fresh asparagus in the grocery store, Brenda whipped up an enormous pot of pasta primavera. But instead of stirring his appetite, today the aroma sent a pang of regret through his chest. All those years, all that love . . .

"Hey there, you!" Brenda sang out as she looked at him from her cutting board. "I just put the water on to boil, and I've chopped up everything but the basil. You should smell this!" Stepping to his side, she lifted a sprig of the fresh herb to his nose.

Steve sniffed and mustered a smile. "Nice," he said.

"Charlie Moore gave it to me." She returned to the counter, but kept talking.

"The asparagus is from his garden too. At the TLC meeting today, Esther heard me mention pasta primavera, and she insisted on giving me the makings for more than we can possibly eat."

"Oh," Steve managed.

"You won't believe what Esther has up her sleeve this time. She wants all of us to stage a protest march in front of the new adult-video store at the Tranquility mall. It hasn't even opened yet, but she's found a megaphone, and she's figured out a way to print flyers. Charlie is going to plaster his golf cart with signs and drive it around and around the parking lot, tooting the horn, while the rest of us walk behind him carrying placards."

Realizing he couldn't escape and shouldn't want to, Steve set his briefcase on the floor. "Who's going to be participating in this protest?"

"The TLC. I told you about us, remember? We meet at Just As I Am. We used to be called the Tea Ladies' Club, but now we're the Tea Lovers' Club, and Cody is a full-fledged member. Does this tomato look fresh to you?"

She crossed the kitchen floor to him again. Steve inspected the tomato, which had a suspicious hole near the stem. "It's either a worm or the birds have been at it."

"I'm not taking any chances," she said, swinging away from him and tossing the tomato into the garbage can. "Speaking of the TLC, did I tell you that Ashley Hanes and I are making bead necklaces? We're going to give them as Christmas presents. Ashley and Brad have invited us to dinner on Sunday, by the way. And Brad has agreed to build a bridge over our drainage ditch."

As Brenda spoke, Steve studied his wife. He recalled the weeks when she had dragged around in her bathrobe, and he almost wished that woman were back. It would make his misery a lot easier.

Today Brenda looked pretty, he had to admit. Her blonde hair was bouncy and soft, cut just the way he liked it. She wore a pale pink top and a pair of shorts. Her bare feet had always intrigued him with their tiny toes and pink polish.

Throughout their courtship and marriage, Brenda's petite figure and shapely legs had always been able to stir something inside her husband. If he weren't so confused, Steve realized, he could almost start feeling that way about her again — his heart beginning to thump and his hands itching to trace over her shoulders and down her silky arms. Brenda had impulsively hugged him once and they made a habit of walking hand in hand, but Brenda still kept to her side of the bed, and Steve never made any attempt to touch her.

"None of us could believe what a fantastic job he had done," Brenda was saying as Steve tried to refocus his attention. "He polished all the mirrors, swept the floor, scrubbed the sinks, and mopped the back room — and that was just during the meeting. Patsy was thrilled to death. Cody wanted to keep working, so I said that was fine and came on home to start the pasta. Patsy's taking him out for supper, and then she'll bring him back here later tonight. Isn't that wonderful?"

"Cody?" he asked.

"You saw how he washed our windows over and over. He's like a cleaning machine once he gets going. Esther is going to have him shake out her rugs and do some dusting. She said she'd pay him minimum wage."

Surprised to hear the animation in Brenda's voice, Steve instinctively responded. "Cody could clean the offices at the agency for me," he said. "That woman I hired doesn't show up half the time."

"Really? That's awful. But good for Cody." Brenda's green eyes shone as she looked at

Steve. "You'd really hire him to clean? I could drive him over in the afternoons —"

"And I'll bring him home with me at night."

"Oh, honey!" Brenda threw her arms around Steve and gave him a kiss on the cheek. As if suddenly catching herself, she stepped back quickly. "That's so nice of you. I think Cody can accomplish a lot if he gets the chance to try."

Still reeling from the kiss, Steve discovered he couldn't make his mouth form any audible words. Brenda had hugged him. Kissed him. Just like the old days.

He had to sit down.

"I'll be in the living room," he called to her over his shoulder.

Did he want Brenda's affection? He sank into his favorite chair and leaned his head back. Trying to please her had meant cutting into his profits at work and annoying some of his agents. One had told Steve he was quitting when he found another place to work. Was all that loss and trouble worth it? Were the sacrifices going to pay off in something he even wanted?

"I don't know what to think about that protest march," Brenda said from the kitchen.

She had always spoken to him while he

thumbed through the lake area's daily newspaper — checking his ads and scanning those of the competition. This felt so normal. Eerily normal, Steve thought as he shut his eyes and tried to relax.

"I don't mind making some kind of public statement," she was saying. "But I doubt a protest march will do any good. Pete Roberts told Patsy that the new tenant is getting boxes of stuff delivered at his store every day. Nothing is going to make that man move. It could affect the school-bus route, you know. Oh, and I have the worst news. Luke Lockwood — one of the cute little twins? — well, it looks like he has diabetes. The worst kind too. Kim told us about it today at the TLC meeting. I felt so awful for her. Our kids had the usual colds and broken bones, but we never went through anything that serious. I promised we would pray for the Finleys, and the club wants to do whatever we can. Do you know much about diabetes? Doesn't your cousin have it?"

Steve cleared his throat. "Yeah, Robbie. He doesn't talk about it much."

"Kim sounded so scared." Brenda's voice grew louder suddenly, and Steve opened his eyes to find that she had walked into the living room. She held out a glass. "Would you like some iced tea?"

He took it and set it on the table beside his chair. "Thanks."

She stood for a moment in silence. Then she squared her shoulders, circled his chair, and dropped down into his lap. "Tell me about your day." She leaned her head against his neck. "Did you sell any houses?"

Steve couldn't move. He had longed for this. Physically ached for it. And now here she was, in his lap, snuggled up next to him. Yet he felt cold, stiff, unable to budge.

"No," he said. "Not today."

"Did you show some?"

"A few."

"Where?" she asked, her voice shaky and slightly breathless. "In town or lakeside?"

He forced his hand up from the arm of his chair and set it on her shoulder. "Lake," he said, feeling as though he were an actor playing a part in a rerun of their former life. "One of them should go in a few days. Price is right."

She was trembling. "Does it have a nice view?"

"It looks out over the main channel," he mumbled, letting his hand slide down to her elbow. "It's on a point, though, and the home's lake access is in a quiet cove just off the channel. It has huge windows, a paved driveway, a stone fireplace, and a two-slip dock with lifts."

"Wow."

As Steve allowed his arm to move around Brenda's back, he felt something damp on his shoulder. She was crying. As hurt as he was — as painful as the reality that wouldn't go away was — he couldn't stand to think of Brenda's tears. Lifting his other arm, he encircled her and drew her close against him. "Oh, honey." He closed his eyes and sighed. "Brenda . . . I've made it my goal to work toward a happier marriage." He looked at her. "I know it may take a long time and be very hard, but I'm determined."

"Thank you, Steve," she whispered. "I'm so sorry. I made terrible mistakes and bad choices. I did everything wrong. I'm just so . . . so sorry."

He stroked her hair, marveling at the silky touch of each strand against his fingertips. Then he ran the side of one finger down her cheek, gathering up tears and rubbing them away. "Shh," he said. "Don't cry, honey."

"Sometimes I hate myself so much that I don't think I can stand it. If my friends hadn't supported me through this, I don't know what I would have done. And you . . .

you finally listened to me. You changed your schedule and reshaped your whole life, and I don't deserve it. I don't deserve anything good after what I did to you."

He swallowed at the lump in his throat again. And suddenly he realized what that lump was.

He had been blaming Brenda for her shortcomings and mistakes, and it was time to forgive. But there was more. He saw the truth in her eyes and allowed it to penetrate his heart for the first time.

He had failed her too.

She had been trying to tell him how deeply his abandonment had hurt her. Instead of admitting the part he had played in their problems, he'd laid all the blame at her feet. Again and again, she had begged him to forgive her, and he felt he was finally ready to do everything he could to set her free from the burden of her guilt.

He was carrying the same burden.

"Brenda, listen to me." He held her as close as he could and kissed the top of her forehead. "I failed you too. I didn't want to admit it, but you were right. I've been trying to deny the truth right up to this very minute, but I just can't do that any longer. I did love my job too much. I gave it first place in my life. The way I feel about it is different from how I feel about you, but the end result is the same. I took you for granted, and I abandoned you. I know I did."

"I forgive you, Steve." Brenda brushed at her eyes, trying to stop the tears. "I've missed you so much."

Steve held her in his arms, feeling the sweet curves and gentle outlines of his wife. Then he cupped her cheek with his hand and turned her face to his. "I forgive you too."

As their lips met, a rush of relief poured through him. The dam of resentment, anger, and hurt had cracked open, and for the first time in ages, joy and peace began to trickle through.

Patsy could have just about died of embarrassment when Cody barged through the front door of the Hansens' house after their chicken-fried steak dinner at Aunt Mamie's. Steve and Brenda were curled up together in a living-room chair, smooching and crying and giggling like a pair of lovebirds. At the intrusion, Brenda gasped and sat up, her cheeks flushed with surprise.

Cody was oblivious. "Guess what!" he announced. "I got a job. A forever job. Patsy's going to pay me to clean her salon every day, and that means you know what — hot dogs!"

As Brenda pulled herself together and Steve raked his fingers back through his hair, Cody marched around the room in front of them.

"Hot dogs every day," he told them. "When you have a job, you can buy hot dogs. I'll share mine with both of you too, because I'm a Christian. And Patsy told me I can sleep in the back room if I want. She's going to get a bed and sheets. A real bed! And there's a bathroom and a shower too. How about *that?*"

"He can't really be living there," Patsy said, wringing her hands together and wishing she could make a discreet exit from the Hansens' house. "It's zoned commercial, you know. But I figured Cody could sleep there one or two nights a week anyway."

"He can stay here, too," Steve offered. "We've got plenty of room."

"Inside?" Brenda asked. "Inside the house . . . with us?"

"I used to think Jesus lived here," Cody said.

"He does, Cody. We invited Him back. But there's room for you, too." Steve smiled and winked at his wife. "Sure, Cody's welcome. You got all the mice out of his hair, didn't you?"

"All gone!" Cody assured him. "And Esther Moore told me I could sleep at her house too. I have more houses than anybody, all of a sudden. I sure do wish my daddy was here. He would be so happy to see me. He would say, 'You made your way, Cody.' And I have."

"You sure have," Patsy echoed. "Well, I guess I'll leave Cody here tonight and head for home. It's going to be a long day at the salon tomorrow."

"Speaking of which," Steve said. Brenda made to stand up, but he pulled her back into his lap and wrapped his arms around her. "A while ago, I was thinking about going into commercial real estate. I considered buying the Tranquility mall as an investment. I thought I had a partner, but eventually we decided not to go through with it. I hope you'll tell the other women that I did make an effort."

"A partner?" Brenda asked. "To buy the mall?"

"It was just an idea. Jackie Patterson wanted to invest in the project, but . . . well, I just felt it wasn't the way I wanted to go."

"You decided not to go through with that?"

Brenda stared at Steve till Patsy began to

434

worry that she was going to get upset with him. Why hadn't she kept Cody out a little longer? He had wanted to go to the Dairy Queen for ice cream after dinner, but she was trying to lose weight as usual, and she had vetoed it. The memory of Brenda sitting in her rocker like an Egyptian mummy and Steve trudging around with a frown on his face brought up a lot of discomfort. If these two were going to start having trouble with each other again, Patsy wanted to be long gone.

"Why don't I be your partner?" Brenda asked. "We could do it, Steve. If we bought the mall, we could cancel that video store's lease. We could bring in good tenants, people who would help the west side of the lake grow."

"Well . . ." He brushed a wisp of hair from her cheek. "It would be a big investment, honey. We'd have to go to a bank and get a loan. It would be a fairly heavy debt to service. There's a lot involved in commercial real estate. And then we would be responsible for keeping the space rented out and cleaned up."

"I could help you with that. I would enjoy it," she said. "Let's do this, Steve."

He gave a laugh. "Are you serious?"

"She is, Steve!" Cody said. "Can't you

tell? She wants to buy the mall."

"All right," Steve told her. "I'll look into it tomorrow. We'll go to the bank . . . together."

Wearing a smile Patsy hadn't seen in ages, Brenda leaned back into her husband's embrace. "Thanks for bringing Cody home," she told Patsy. "Cody, it's late. Go put on your pajamas and head out to the porch swing."

"But you said I could sleep inside your house," Cody told her. "You did say that. You said inside the house."

"Not tonight, Cody. You sleep outside one more time." Brenda spoke firmly, but she was looking into Steve's eyes.

He grinned and kissed her squarely on the lips, and that was enough for Patsy. Clutching her purse under her arm, she hurried through the front door, across the porch, down the steps, and into her car.

As she switched on the ignition, she noticed a small square package on the passenger seat. Odd. That hadn't been there when she and Cody got out a few minutes before. Had the boy left it for her?

Her heart warming, Patsy took the package and tore away the badly folded wrapping paper. But when she lifted the lid of the box, she knew immediately that someone else had left her the gift. Inside sat a beautiful white teacup and matching saucer trimmed with soft pink roses and a gold rim.

She glanced out the windshield in time to see a truck vanishing around the curve at the upper end of Deepwater Cove. "Well, that's one," she murmured. "But as I recall, mister, you broke a whole shelfful."

Still, she held the cup up to the streetlight and admired the thin bone china. *It's a real antique,* she thought. *What a perfect beginning.*

DISCUSSION QUESTIONS

The principles and strategies illustrated in this novel are taken from *The Four Seasons of Marriage* by Gary Chapman. In this book, Dr. Chapman discusses marriage as a journey back and forth through different "seasons."

- **Springtime** in marriage is a time of new beginnings, new patterns of life, new ways of listening, and new ways of loving.
- **Summer** couples share deep commitment, satisfaction, and security in each other's love.
- **Fall** brings a sense of unwanted change and nagging emptiness appears.
- **Winter** means difficulty. Marriage is harder in this season of cold silence and bitter winds.

1. In *It Happens Every Spring,* which season of the year is it in Deepwater Cove, Missouri? Which season of marriage do you think Steve and Brenda Hansen are experiencing in their marriage? What are the signs that let you know?

2. In the scene in which Brenda and Steve eat dinner together and try to make plans for spring break (pages 120–132), they could have begun to thaw their winter marriage. What went wrong? What could each of them have said or done differently?

3. In the same scene, Brenda's repeated references to Nick LeClair should be a clue to Steve that trouble is afoot. Why doesn't he notice? How might it have helped if he had? Give an example of a helpful way in which Steve could have responded to his wife.

4. To Brenda, Steve's work schedule means he has intentionally rejected and abandoned her and their marriage. This kind of all-or-nothing thinking is common. Is there another way Brenda could try to look at Steve's choices? When and how does Brenda begin to see Steve's job in a different light? Is there a situation in your

marriage where you need to try to see things in a more balanced way?

5. When Steve is walking to the dock with his daughter Jessica (page 198), he explains his approach to solving problems in a marriage. What does he think a couple ought to do if they're having trouble? How does Jessica respond? What does she think her parents need to do to improve their relationship? Which one of them do you think is right? Why?

6. When Brenda visits their pastor, he asks the couple to come in for joint counseling (page 256). What do Steve and Brenda do regarding this advice? Why do you think they chose the course of action they did? How would you respond if given this advice? Why?

7. Kim Finley tells Charlie and Esther Moore about a time in the past when she suffered from depression (page 372). What caused Kim's depression, and what did she do about it? What is Esther's view of depression, and how does she think it should be handled? Which woman do you tend to agree with? Why?

8. Strategy 1 in *The Four Seasons of Marriage* challenges couples to deal with past failures. Failure alone will not destroy a marriage, but unconfessed and unforgiven failure will. Couples are urged to identify past failures, to confess and repent, and finally to forgive. How has Steve failed Brenda? How does Brenda fail Steve? When does each of them identify their failure? When does each confess it? When do they forgive each other? In what ways does this strategy help Steve and Brenda begin to heal their winter marriage?

9. Strategy 3 in *The Four Seasons of Marriage* encourages couples to discover and speak each other's primary love language. The five love languages are (1) words of affirmation, (2) acts of service, (3) receiving gifts, (4) physical touch, and (5) quality time. What is Brenda's primary love language? What is Steve's? How is each one failing to speak the other's language? When and how do they begin to communicate with each other through their primary love languages?

10. Strategy 5 in *The Four Seasons of Marriage* urges couples to discover the joy of helping each other succeed. Practical ways

to do that include (1) offering encouraging words, (2) taking supportive action, (3) providing emotional support, and (4) expressing respect for your spouse. When and how do Steve and Brenda begin to use this strategy to warm their winter marriage? In what specific ways does each of them help the other?

11. Think about the other couples in *It Happens Every Spring.* Along with Brenda and Steve Hansen, you have met Ashley and Brad Hanes, Kim and Derek Finley, and Esther and Charlie Moore. Patsy Pringle, viewing her salon as a garden, describes the season she believes each woman is experiencing in marriage (page 71–73). From what you have learned about these marriages, would you agree with Patsy? Why or why not?

12. Psalm 8:1–2 says, "O Lord, our Lord, your majestic name fills the earth! Your glory is higher than the heavens. You have taught children and infants to tell of your strength, silencing your enemies and all who oppose you" (NLT). In this book, the character of Cody is childlike in his faith and understanding. Recall some of the truths he speaks and how they affect

the other characters. What was your favorite "Cody-ism"?

ABOUT THE AUTHORS

Dr. Gary Chapman is the author of *The Four Seasons of Marriage,* the perennial best seller *The Five Love Languages* (over 3.5 million copies sold), and numerous other marriage and family books. He is the director of Marriage & Family Life Consultants, Inc., an internationally known speaker, and host of *A Growing Marriage,* a syndicated radio program heard on more than 100 stations across North America. He and his wife, Karolyn, live in North Carolina.

Catherine Palmer lives in Missouri with her husband, Tim, and sons, Geoffrey and Andrei. She is a graduate of Southwest Baptist University and holds a master's degree in English from Baylor University. Her first book was published in 1988. Since then Catherine has won numerous awards for her writing, including the Christy Award — the highest honor in Christian fiction —

in 2001 for *A Touch of Betrayal.* In 2005 she was given the Career Achievement Award for Inspirational Romance by *Romantic Times BOOKreviews Magazine.* More than 2 million copies of Catherine's novels are currently in print.